D0725396

DOOLEY'S BACK

ALSO BY SAM REEVES

A Long Cold Fall

Fear Will Do It

Bury It Deep

Get What's Coming

AS DOMINIC MARTELL

Lying Crying Dying

The Republic of Night

Gitana

DOOLEY'S BACK

SAM REAVES

An Otto Penzler Book

———————

CARROLL & GRAF PUBLISHERS
NEW YORK

Dooley's Back

Carroll & Graf Publishers
An Otto Penzler Book
An Imprint of Avalon Publishing Group, Inc.
245 West 17th Street, 11th Floor
New York, NY 10011

AVALON
publishing group incorporated

Copyright © 2002 by Sam Reaves

First Carroll & Graf edition 2002

First Carroll & Graf trade paperback edition 2007

All rights reserved. No part of this book may be reproduced in whole or in part without written permission from the publisher, except by reviewers who may quote brief excerpts in connection with a review in a newspaper, magazine, or electronic publication; nor may any part of this book reproduced, stored in a retrieval system, or transmitted in any form or by any means electronic, mechanical, photocopying, recording, or other, without written permission from the publisher.

All of the characters in this book are fictitious, and any resemblance to actual persons, living or dead, is purely coincidental.

Library of Congress Cataloging-in-Publication Data is available.

ISBN-13: 978-0-78671-988-4
ISBN-10: 0-7867-1988-5

9 8 7 6 5 4 3 2 1

Interior design by Sue Canavan

Printed in the United States of America

Distributed by Publishers Group West

What made this book was talking to cops. First and foremost was Frank Cappitelli, who patiently set the author straight on many points and then generously took the time to review the manuscript. Others who helped to educate the author were Phil Cappitelli, Robert M. Lombardo, Hugh Holton, and Dave Salter. Many thanks. Any errors that remain are emphatically the fault of the author's fevered imagination.

DOOLEY'S BACK

1

"DOOLEY'S BACK." RODDY MCSHEA SAID IT IN FLANIGAN'S AND NOBODY could think for a second who he was talking about, staring through the smoke at him. "Frank Dooley, I mean. Kevin's kid brother. Jack Augustine said he saw him, in the bar at the Holiday Inn downtown."

After a silence, someone farther down the bar said, "No. No way."

"What the fuck does Jack Augustine know?" said Jim Dimas. "If it was in a bar he wasn't sober, and if he wasn't sober I don't believe a word the guy says."

"If he *is* back, he's an idiot," said Bill McPeak, and everybody in the place sank into melancholy reminiscences. "Dooley, Jesus Christ." McPeak waved for another shot.

"Can't be," said Mike Duggan. "Dooley's too smart to ever come back."

Roy Ferguson, who had known Dooley best, let a few seconds go by and said, "Smart was never the problem with Dooley. If he's back, it ain't because he's stupid."

"Western Avenue," said John Spanos, as he strolled across it in the middle of the block, hands in the pockets of his raincoat, coattails flapping in the wind. "I like Western Avenue." A car swerved to miss them, horn dopplering away down the block, tires hissing on the wet pavement. A step behind Spanos, Terry shouted the customary fuck-you after it, without passion. "Did you know this was the longest straight street in the world?" said Spanos.

Terry looked south to the vanishing point under the flat gray sky, past numberless used car dealers, liquor stores, restaurants that were never in anybody's dining guide, garages, bowling alleys, and bars. "This? Who the hell says?"

"I read it somewhere. The longest straight street in the world. There might be a longer one someplace, LA, maybe, but not straight. Look at it. Goes all the way from the North Side to the South Side. Twenty-some miles. Cuts through the whole fuckin' city of Chicago."

Reaching the sidewalk, Terry shook his head. "It ain't even straight the whole way. Where is it, down around the ship canal someplace, it like jogs."

"Jogs, my ass. So it jogs twenty feet one way and back. Look at it on a map sometime. It's straight as a fuckin' arrow."

Spanos pushed through the door of the bar. It was a long dim room walled in light-colored composition paneling, with two pool tables under low-hanging shaded lights at the very back. There were booths to the right, tables farther back sharing space with pinball and video games, and a long bar down the left-hand wall with liquor bottles stacked in front of a mirror. Neon beer signs hung on the walls, and sports trophies were ranged along a shelf high above the bar. There was one early customer at the bar and the owner behind it, smoking a cigarette and watching the four o'clock news on the TV at the far end. He nodded at Spanos and Terry and reached for the beer mats.

"How ya doin'," said Spanos. Terry wandered on down the room, just strolling, but Spanos put his elbows on the bar. "What you got on tap there, Old Style? Fine, draw one for me. Terry, want a beer?"

"Sure," said Terry, looking at the video games.

"Make it two."

"You got it," said the owner quietly. He was a lean man with sparse gray hair and a sparse gray beard. He had been around the block a couple of times and it had left him with a hard fleshless face and blue eyes that didn't get excited for anybody or anything. He drew the beers with his cigarette dangling from his lips. At the back of the room Terry was rolling the cue ball across one of the pool tables to bounce against the far rail and return. Bounce, catch, roll again. The old man ten feet down the bar from Spanos was watching the news too. His spine was bent and Spanos could hear the wheezing as he breathed.

The owner set the beers on the bar. "Nice place," said Spanos.

"We like it."

"Good neighborhood type of place. Love this kind of place."

"Thanks a lot. That's two bucks."

"You got a beer garden out back?"

"In the summer."

"God, that's great. I bet you get a good crowd in here. Pack 'em in on Sunday for the Bears, do you?"

"We do OK."

"Softball team?" Spanos pointed at the trophies above the bar.

"Sixteen-inch, league ball, bowling. We got a lot of teams. You want to run a tab?"

"Sure, we'll run a tab."

The owner shrugged and tapped ash off his cigarette. As he started to move away Spanos reached inside his overcoat. "Wait a second." Spanos brought out the paper and unfolded it, shook out the creases, laid it on the bar. "This is for you."

The owner's expression didn't change but he looked Spanos in the eyes before he came back and picked up the paper. He reached into the pocket of his denim shirt and pulled out a pair of reading glasses and set them on his nose. He looked at the paper and then looked up at Spanos with an irritated expression and said, "What the hell is this?"

"It's a bill." Spanos smiled at him.

"A bill for what?"

"That's your tax bill."

"My tax bill? Bullshit." He flung the paper down on the bar. On it was written in big black letters:

U. O. ME

$24,000

BACK TAXES

"Bullshit? I don't think so. Terry, the man says bullshit."

Terry had come quietly back up the room, hands in the pockets of his leather jacket. "He thinks it's bullshit, does he?"

The blue eyes narrowed and for the first time there was just a touch of wariness there. Spanos could see him thinking, could practically hear the thought processes of a man just now fixing on the way Terry looked, a big dark good-looking kid with three days' stubble and very broad shoulders under a Hawks jacket and eyes that could get excited fast. The blue eyes flicked to Spanos and Spanos knew all he had to do was stand there and let the wheels turn in the bar owner's head. "Who the fuck are you?"

"It don't matter who I am," said Spanos. "What matters is the number on that piece of paper. You've been taking action here for almost a year, big action, and anybody that takes action in this part of town has to pay for it, 'cause, see, you're in our business. I asked around a little and that's what I figure you owe me."

"Who says I'm taking bets?" said the owner, voice starting to go raspy.

"You trying to tell me you ain't? You gotta learn to keep secrets better than that."

"So what if I do? So what if a few friends put a buck or two on a game now and again? Is that any of your god damn business?"

The old man was watching them now, distracted from the news.

Spanos looked at him and said, "Hey. Don't you have to take a piss or something?"

The old man blinked at him for a couple of seconds and then looked at the owner and finally slid off the stool and made for the back of the bar, grumbling in a breathy incoherent rumble.

Spanos turned back to the bar owner. "You got three guys working for you. You collect on Tuesday and pay on Thursday. You got two phone lines, and you laid off nearly ten thousand dollars last week with another book that happens to belong to me. Did you really think you could get away with it?"

The bar owner sucked the last life out of his cigarette and stabbed it out in an ashtray. "Where does it say I got to ask your permission to take a few bets?"

"Right here," said Terry. He brought the white cue ball out of his jacket pocket and while the bar owner was still gaping Terry wound up and whipped it. The ball made a dry *tock* sound bouncing off the owner's skull and then a huge *crash* as it took out one panel of the mirror behind the bar. Glass tinkled to the floor. The old man had frozen halfway to the john; when he saw Spanos and Terry looking at him he turned and hustled toward the rear like an ostrich in a panic.

The bar owner had steadied himself with one hand on the bar, the other hand to his head. His eyes were squeezed shut. "Jesus," he said.

"Jesus won't help you," said Spanos. "Only thing that'll help you is twenty-four thousand dollars. Legal tender, in cash, in an envelope right here on this bar one week from today. And every month after that, two thousand, on the first day of the month. Me or one of my people will be by to collect it. Welcome aboard."

"OK, you made your point." The bar owner had backed away, edging instinctively toward his cash register, moisture making the blue eyes glint. He had both hands to his head now and his grimace bared yellow teeth. "I'll stop. I'll get out of it."

Spanos leaned across the bar. "Nice fuckin' try, jag-off. You think you can just blow off the twenty-four thousand? Sorry, pal, but that's what you already owe me for the past year. That twenty-four thousand I get if you never take another bet."

"That's too much. I can't do it."

"Can't do it? Don't say that. This bar's a fucking gold mine. Terry, look at this place. What do you see?"

"Gold mine."

"See? Look, maybe you got the wrong idea. I'm not here to put you out of business. I want you to do all kinds of business. I want you to get rich." Spanos waited a beat, let the man register that before he hit him with the punchline. "'Cause, see? When you get rich, I get rich."

Spanos could see realization dawning through the pain in the man's head, the man recognizing the facts of life too late. In a voice without much breath behind it the man said, "You'll get your money. But I'll close the place down before I let you take over."

"No you won't," said Spanos. "Not after you think about it for a while. Best thing for me and you both is to go on doing just what you're doing. Have my money ready for me next week and we'll get along just fine." Spanos reached into a pocket and pulled out his roll. He peeled off a hundred and threw it on the bar. "Get the fucking mirror fixed. We want to do decent business, the place has to look nice. See you in a week, partner."

Spanos looked back from the doorway and saw the man trying to get a cigarette out of the pack, a tough thing to do with shaking hands.

So far, thought Dooley, it's been about as much fun as a funeral. Welcome home.

Dooley was the only one left in the café, sitting with his thoughts, a stranger in a strange land. He would rather have been in a bar but he had had the sense to avoid that tonight; one hangover in twenty-four hours was enough. Where he would really rather have been was at Kathleen's kitchen table, or Kevin and Mary's, but he wasn't ready for that. Why not, he couldn't say. But six times in approximately forty-eight hours he'd had the phone receiver in his hand and the coins ready to go in the slot, and every time he'd hung up again and put the coins away. Dooley was starting to think the whole thing was a mistake.

"Sir? I'm afraid we're closing." The pretty blonde behind the counter gave him a quick smile, apologetic and a little nervous, as she said it.

Dooley got up from the table and carried his empty cup toward the bus tray. The blonde intercepted him and gave him the smile again as she took the cup from his hand. She had warm brown eyes and Dooley thought she looked like the type who might be willing to sit over a cup of coffee and listen as he poured his heart out. Suddenly there was nothing in the world he would have liked better, but it was closing time and he could see he made her nervous. It was a lonely place to have to work late at night, up here on the fifth level of the mall; Dooley wondered if the security guard he'd seen down at the street entrance ever found the initiative to take a ramble to the top. "Thanks," he said. "Sorry to hold you up."

"That's OK, I have to be here anyway. G'night." She gave him that smile again and Dooley left, wondering why he couldn't talk to people anymore. He was back in a place where everybody spoke English, but for all the good it was doing him he might as well be in China.

The mall was a gutted warehouse five stories high, shops around a central core open all the way up to a skylight, with the ramp winding around the well and a bank of elevators shooting up one side. The other shops were already shuttered. Dooley headed for the ramp, thinking he could pick up a pint of bourbon after all, see what was on cable at the Holiday Inn, put off a decision till tomorrow.

Dooley had been a cop, and he still saw things through a cop's eyes. So when the two bad guys came up the ramp past him toward the top level of the mall, he noticed. There was no doubt they were bad guys; even after eight years away Dooley could tell without thinking about it. Maybe the tattoos, murky blue tattoos that shouted jailhouse; maybe the general style, Latin gang-banger chic with the baggy pants and close-trimmed goatees. Maybe the careful avoidance of his eyes.

Dooley worried about it for the time it took to go down one level, thinking he was wrong, he was on edge, it was not his god damn job anymore. And when he reached the elevators he punched the button and stood listening while a car whined up the glassed-in shaft toward him. He took it back up to the fifth level and stepped off, hearing nothing that alarmed him. He walked around to the café and saw the steel latticework shutter over the entrance halfway down, as the pretty blonde had pulled it when he left the place; there was no sign of the bad guys.

Dooley couldn't see the blonde or anyone else inside, just the long counter with the espresso machine and the bottles of Italian syrup arrayed behind it, the bench along the wall, the bags of beans stacked on display. There were whispers and a scuffling noise from the back room of the café, out of sight around a corner at the rear.

Dooley ducked under the shutter and walked quickly toward the back. The big one came around the corner with a startled look on his face, maybe six-two, two hundred and forty pounds of overfed delinquent quickly zipping up his pants, and his eyes lit up as he saw Dooley approaching. "We got company," he said.

Dooley said nothing. He made no move, no gesture other than to keep walking; when the big one saw how it was going to be he just stepped into his path and reached out to grab his shirt. Dooley sagged, making the punk take his weight on the outstretched arm, and then reached out and grabbed a handful of testicles through the loose jeans.

The punk managed to deliver one shot to Dooley's head, but then he screamed and let go fast as Dooley squeezed. The punk was beating on his back but Dooley was doing bad damage, and after a couple of seconds he let go and the big punk sank to his knees as the little one came around the corner. Chairs were falling over and somewhere just around the corner the woman was screaming now with every breath, *Help me, help me, help me!*

The little one had a knife, a six-inch stiletto switchblade which he had probably been holding to her throat; when he saw his partner on the floor bellowing like a gelded steer, he came at Dooley with the knife waving, back and forth in front of him like radar. He had a Kings crown tattooed on his knife arm and a teardrop inscribed under one bloodshot eye. Dooley had picked up a chair and as calmly as he could with adrenaline jacking him up he said, "You drop the knife and run, we'll call it quits. Otherwise I'm going to kill you and that's a promise."

"You got it the wrong way around, motherfucker." The punk was scrawny, an abused and twisted whippet, and his code said you never ever backed down from anyone. He made a lunge and Dooley parried with the chair, backing away a step or two. The punk kept coming; Dooley led him down the long counter toward the exit. Behind the little punk he saw the big one crawling, moaning now, and then the terrified blonde staggered into view, bouncing off tables; they'd gotten her pants off and she was bleeding from the nose.

The punk with the knife knew more people had to show up soon and it was time to ditch his partner and run. Dooley hit the lowered shutter with his back, ducked, and backed out onto the concourse. He gave the punk enough space to encourage him to come out, then jumped forward as the buzz-cut head with the rat tail in back emerged, vulnerable for one crucial second, and brought the chair down hard. It caught more shoulder than head and the punk went to his knees but kept the knife; Dooley backed away, giving him a chance to say uncle. Instead he charged again, and Dooley had to jam the chair down on top of him; that was enough for Dooley. He jettisoned the chair and picked the punk up by the rat tail and the back of his waistband, Dooley spun like a hammer thrower, the punk taking a pointless swipe with the knife, finding nothing, and then screaming *No!* as he saw where Dooley was taking him.

The punk's heels hit the railing as Dooley swung him out over the void and he tumbled as he fell, clawing at the air and working his legs like a long jumper straining for the extra inch; his scream filled the gallery, all the way down. He hit the umbrella over one of the tables on the food court five stories below. In a cartoon he would have bounced off and landed on his feet but this was real life; neither the umbrella nor the table slowed him much and they collapsed with a booming crash that masked the sound of the punk's head cracking on the tiles. The punk had let go of the knife in midair, and it hit the floor and bounced at the same time he did, proving Galileo right once again.

2

SPANOS PARKED ON THE CHICAGO SIDE OF HARLEM AVENUE AND crossed the street to the deli, briefcase in hand. The deli was nearly empty; there was an old man drinking coffee over the *Sun-Times* and old Mrs. Amonte was wandering the room, clearing napkins and straw wrappers from tables. Spanos went to the counter and got a cup of coffee from Laurie. She was looking haggard in her makeup and white apron, a good-looking woman run into the ground by hard work. "You look like you could use a vacation," said Spanos.

"I could use a new life. But who's complaining?"

"Don't do no good anyway."

"Not around here it doesn't." She returned Spanos's smile and he wondered again how she was dealing with the personal aspects of Mario Amonte's enforced absence. He was getting into taboo areas here but he loved to watch her walk.

"Vince back there?" he said.

"I think so." The smile flicked off and Laurie went away down the counter; she'd been a connected guy's wife long enough to know when the small talk was over. Spanos pushed through the swinging door at the end of the counter and went down a short hall to a small room with two folding tables and a half dozen chairs and a window with blinds that were never opened even on the brightest summer day.

Vincent Bonifazio wore his customary sweatshirt and jeans; dressing up for Vince was a polyester sport jacket over a polo shirt.

Bonifazio was a scrappy flyweight who had grown old instead of growing up; instead of swelling up with age he had just dried out. He had white hair combed into a modified ducktail and a seamed face that had looked at lots of unpleasant things and recorded them all with eerie blue eyes that didn't quite go with anything else in the face. He looked like a gust of wind could blow him away but not before the wind sustained some nasty cuts.

Spanos took a chair. Bonifazio was deep in conversation with Terry, leaning across the table and jabbing a finger at the kid sitting there in his Blackhawks jersey. "You showed real disrespect there, pal. That was not good."

"How in the fuck was I supposed to know?" Terry was holding his own, looking back at Bonifazio with resistance and a little amusement in his face.

"You just know. Friends of mine don't pay for shit here."

"How am I supposed to know who's a friend of yours?"

"The man says he don't pay, he don't pay."

"And I just take his word for it."

"That's *right* you take his word for it." Bonifazio lowered the finger and leaned back, easing up.

Terry nodded a few times. "OK, I read you. I'm just trying to run a god damn business here."

"Let your mom run the business. You just pour the fucking coffee."

Terry's look took in Spanos and a third man who sat at the head of the table. He stood up, nodded, and went out, never losing the slight smile.

"He's a good kid," said the third man, when the door had closed. Pete Bianco was a weathered and collapsing seventy or so, eyebrows running riot as the hair on his crown thinned.

"He'll be OK once he learns the rules. Trouble is, Mario don't want him to get involved with things. Wants him to go to college and all. Gave the kid ideas. Johnny, can you believe this shit? Angelo was in here the other day and this fucking kid tries to make him pay for lunch. Says he didn't know who Angelo was."

"Maybe he *didn't* know," said Spanos.

"He don't know a god damn thing."

"He's a good kid. He'll learn."

"He needs a father. Fucking Mario had to go and get himself scooped."

"He got a bad break," said Bianco.

"He fucked up." Bonifazio waved a hand in dismissal. "So Johnny, what you got for me today?"

Spanos opened his briefcase and slid it down the table to Boni-fazio. Bonifazio reached inside and started pulling out rubber-banded stacks of bills. "The usual and then some," said Spanos. "Joey finally got that five grand from the guy, that guy at the Board of Trade. But he still has to give me the juice on it. He gave me the usual bullshit, swore he'd have it in a week. I told him he fucking better."

"Well, that's good. I can't believe how long he let the fucking guy slide."

"I had a little talk with him. I think he's got a little better idea now what he has to do. I mean, if you're going to put money out on the street, you have to be prepared to do what's necessary."

"Yeah. He don't pay the juice, you go and put a fucking turban on his head or something. If he can't do it himself, all he's got to do is come to you."

"That's what I told him."

"Christ, you give a guy a bankroll to put out, it's with the under-standing he's grown up enough to do what he has to do."

"I think I got through to him today."

"I fucking hope so." Bonifazio riffled through a couple of stacks of bills and shoved them down the table to Bianco. "We cleaned up on Sunday, huh? Thank God for the fucking Bears. You'd think we paid that guy to throw that fucking ball away there."

"Why bother? He's gonna do that anyway. You get the count from Charley?"

"Yeah. We did unbelievable."

"And I made an arrangement with that guy on Western Avenue, remember? Two grand a month. I think he's gonna go for it. That or close the fucking place, which I don't think he's gonna do."

Bonifazio nodded. "Johnny, for a Greek you're a hell of an Italian." For a while nobody said anything, watching as Bianco counted bills, stacked bundles. Spanos lit a cigarette. Bonifazio rose and went to a radio sitting on a shelf by the door. He turned on the radio and the room filled with swelling strings and an anodyne beat, music that was almost white noise turned up to a volume that was almost uncomfortable. "Johnny, you're a fucking gold mine, you know that?" he said over the noise.

"Just trying to make a living."

Bonifazio came back to the table and sat down. "We got a situation, Johnny," he said.

"What kind of situation?"

"You tell him." Bonifazio nudged Bianco.

Bianco cleared his throat. He looked startled, as if he couldn't quite remember what he was supposed to tell Spanos. "Herb Blumberg got his fuckin' hymie ass indicted downtown," he said.

Spanos smoked. "Who the hell is Herb Blumberg?"

"Johnny don't know him," said Bonifazio.

"Ah yeah. OK, Blumberg takes care of Angelo's money. He's an accountant, investment advisor, some fucking thing. Except he just got indicted."

Spanos shrugged. "How bad is that?"

"It's bad."

"It's potentially a motherfucker," said Bonifazio. "Angelo's shitting bricks."

Bianco had remembered where he was now, leaning over the table.

"Blumberg's been Angelo's guy for twenty years. You gotta know the G is gonna try and get him to deal."

Spanos reached for an ashtray. "What's he looking at?"

"Fuck, you know how it goes. He's *looking* at dying on government time. They're hitting him with tax evasion, mail fraud, the usual bullshit. But he won't do anything close to what they're talking about."

"Not if he cuts a deal," said Bonifazio. He was leaning back with his arms folded, looking steadily at Spanos.

"And if he cuts a deal, Angelo's fucked," said Bianco. A silence fell.

John Spanos smoked, took a sip of coffee, smoked some more. He nodded. "OK."

Bonifazio smiled. "You're coming up fast, Johnny. You know that?"

"Is that so?"

"Yeah. For somebody that ain't Italian you're doing unbelievable."

"Is that so."

"Now you need to take on some responsibility, something important. Something to impress Angelo, make him sit up and take notice."

Spanos blew a smoke ring and watched it dissipate under the harsh fluorescent light. "I said OK," he said.

The city didn't look much different; they hadn't found a way to keep the streets from crumbling and people still lived in the same houses, looked at the same hazy skyline far downtown. The weather was lousy, cold and gray, and for Dooley that was appropriate. For eight years down in Mexico the one thing that was most likely to bring on an attack of homesickness was a touch of cool weather, a little rain. In his mind's eye Chicago was a bad-weather town.

Dooley had nearly cried looking at the city from the airplane on its approach, coming in over the lake toward the vast sprawl along the shore, picking out landmarks and remembering. He had never imagined, down there in Mexico, how deep in his bones he had missed the city.

Out here on the Northwest Side nothing had changed. This was a long way from inner-city blight, with rows of solid well-kept bungalows, but it was a long way from Rush Street and Lincoln Avenue too. You didn't move out here to have fun; you moved out here to raise kids. Cop kids, Dooley thought; we grew up out here and we went away to college or the service or whatever and then we all became cops just like our old men and moved back. And we all lived happily ever after on the Northwest Side.

Dooley steered the rental car along quiet streets just south of Foster, navigating from memory. Kathleen's house had, he thought, a different color paint on the trim, yellow instead of white. He drove on past and parked in the next block and watched for a while in the mirror. Today he'd woken up without a hangover and with a sharp new sense of resolve, even urgency.

The morning drive-time radio reports had had it: death at the Century Mall, gang activity suspected. Nothing about an attempted rape or a white male in his forties. Dooley knew that didn't mean they didn't have it all; they would just play it close. Whether or not the girl had seen him pitch the punk over the rail, she would tell the dicks about him and give them a description. He had gotten away clean through the parking garage and it would take a hell of a lot of luck to get further than the description, but Dooley knew he didn't have a lot of room for error.

One wasn't enough, he thought; I had to go and do another one. What Dooley felt was not remorse exactly, not regret; he knew he had saved untold numbers of cops and state's attorneys work for years to come by pitching the creep over the rail. What he felt was a burning annoyance that he had made things hot for himself. He had always prided himself on his poise but certain things were beyond his control. Ever since Consuelo, Dooley wasn't quite rational about women in peril.

It's not too late to drive straight back to O'Hare and catch the next flight out, he thought. Instead, he got out of the car.

On the phone he had told her he would come to the back and she must have been watching for him at the window; two seconds after he knocked at the back door she tore it open. When he got inside she threw her arms around him and squeezed. Dooley held her up as she swayed, patting her on the back once every few seconds as she sobbed. She said his name again and again, calling him Franny, the name he had not let anybody but her call him since he was about six.

Finally she stepped back and Dooley got a good look at her; her hair had started to go gray and her figure had gone. In eight years his sister had moved over that line from young mother to middle-aged lady with teenagers.

"I like the beard," said Kathleen, wiping her eyes with her fingers and forcing a smile.

"I got tired of shaving." Dooley ran a hand over his jaw. "You had the kitchen redone."

"Yeah, you like it? God, that was, let's see, five years ago already. Cost us a fortune."

Dooley paced, touching the counter, rapping his knuckles on the table. "How's Bob?"

"He's fine. They work him too hard and don't pay him enough. But he's fine."

"Christ, is this Patrick?" Dooley was looking at pictures on the refrigerator.

"Yeah. And that's Maureen there."

"Damn. She's gonna be a beauty. How'd they grow up so fast?"

"Eight years is a long time with kids."

Dooley nodded. "Yeah."

There was a moment of awkwardness and then Kathleen took the carafe from the coffeemaker and pulled a mug out of the cupboard.

"Well, have some of this. I'll put a little Jameson's in it and we'll celebrate like Irishmen."

"Sounds good."

She produced the bottle and they said nothing for a while, sitting at the table and doctoring their coffee. The smell of the whiskey cutting through the coffee aroma hit Dooley in a good place.

Kathleen took a sip and said, "I can't believe you're here. You get in last night?"

"Day before yesterday."

"You've been here two days? What the hell have you been doing with yourself?"

"Driving all over the city. Walking around downtown. Sitting in bars. I even went to a movie."

Her look was astonished, shading to wounded. "Why the hell didn't you call?"

"I don't know." Dooley set down his mug and raised his eyes to hers. "Shame. Fear. Whatever."

Kathleen's eyes were clouding again and her lips were tensed. She reached across the table and grabbed his hand. In a strangled voice she said, "Francis. I'm so glad you're home." All Dooley could do was squeeze back and watch his sister cry. Finally she let go, got up to get a tissue, blew her nose, and sat down again. Composed, voice under control, she said, "Tell me something."

"What?"

"Did you kill him?"

Dooley took a deep breath. "Kill who?"

She opened her mouth to answer and then closed it again and just nodded. "OK. Kevin always said if you showed up they would haul you in to question you, for sure. But he says if you kept your mouth shut they would never have enough to charge you. You were the number one guy they wanted to talk to, but there was absolutely no evidence. Nothing but motive and the fact that you flew out the night he got shot."

Dooley nodded slowly. "I gotta talk to Kevin."

"Are you back for good?"

"I don't know. It all depends." As he had for half the night, Dooley saw the punk again, sailing out over the rail. I screwed up bad last night, he wanted to tell his sister, but said nothing.

"Kevin always said if you kept your head down and your mouth shut, there was no reason you couldn't come back."

Dooley shrugged. "I'll see how things stand."

Her eyes dropped away from his and she said, "So. What's Mexico like?"

Dooley felt knots easing. "Pretty wild. A lot of it I liked, a lot of it I didn't. It's poor. But the rich folks are very, very rich."

"How's your Spanish?"

"It's good."

"I bet. What did you do for a living down there?"

"Different things. The last five years I worked for a politician. I was a bodyguard, gofer, errand boy. Muscle sometimes. Politics is a little rough-and-tumble down there."

"More than here?"

Dooley shook his head. "You wouldn't believe it."

Over the rim of her mug she said, "We missed you."

"I missed you too. I missed a whole lot of things."

"Well. We've got a Hide-a-Bed in the living room. It's pretty comfortable. You have any bags or anything?"

Dooley drank; he was already feeling the fiery effects of the whiskey. "Don't take it wrong, but I'd rather stay at the hotel. I want to play things close to the vest for a while. And kids talk, even if you and Bob don't."

"What are you worried about?"

"Contamination, complication. Explanations. I'd just as soon be on my own until I scope things out."

"Can I tell them you're here? Or is that a big secret?"

"Sure, tell 'em. I'll come over for dinner or something. Just tell them not to spread it around."

She nodded, resigned. She had married a civilian, but Kathleen knew all about arguing with cops. "Talk to Kevin. He's on days now, down at Maxwell Street. Gang Crimes and Intelligence. He made lieutenant."

"Was there ever any doubt?"

"Don't start playing little brother again. Kevin's all right. He'll go to bat for you."

"I know."

"He really will. We all want you home again."

Dooley looked out the window over the sink into the gray sky. Home again. For a second he thought about it. "I don't know," he said.

"What?"

"I think I may have blown that."

They sat in silence and a tear fell from Kathleen's face—*plop*—into her Irish coffee.

3

Dooley figured Kevin would keep for a while. That left Roy. Dooley cruised looking for a phone, wishing he'd thought to call from Kathleen's, finally deciding he was close enough that he might as well drop in cold. If Roy was still on evenings he'd be just getting up, unless he had to be in court. If he missed him he could get the lowdown from Andrea. Unless she was at work; would she have gone back to work? Sean would be what, ten or eleven now? And there would be other kids; he was starting to see how much could change in eight years. Andrea might be at home with a baby, number three or four; Roy had always said he wanted lots of kids. After two wasted days Dooley was anxious now, anxious to see people.

Roy had a house on one of those blocks squeezed between Devon and Caldwell near the forest preserve. Dooley pulled up across the street and switched off the engine. Nothing looked different. The garage door was shut, curtains were drawn in the big front window. The lazy son of a bitch was sleeping in. Andrea would have got the kids out the door to school and gone off to work herself, everybody being careful not to wake Daddy.

Dooley leaned on the doorbell. He gave Roy a good minute or so, standing on the porch looking up and down the street, then leaned on it again, starting to think nobody was home, disappointed. He had taken a step back toward the car when locks started clicking behind him.

It took him a moment to recognize Andrea. His first thought was damn, they moved; his second thought was oh shit she's sick and I've gotten her out of bed. Andrea Ferguson stood there looking at Dooley around the half-open door with the dazed, defensive expression of somebody who has just woken up. She had on a blue terry-cloth bathrobe and her sandy blond hair fell in strands around her face.

"Andrea?" said Dooley, after a long moment.

She stared back and then finally the door came open a little wider and she stepped up to the screen, starting to take on a look of wonderment that brought a little life to her face. She ran a hand through her hair to get it out of her eyes and said, "Frank?"

"The one and only." Dooley gave her a tentative smile. "I didn't mean to get you up."

"That's OK." She pushed the screen door open. "Come on in. God, where have you been?"

"Long story." Andrea pulled on the cord to open the drapes and the living room filled with light. Dooley took a couple of steps, just taking things in, and turned to face her. "I guess I'm not much of a letter writer."

She brushed her hair back again and stood with her hands in the pockets of her robe, looking at him blankly. Here was one woman who had lost weight in eight years; Andrea had never been plump but this was a new look, too thin almost, the bones in her face showing more than he remembered, the gray eyes wide above the dark circles. "Roy on days now?" said Dooley.

He knew what she was going to say from the time it took to answer him. "Roy doesn't live here anymore. We got divorced."

And suddenly it was all wrong. He should have found that phone and called first. "I'm sorry," he said.

Andrea gave a little shrug. "I think he is on days now, as a matter of fact. He got an apartment in Wrigleyville somewhere. I can give you his phone number. He's got a cell phone, too."

Dooley nodded a couple of times. "When did all this happen?"

"It's been a couple of years." Dooley waited but no more came out. He was feeling for an exit line when she said, "Want some coffee or something?"

He thought about it for a second; the honest answer was no but the implied offer of conversation interested him more. "If I can use your bathroom first. I just took in a couple of gallons over at Kathleen's."

When he got back to the kitchen Andrea was standing at the stove, arms folded, watching a kettle on a burner. It took her a couple of seconds to look up. "I don't have any coffee. I'm sorry."

"That's OK. I didn't really want any."

"I might have some tea."

"Don't worry about it."

"Wait, I think I've got some instant somewhere. Have a seat." She pulled open a drawer. Dooley sat down at the table, wincing as she produced a jar of instant coffee. This kitchen was different from Kathleen's; there were no pictures on the fridge, no calendar by the phone, no fruit in hanging baskets. This kitchen looked a little empty. "So where have you been?" Andrea said, rummaging for spoons.

"Mexico."

"Mexico."

"Yeah. Started out as a vacation and turned into eight years."

She looked at him for a long time then, eyes searching his face. Dooley thought she looked a little older, not much, but mainly harder, worn and tired. "Vacation's over, huh?"

"I guess so."

Her eyes lingered for a moment and were gone; Dooley wasn't quite comfortable with that look. "Listen," he said. "I didn't mean to bother you. I'll just get Roy's number and go bother him."

"No, really. It's good to see you. I'm sorry I'm such a mess. I work late at night, I sleep in."

Dooley shrugged. "OK."

"You want something to eat?" She was opening a cabinet.

"No, I'm fine. Hey, how's Sean?"

And once again there was no need for her to say anything; Dooley couldn't believe he'd missed all the signs. He could tell from the way she froze, head sunk, hands still on the cabinet doors, exactly what she was going to say, and he would have given anything never to have darkened her doorway.

"Sean's dead." She looked at him over her shoulder, and her look was empty. "That's what happened to Roy and me. Sean drowned when he was seven years old. He drowned in a lake up in Wisconsin, with his grandma and five or six cousins and his mother sitting there watching." She shuffled to the table and sank onto a chair. She sat with her hands in her lap staring across the table at him, blinking a couple of times. "Don't worry, I'm not going to cry." Dooley stared back and found nothing to say. He stared into her gray eyes until finally she said, "You've been there, haven't you?"

"Yeah."

"It tore my heart out. I thought I would die, it hurt so much, and Roy wasn't much help. I guess we found out that Sean had been pretty much what was keeping us together. I guess that's why we never had any more kids, we must have figured it would be a mistake. Anyway, we never got over it." In the silence the kettle started murmuring. Andrea pushed away from the table. "So that's the news here. Sorry it's such a downer."

He watched her make for the cabinet again. "Why don't you give me Roy's number? I'll get going."

"No, please." She spun to look at him. "I didn't mean to chase you away." Dooley could see she meant it; this was a different look. "Stay and tell me about Mexico. Tell me—" She stopped and suddenly it was all out there, everything that both of them had been through, and he could see the same thought in her eyes that he had: anything but that, talk about anything but that.

"Mexico was a trip," he said. "A real trip."

"You son of a bitch, I thought you were gone forever." Roy Ferguson hadn't stopped grinning since he'd walked into the diner and picked Dooley up off his feet with a bear hug. "Passed right into legend, never to return." Grinning across the table now, Roy was shaking his head in wonder. Behind the counter, grease sizzled and a radio tuned to a schlock rock station labored to be heard. Besides Dooley and Roy there was one other customer, at the far end of the counter. Outside the fogged-over windows, traffic oozed by in the drizzle on Belmont.

Dooley smiled back. "It gets lonely up there in Valhalla. I got tired of waiting for the rest of you mopes."

Roy was older like they all were, a little heavier maybe, a little gray showing at the temples, but still with the long handsome face, matinee-idol eyes and tousled dark-brown hair, the big athlete's body, broad-shouldered and long-limbed. "Augustine saw you downtown. I didn't believe it at first."

"He recognized me, huh? I wasn't sure. I didn't want to talk to him."

"Well, it ain't no secret you're back. But I don't think anybody's gonna go to the State's Attorney."

"Now why would they do that?"

The grin had finally faded. "OK. Don't ask, don't tell. But I'm assuming you had a good reason to disappear."

Dooley shrugged. "As far as you can tell, is there any reason why I couldn't spend a week or two here, catch up with a few people?"

"You mean is Bill McPeak likely to get the file out, see a chance to clear an eight-year-old case? He may have to go through the motions just to cover his ass."

"McPeak, huh?"

"Yeah. And I'm sure you're his first guess. But I don't know what he's got, if you keep your mouth shut. You want to know the truth, I think you did what every copper in the world wishes he could do once in a while. I think the only way he'd go after you is if somebody raised a stink, and as long as you don't advertise you're back I don't see who's going to raise it."

Dooley nodded slowly. "Well, I guess that's good news. So, is Area Six still as much fun as it always was?"

"Man, you missed some changes. No more Area Six. They reorganized everything a few years back. There's only five areas now. Belmont and Western's Area Three."

"No shit. Who you working with these days?"

"Guy named Tommy Crane. Came up out of the twenty-fourth. Only been a dick a couple of years."

"How is he?"

"He's OK. Pretty good workman, decent guy. Serious, real serious. I miss your sense of humor."

"So do I."

Roy watched him sip coffee and said, "So, you ready to come home?"

"I don't know."

They sat and listened to street sounds, the lousy music, the fry cook passing the time of day with the customer at the counter. Roy said, "You find what you wanted down there in Mexico?"

"I guess so." Dooley stared out the window. When he spoke it was very quietly. "I went down there to tell Consuelo's parents . . . well, I went down there to see them, and then I just stayed. It was someplace to be, something to do. I never found Consuelo, though."

"If only it was that easy." Roy's look had a melancholy cast Dooley couldn't remember ever seeing.

"Andrea told me about Sean."

"Yeah. That kinda took care of that marriage. She went to pieces and I just couldn't put her back together. She blamed herself and she was afraid I blamed her too and she wasn't going to get over it. Finally I split."

"I'm sorry."

"Hey. It hurts but you get over it, you know?"

"Yeah."

"She tell you what she's doing now?"

"No."

"She's a cocktail waitress. She works at some hotel out by O'Hare. She's got a fuckin' master's in education and she's waiting tables, letting drunks feel her up and sleeping all day. She went to pieces, like I said."

"She had a rough time."

"She ain't the only one." In Roy's face Dooley could see a hurt that went down to the roots. "But you keep on humpin'. You don't just lose it and refuse to fight for it. Do you?"

Dooley looked at him for a while and said, "I don't know. There's not a lot you can do sometimes."

Roy looked at him, and a lot of unspoken words went back and forth. "No. Still, if there was any way I could have drained that fucking lake, wiped it off the map, you better believe I'd have been out there pumping. I wanted to take somebody's head off, but there wasn't anybody to go after except Andrea. And she was hurting bad enough already."

Some kids came in, boisterous in NFL jackets and unlaced basketball shoes, and Dooley and Roy watched them out of long professional habit until they settled at the counter. "Maybe it's not too late," said Dooley.

"What?"

"I don't know, try and patch it up with Andrea."

"No. It's too late. Too many things got said." In the silence Roy's pager went off. He pulled it off his belt, looked at it, and said, "Duty calls, man. What are you doing now?"

"I don't know. I guess I'm going to see Kevin next."

"You haven't talked to him yet?"

"Nah. I saw Kathleen this morning."

"Kevin's headed upstairs, man. They're talking about Deputy Chief for him. Maybe right here in the Area."

"That's my big brother."

Roy paused, sliding out of the booth, and said, "Pretty good brother to have, if you want to come back and live here again."

"Maybe."

Out on the sidewalk, Roy said, "Where you staying?"

"I been at the Holiday Inn, downtown."

"What the fuck, Kathleen wouldn't put you up?"

"I didn't want her to. I don't think I'm fit for family life."

"Hell, come stay at my place. I got lower standards."

Dooley considered it. "I'm not gonna do your laundry for you."

"Shit, Dooley, just keep the refrigerator full of beer, you can stay forever."

When Kevin walked into the bar, Dooley thought his father had come back from the dead. Kevin paused in the doorway and heads turned; even though he'd thrown a windbreaker over his uniform shirt and ditched the gold-banded lieutenant's cap, he projected a certain presence. Kevin could walk into a place and own it. Dooley had a spot about halfway down the bar and when Kevin caught sight of him Dooley smiled, all the doubts gone for a moment.

Kevin walked down the room without giving anything away; the look on his face was more one of amused wonder than anything else. Dooley would have slid off the stool but he knew there wasn't going to be any bear hug.

"I'll be damned," said Kevin. "You came back." He held out his hand.

"Jesus Christ, you look like the old man," said Dooley, shaking it.

"That's what they tell me." Kevin shook his head, still faintly smiling. "Where the hell have you been?"

"You didn't get my postcard?"

Kevin snorted, as close to laughter as he ever got. The barkeep was hovering and Kevin said, "Gimme a draft." The barkeep hustled away.

"I called Kathleen every Christmas," said Dooley. "She must have told you where I was."

"Mexico." Kevin shook his head again, the smile gone. "How'd you like it down there?"

Dooley had to grin at the skepticism in his voice. "I liked it OK. The beer's cheap."

Kevin leaned on the bar. "You see Consuelo's people?"

"Yeah. Once in a while. I wound up in Mexico City. They're in Guanajuato."

"What the hell'd you do for eight years?"

"A little of this, a little of that. Traded on my expertise as a gringo cop. Worked my way up to bodyguarding a senator. Looked under the bed for assassins, swept his office for bugs, delivered a message now and then. That kind of thing."

Kevin nodded, not looking at him. "I bet you got some stories to tell."

"A few good ones, yeah."

"And now you're back."

"For a little while, anyway." Dooley took a drink of beer. "I got homesick."

"Eight years, I guess so. I'd last about a week down there."

"You're getting set in your ways, like the old man."

Kevin smiled; he looked for all the world like the legendary Commander Michael Dooley, with his hair gone gray and the piercing blue eyes in a face chiseled out of granite. "Maybe."

"'Why would I wanna go to Florida to die'; remember that?"

"Yeah. Adaptability wasn't exactly his strong suit."

"He didn't even have fun in Ireland."

Kevin snorted again. "Remember what he said? 'Now I can see why they left.'"

"Poor Ma. She must have got tired of apologizing for him."

They shook their heads, grinning, and Dooley knew it was going to be all right. "Hell with this place," said Kevin quietly. "Why don't you come out to the house?"

"Had to check me out first, huh?"

Kevin threw money on the bar. "Well kid, I wasn't real sure who I was gonna meet here."

Kevin lived in Sauganash, a thickly wooded and well-monied corner of the Northwest Side with a heavy population of cops and other city employees who wanted suburban comfort but had to live in the city. The house was brick and substantial, the image of its owner.

Late that night, Kevin thumped a bottle of Jameson's onto the bar of the finished basement and said, "You get tired of tequila down there?"

"You get tired of anything after a while."

"I'll never get tired of this."

"No, not this." Dooley watched as Kevin poured. "Mike like it OK down there at Notre Dame?"

"I guess so. I don't know if he does much studying. His grades weren't worth shit last term. Here's to ya."

They clinked glasses. "May the road come up to meet you when you fall," said Dooley.

Kevin drank. "Colleen's the smart one. She's gonna do great at DePaul. Rose, it's too early to tell. She may be too good-looking for her own good."

"She's pretty, all right."

"She's just found out about boys, too. I'm gonna have to chase 'em away with a baseball bat."

Dooley laughed through his nose. "Mary looks great. She's aged better than Kathleen."

"Yeah, Kathleen's starting to look a little worn around the edges."

They drank and mused. The den was in shadow except for the fluorescent light above the bar. Upstairs the floor creaked gently as people settled in for bed. Outside the streets were quiet. "I missed a lot," said Dooley.

"You did." Kevin was absorbed in something he saw in his glass. "Say, listen."

"What?"

"I'm not gonna ask you any questions, OK?"

"All right. I'll try not to give you any answers."

"I'm your brother, but I'm also a cop. You are too."

"I resigned, remember?"

"Two days before you disappeared. I remember. Makes no difference. You're a cop for life. That's why I'm stepping carefully here."

Dooley gave him a long look across the bar. "OK, what do you want, a confession?"

"Christ no, don't say another word." Kevin was staring at him, blue eyes intent in the broad heavy face. "Just listen. I'm gonna tell you how things stand here. It's still an open case. All right?"

"Uh-huh."

"But there is no evidence, you understand? Nothing. They may haul you in and ask you all about it, but if you keep your mouth shut there is no way in hell they can make a case. No state's attorney would take it. You deny everything and you walk, because there is no evidence. I know, I've looked at the files. People will wonder, but they'll never be able to prosecute you. All right?"

Dooley was silent, twirling the glass on the smooth polished bar. "All right." He looked up at Kevin. "I've made some mistakes. Some big-time mistakes."

Kevin shrugged, frowning, a massive broad-shouldered shrug. "That's all over. You're back home now, aren't you?" Dooley shrugged. Kevin picked up the bottle and poured him another two fingers of whiskey. "So it worked out OK, didn't it?"

Dooley raised his glass, knocked it against Kevin's. "If you say so, big brother. If you say so."

4

DOOLEY WOKE UP WITH A HANGOVER. NOT A BAD ONE, JUST A FAINT sour reminder in head and stomach of the beers he'd downed with Roy on top of Kevin's whiskey late last night. Near midnight Dooley had found the yellow brick three-flat a couple of blocks north of Addison on Wayne, and Roy had been sitting up waiting.

Dooley got his feet off the couch and onto the floor, gingerly pushing the blanket aside. Sunlight was coming in through the front window and making the clean wood floor glow. Dooley had a vague impression of Roy leaving early, the sound of the front door closing. He stood up and pulled on his jeans, wobbling only a little. He felt cleaner and a little better after a few minutes in the bathroom. There was a key lying on a note on the kitchen table: WORKING TODAY. MI CASA ES SU CASA. KEY TO BACK DOOR. LATER. R. Dooley found the coffee and the coffeemaker and set things in motion.

He dressed, groomed himself a little, made some toast. He turned on the radio on the kitchen counter and listened for the news. It came and went with no mention of the Century Mall. He sat down with the coffee, the toast, and a three-day-old *Sun-Times* he had found on the floor in the living room. Dooley was out of touch; he'd followed U.S. and international goings-on pretty well down in Mexico but the Chicago news was full of issues and names he didn't have a clue about. Richie was still mayor, no surprise there. The Bears had won a couple and lost a couple, and Dooley didn't recognize any of the names on the roster, not one.

With his second cup of coffee he stood in the living room and looked at Roy's place. It took him back. He'd lived in apartments, hung with people who lived in apartments just like this, old Chicago three-flats or six-flats with the rooms laid out along a long meandering hallway that stretched to a back porch where the garbage cans were. He and Consuelo had lived in an apartment like this, just starting to think about houses when it happened. Dooley sucked down coffee, trying to get his mind around the idea that he was home.

It was a bachelor place for sure, not too messy but with that hap-hazard decoration scheme that says *unattached male*: mismatched furniture from the Salvation Army, softball trophies instead of house plants, a bad print of a bad landscape that had come from a garage sale and was hanging there because it looked like something ought to hang there. There were jackets draped on closet knobs, stray coffee mugs. Dooley wandered over to look at the books Roy had put on the built-in shelves on either side of the bricked-up fireplace. For years Roy had kidded him, called him the egghead; Dooley was curious to see what an anti-intellectual read. There were some swollen drugstore novels, Ludlum-variety intrigue, some self-help books betraying a dabbling interest in business and investing, a biography of Eisenhower, Shirer's *Third Reich,* and a hardcover book about Michael Jordan. With a couple of exceptions, the books looked as if they had actually been opened.

Dooley took off down the long hallway toward the back, just wandering. The first room he came to was Roy's bedroom; Dooley cast a glance in through the door at an unmade bed and lowered blinds and kept walking. Next was the bathroom, and then there was a second bedroom before the kitchen. The door was closed but not locked and Dooley stuck his head in.

This was the junk room. There were some cardboard boxes stacked along the wall, things that had never gotten unpacked. Other than that the room was bare except for the computer. That surprised Dooley a little; he'd always figured Roy would be the last holdout against the information age. The computer sat on a scarred wooden table, keyboard and monitor beside a telephone, with the cpu on the floor. Dooley pulled the chair away from the table and sat down. He put down his mug and rummaged among the papers on the tabletop. Bank statements, bills, an investment newsletter. There was a plastic disk file with a flip-up lid; inside were a dozen or so floppy disks, a miscellany of games, personal finance software, an encyclopedia. At the back of the file was a disk that was labeled HANDICAPPER'S POINT SPREAD ANALYZER. Dooley frowned at it, closed the file, and took a drink of coffee.

His eye ran over the boxes. Some of them were taped shut and some were open, things poking out. Dooley stood up and crossed the room. In one box there were letters, ragged tops of envelopes. In another box Dooley saw photographs. He looked for a moment at a picture of a very young Sean on his father's shoulders. In a third box were magazines and newsletters. Dooley saw *Money, Personal Finance, Cutting Edge Investing.* He rooted idly, just poking, and saw *The Vegas Silver Sheet.* Dooley pulled it out and looked at it. There was a graphic of a football sailing through the goalposts and a headline: BEAT THE LINE, EVERY TIME. Dooley dug deeper. Under the money magazines was a stack of gambler's sheets, three or four different tout services. They were dated a year or two back.

None of my fucking business, thought Dooley, and went back to the desk. He took a drink of coffee and stood looking at the boxes. Son of a bitch, he thought; people surprise you. He set down his coffee and went back to the boxes. There were more tout sheets in a second box; at the bottom of the box was a spiral notebook with a blue cover. Dooley glanced inside and took it back to the desk.

He opened the notebook and saw *9/8 NYG10-Dal $500NY* in ballpoint pen at the top of a column on the left. At the top of the right-hand column was the figure *−8700*. Below that was written *−550* and on the next line *−9250*. The second entry on the left was *9/8 LA-KC3 $200KC.* On the right was *+200*, making *−9050*.

It took Dooley a while to scope things out, paging through the notebook. There were no years with the dates, but it looked like the two previous football seasons were there, with both college and pro teams represented. In between the football seasons was what looked like basketball action, especially heavy in the spring. There was even baseball, and Dooley didn't think anyone in his right mind bet baseball other than the odd sawbuck on the Series.

Dooley went through it again, an archaeologist patiently sifting. Year round, somebody was putting down money on anywhere from a couple to seven or eight games every week. He won a few, but the minus figure in the right-hand column kept growing. Once in a while there was a line through it and a reduced figure below it, but it always started growing again.

Up to a point. Dooley closed the notebook and tossed it back on the table. He finished his coffee and listened to street sounds. Finally he walked slowly back to the kitchen. If he was reading things right, Roy Ferguson had been a net loser for a year and a half, the vigorish chewing a hole in him. If the figures in the blue notebook were accurate, he had been nearly sixteen thousand bucks in the hole when he'd come up with fifteen grand six months ago to knock the debt down to size. After that there was no more action recorded. Either Roy had stopped, or he had stopped keeping records.

Dooley poured himself another cup of coffee but didn't drink it; instead he sat at the table and thought, with the coffee cooling in front of him. People can surprise you, he thought.

Spanos called Mike Siminowicz from a phone in the entranceway of a drugstore on Augusta Boulevard and then drove on over. The house was one of a row of neat brick boxes on a quiet well-kept block. Siminowicz's mother opened the door, a frail bent-over old woman with tight gray curls. The inside of the house smelled like week-old cabbage. Siminowicz, a big untidy man getting larger and untidier with every passing year, came down the stairs and shook Spanos's hand, ignoring his mother, who stood there blinking at them with a worried look on her face. "This is Johnny," said Siminowicz, barking at her. "Business." The old lady nodded and went back to the kitchen, baffled by the comings and goings in a house she had lived in for sixty years.

The basement was unfinished, with mortar falling out from between the bricks in the foundation, but one end had been made into a machine shop. Drills, punches, lathes, things Spanos didn't recognize sat on benches. Toolboxes, some padlocked, were stacked one on top of the other. Siminowicz hauled a couple of chairs closer to a workbench and Spanos sat down. Siminowicz reached into a drawer in the workbench and pulled out a pair of latex surgeon's gloves. He wrestled them onto his hands. He went to a locked gray steel cabinet, sorted a key out of the bunch at his waist and opened the cabinet. He reached inside and pulled out a pistol and laid it on the workbench.

"You don't take any chances, do you?" said Spanos.

"Nope. My prints show up nowhere."

Spanos picked up the .22 Colt Woodsman and worked the slide. The action had a nice smooth solid feel. "I don't want to have pick up the shells," he said. "You wouldn't have a revolver in there, would you?"

"Any ammunition I give you will be clean. You want to go to a revolver, you can't silence it."

Spanos nodded, sighted down the blue steel barrel. "OK. What about the silencer?"

Siminowicz pulled a locked tool kit down off the top of a cabinet on the wall and opened it. He took out a four-inch steel cylinder about an inch in diameter and handed it to Spanos. "This will take care of it," he said.

Spanos examined the two objects in his hands. There were interrupted threads set into the end of the pistol barrel and he fitted the silencer onto it and gave a quarter turn. "You're all set," said Siminowicz.

"Except for something to shoot."

Siminowicz went back to the cabinet and pulled out a loaded magazine. "Twenty-two long rifles, standard load. Subsonic, so with the silencer there'll be nothing to hear. It'll sound like a cough, a nice ladylike cough. The cartridges are clean but you'll need to wipe down the gun and the clip if there's a chance anyone's going to find it."

Spanos shoved the magazine home, flicked the safety off and then back on. "They'll go into deep water first chance I get."

"That's the recommended procedure. I'd wipe 'em anyway."

"OK. Six hundred with the silencer?"

"That'll do it."

Spanos pulled a roll out of his pants pocket and counted off six hundred-dollar bills onto the bench. "You got a bag or something I can carry it in?"

"Sure." Siminowicz rummaged on a shelf and handed him a plastic T. J. Maxx shopping bag.

Spanos slipped the automatic inside. "Does your old lady ever wonder what goes on down here?"

"She thinks I sell sports collectibles." Siminowicz nodded at a set of shelves along the wall. "I got hundreds of baseball cards over there. Trouble is, she kept 'em in the basement all these years and they're fucking worthless, with the damp and shit."

"At least she kept yours," said Spanos. "My old lady threw all of mine away."

Twenty minutes later Spanos pulled to the curb half a block

beyond an auto body shop just off Chicago Avenue in Melrose Park. He got out and locked his car and walked back to the garage. The big overhead door was open and Spanos strolled through into the dimly lit interior. There were five or six cars inside, some with bashed-in panels and others with missing doors, but it didn't seem as if much work was going on; the place was silent. In a partitioned-off cubicle in the back corner two men were drinking coffee. One of them wore coveralls and was smoking a cigarette. When he saw Spanos in the doorway he doused the cigarette in his coffee and pushed away from the desk. "Morning," said Spanos.

"How ya doin'." The man in coveralls had suddenly remembered his business; he slipped by Spanos and walked briskly up the garage toward the open door. Spanos looked at the second man. "All set?"

"Ready to roll." Bobby Marino looked like a bulldog with sore feet. It was pushing it to call him five-six, but he carried nearly two hundred pounds. He walked gingerly and scowled at the world, and on Bobby Marino's square heavy-browed face a scowl carried some weight. He scowled now as he rose to his feet. "Just me and you?"

"You think we need somebody else?"

"I thought maybe you were gonna bring the kid along."

"You kidding me?"

"Hey. Vince just said, Make sure he don't involve the kid."

"He think I'm nuts or something?"

"He's just looking out for the kid, that's all."

"He doesn't have to tell me."

"OK, he didn't. I did."

"Fuck it. What you got?"

"We got a '96 Taurus, so hot it's still steaming." Marino led him toward the back of the garage.

"You change the plates?"

"Of course I changed the fucking plates. What do you think, I'm senile or something?"

"OK, I guess we can ease off a bit, huh?"

"Suits me." Marino was opening the driver's side door of a blue Ford Taurus parked at the very back of the garage.

Spanos tried the passenger side door and found it unlocked.

"Where we goin'?" Marino was fiddling with wires under the steering column.

"Touhy. The twenty-six-hundred block."

The engine caught and Marino pumped the gas a couple of times. He put the car in gear and backed carefully out of the slot, then pointed it toward the bright opening of the garage. The man in coveralls had found something to do on a red Pontiac Grand Prix and didn't look up as they eased past.

"So Touhy, huh?" Bobby scowled out the windshield as he turned east on Chicago, driving one-handed, doing what he liked best. "What's that, seventy-something north?"

"Seventy-two. He's near Touhy and California."

They said nothing for a while as Bobby drove. It was getting dark and Bobby put on the headlights. "You know the guy?" he said.

"No."

"You'll get the right guy, right?"

"I'll get the right guy. I went to his office this morning. Tried to sell him some insurance. I looked him in the eye, made sure he was the guy I wanted. He threw me out of the office."

There wasn't any more talk after that. It was five o'clock by the time they reached Touhy and California, and Spanos started looking for the low brick facade of the office building. It was on the north side of the street, a low-rent address for low-rent lawyers, accountants, and maybe a dentist or two. Touhy Avenue was a quiet commercial strip for a quiet Jewish neighborhood, with Chinese restaurants and kosher delis elbowing for position. "There it is," said Spanos.

Bobby went up a side street and came along the alley. Spanos spotted the recently indicted tax accountant's blue Mercedes 300 at the rear of the office building next to a dark green Dumpster. "Whoa," he said. He got out of the car. The alley was more brightly lit than he would have liked, but he had driven down it that morning and seen that there were garages on one side and the blank back of the office building with a lot of drawn blinds on the other. He knelt at the right front tire of the Mercedes and took a hammer and a ten-penny nail out of his jacket pocket. He drove the nail into the side of the tire with two firm strokes and then wiggled it a little. He stood up and slipped the hammer back in his pocket and walked back to the Taurus, hearing the steady hiss of the flattening tire behind him.

Bobby drove around a few corners and pulled up in the alley a block west of where the Mercedes was parked, along a blank back wall. He cut the lights. "What if he don't pull it out of the slot? We won't see it," he said.

"He won't notice the tire's flat until he tries to drive it. He'll get out in the middle of the alley and stop."

They had only waited ten minutes or so when it worked just like Spanos had said. They saw the Mercedes come out into the alley, listing and wobbling just a little, straighten out and go for maybe ten feet before the accountant figured out what the problem was.

Spanos took the automatic out of the plastic bag and racked the slide. "OK. You go around and wait for me at the other end." He got out of the car. He tried to put the pistol in his jacket pocket but with the silencer on it was too long. Instead he loosened his belt and slipped it into his waistband inside the jacket, checking the safety with his thumb, not wanting a slug in the thigh or the nuts. He could see the accountant looking at the flat tire now, throwing up his hands in disgust. He started walking.

Coming up the alley, Spanos watched the accountant wrestle the heavy spare out of the trunk and roll it along the side of the car. He watched him take out the jack and the tire iron. The accountant was a pudgy man who was as worried about the trousers of his nice dark suit as he was about the tire. He knelt with some difficulty and finally had to put one knee on the ground after all to steady himself while he fitted the tire iron to the first nut.

When Spanos got close enough to catch his attention, he got all of it. In the light from the lamp on the back of the building his face was washed out except for the dark worried eyes, riveted on Spanos.

"Trouble?" said Spanos.

The accountant squinted at him. "Who's that?"

Spanos kept walking. "What's the matter, you got a flat tire?" He came into the light, letting the accountant see him.

The accountant had gotten to his feet, tension making his movements stiff. This was a very nervous man. He still had the tire iron. "Flat as a pancake," he said. "I don't know what happened."

Spanos was ten feet away now, hands in his jacket pockets, holding the jacket closed over the pistol. "Need a hand?"

The accountant had a round face with a sharp chin and a sharp nose and a lot of shiny head where the hairline used to be. He peered at Spanos and his eyes got a little wider; whether he had put two and two together and gotten all the way to four or just recognized somebody he'd said some curt words to this morning, Spanos saw something had clicked. "No. Thanks, I got it covered."

Spanos was four or five feet away and he figured it was time; the gun came out of his belt with only a little hitch as the silencer caught and then the light of panic went on in the small dark eyes and the accountant raised the tire iron and jumped at him. Spanos managed to avoid the blow but the little round man caught his shirt and tore it and almost pulled him off balance, flailing, before Spanos managed to jam the gun into his belly and squeeze. There was no sound at all but the accountant's eyes went very wide and Spanos squeezed again, twice, two little puffs of air into the soft fat. The look of horror contracted to one of pain as the accountant slid to his knees and then keeled forward onto his face, the tire iron clanking on the concrete.

42

Spanos kicked the accountant's hand away from his leg and leaned down to put the silencer at the back of the bald head. Squeezing the trigger as quickly as he could, he emptied the magazine into the accountant's head, making sure they were good solid punches in through the skull, no miracle bounces. The holes were very small and began to bleed immediately, though feebly. The accountant subsided into a huddle, no longer concerned about his suit.

Spanos put the gun back in his waistband and started walking, trying not to look around. He knew the odds were very good nobody had seen a thing. He pulled his jacket closed, covering the gun and the damage to his shirt. He walked calmly down to the end of the alley and saw the Taurus waiting at the corner. His nerve gave out right at the end and he practically dived into the car. Bobby pulled away and Spanos wrestled the gun out of his waistband and tossed it on the floor next to the hammer. "Son of a bitch put up a fight," he said.

"Make any noise?"

"No." Spanos watched the storefronts go by. His heart was still racing. "Go out Wilson," he said. "There's a bridge over the river where we can toss this thing."

Bobby nodded and drove. At a stoplight Spanos opened his jacket and saw the pocket of his shirt nearly torn off, a button missing. "Son of a bitch," he said.

Bobby looked over and said, "You have anything in that pocket?"

Spanos froze the second he said it, the nagging feeling at the back of his mind jumping up and screaming at him. "Fuck," he said, bitterly.

"We had a drive-by right on Belmont today," said Roy, feet up on the coffee table, mouth full of pizza. "Missed all the gang-bangers, killed a twelve-year-old schoolgirl a block away. One slug from a .22

pop-gun, went into her head and killed her. There's justice for you. Remember the mob guy a few years ago who took three shots to the head from the backseat and lived? That fucker's still walking around, and this little girl's dead. Go figure."

Dooley shook his head and took a sip of beer. "Remember what Tyrone used to say about how to solve the gang problem?"

"'Teach 'em to shoot.' Right on."

"So, did you get the trigger?"

"Took us about half an hour. Everybody on the fuckin' block knew who did it. We found him at his mama's house with the gun in his jacket pocket. Dumb fucker had no idea he'd hit anybody."

"Damn."

"Yeah, they're not just getting more vicious, they're getting dumber too."

"Thank God for small favors."

"No shit." Roy reached for his beer. "Roddy McShea's got one that goes in the thanks-for-the-help file. You hear about the guy at the Century Mall?"

Dooley sucked on his beer for dear life. He swallowed and said, "I heard something on the radio about a dead King."

"Yeah. Wilfredo Soto, an LK hard case. I remember him, had him in for a talk a few times. Somebody tossed his ass over the rail there the other night. Five flights down. Splat. Wish I'd a been there to see it."

"That's pretty good. They know who did it?"

"No, they ain't got a thing. McShea says who the fuck cares, they should give the guy a medal. Soto and some no-good friend of his had been up in the café on the top level earlier in the evening and had some kind of a run-in with the girl that worked there. So they went up after hours and tried to rape her. Except somebody came along and broke it up."

"What, some citizen?"

"Nobody knows. The girl thinks it was a guy that had been there earlier but she was pretty hysterical. And Soto's friend ain't talking. He took a pretty good whack in the nuts and he's still at Cook County with a ruptured testicle. They'll never get this one sorted out. I'd like to meet that Good Samaritan though, I really would."

Dooley shook his head. "Damn." He studied the label on his beer bottle as if it were the Rosetta Stone.

Roy drank and said, "So, you miss it? That why you came back?"

"What, the job?" Dooley gave one slow shake of the head. "Dead babies, ten-year-old rape victims, old ladies beaten to death with claw hammers? Paperwork till your eyes cross, grab an hour of sleep and then get to 26th and California by nine, wiseass defense lawyers that were state's attorneys last week? Fuck. Ask me a hard one."

"Well, nothing's changed. Right now, all this overtime, what I was doing this evening was knocking on doors up in Rogers Park. They got themselves a serial rapist up there, jumping Loyola coeds. Three so far and not a clue. Vicious and smart. The worst kind."

Dooley brooded. "Catch him. And do everything right. For me."

Roy shot Dooley a look. "We'll nail him. We'll make it ACLU-proof." There was a silence and Roy said, "That fuckin' guy's still around. I saw him the other day down at 26th and Cal."

"Who?"

"The lawyer that got Dickens off. He's still making a nice living at it."

Dooley shrugged. "I never particularly blamed him." Dooley mused on it for a while, took a drink of beer. "Would I have felt better if they'd convicted him, if he was sitting down in Stateville researching a lawsuit? I don't know that I regret anything. Except not being there to protect Consuelo in the first place. That I regret."

The silence became prolonged. Roy sighed, deep and long. "Well, there you go, man. You can't go around for the rest of your life beating yourself up about it. It wasn't like you did anything wrong."

"No. Still."

Roy drank beer. After a moment he said, "Me, what I gotta live with is why did I tell Sean he couldn't come fishing with me and his uncle? I didn't want him along because he always got bored and wanted to come in early. He begged and begged and I got pissed off and yelled at him, and finally we went out in the boat and when we came back he was dead."

Dooley finished his beer and went slowly down the long hallway into the kitchen to pitch the bottle. He came back into the living room and stood looking out the front windows into the street. He said, "Down there in Mexico, near Oaxaca, there's a complex of ruins called Monte Albán. There's a pyramid there you can climb up, if you got a good head for heights. I was in Oaxaca one time, between jobs, just wasting time, drinking a lot. I hiked out there one night, all by myself, climbed up the pyramid. Dumb-ass thing to do, what with snakes and bandits and God knows what all. Sat up there all night feeling sorry for myself and looking into this unbelievable night sky and cursing God and all the rest. And then, maybe it was just the booze or this strange place or I don't know what, but it was like I heard Consuelo. Not like a nutcase hearing voices, just a sense somehow of what she would say to me if she was there. And she said basically hey, I'm OK now. Move on. So I did." Dooley turned from the window. "So listen for your boy. 'Cause he's OK now."

"Yeah." Roy passed a hand over his face. "I sure hope so, 'cause his old man can't help him anymore. Fuck, I'm tired. Gimme a hand up and I'll let you have your bed here."

5

DOOLEY TURNED IN THE RENTAL CAR; IT WAS GOING TO BLEED HIM dry. He had made no decisions whatever except that he wasn't going to leave town tomorrow. Kevin's boy Mike had gone back to school and left an old Chevy Nova parked in front of Kevin's house and Kevin was happy to have Dooley take it off his hands. The next time Mike came home they could work out a deal. The thing was rusting out but it ran OK.

Dooley spent a lot of time just driving around the city, visiting old favorite places, getting a feel for the town again. He'd forgotten the sprawl of the place; in comparison to the metastasizing blight of Mexico City he'd thought of Chicago as a nice compact town, a tight cluster of memories, an easy drive-around. He was surprised to rediscover how vast it was, block after block of bungalows and three-flats, endless stretches of taquerías and insurance agencies and currency exchanges, all centered on the massive brooding upthrust of the Loop.

Sometimes he drove past good times: a bar where he'd hung out for a summer, an old friend's apartment where a memorable party had gone all night. Too often, though, he saw the cop's landscape: the courtyard building where they found the pretty legal secretary strangled, the alley where a fourteen-year-old honor student bled to death. The city for Dooley was invested with ghosts.

COPS SEEK GOOD SAMARITAN IN CENTURY PLUNGE said the *Sun-Times*

47

headline. Some of the ghosts were with Dooley when he closed his eyes at night. He wasn't bothered by pangs of conscience but he found himself looking over his shoulder a lot.

Dooley hoped he was timing it a bit better this time, giving Andrea a chance to get up and get her hair combed. He wasn't entirely sure why he was heading out Devon toward her house, but he had left Kathleen's after a quick lunch with the excuse that he had some people to catch up with.

This time he'd missed her; he gave her three long peals on the doorbell but she didn't appear, groomed or otherwise. Dooley went back and sat in his car across the street for a moment and wondered what to do next. He didn't come up with anything, so he just sat there listening to the radio for what seemed like a long time until a gray Volvo pulled into the driveway and Andrea got out.

She pulled a couple of small bags of groceries off the seat and headed for the house. Dooley got out of his car and crossed the street. She turned and saw him coming as she was unlocking the door. "Need a hand?" said Dooley.

Andrea paused and just looked at him; finally she said, "Hi." Her hand was still on the key. Dooley could see the question in her eyes: What are you doing here?

"I had some time to kill," he said. "I wanted to talk to you."

She looked better today, clothes and grooming doing wonders; if she was harder and thinner, today there was at least a glimpse of the stunning strawberry blonde she'd been when Roy married her. She had on black tights under a long loose sweater that hugged her flanks below the waistline of her jacket, and her makeup was there but not obvious, highlighting the gray eyes and fine curved mouth. "Sure," she said. "Come on in. I just got some real coffee." He followed her to the kitchen and sat at the table as she put away the provisions. "So which is it?" she said.

"What do you mean?"

"You said you had time to kill and you said you wanted to talk to me. Those are two different things."

Dooley couldn't think of anything to say to that. "I talked to Roy," he said.

"Oh? How's he doing?" Andrea didn't look up from the tumble of groceries on the counter. Her tone told Dooley she didn't much care about the answer.

"OK. Still chasing bad guys."

"Well, he's doing what he does best, then," said Andrea, opening the refrigerator.

She's waiting for it, Dooley thought. And she really isn't too happy to see me. "Did you know he was gambling a lot?" he said.

Andrea closed the refrigerator and turned to face him. She folded her arms and said, "Did I know? Yeah, I figured it out when things started disappearing."

Dooley blinked at her. "I see."

"He sold some silver that had been in my family. I guess he thought I wouldn't miss it. That was the first time I took a swing at him." She went back to the counter and Dooley sat in silence until she had finished putting the groceries away. She closed the cabinet, turned and said, "I'll give Roy credit. He never hit me back. You want that coffee?"

"No. Not really."

Andrea gazed at him for a few seconds and said, "I guess we needed something to dull the pain. With him it was throwing his money away on ball games. It gave him an excuse to spend even more time out of the house, hanging out in bars, away from me." She smiled, wanly. "With me it was booze. That's a nice solitary pursuit. I guess we reverted to form. The extrovert and the introvert." The smile was gone and there was nothing but sadness left. "It's too bad we couldn't have found our consolation in each other. That's what's supposed to happen, isn't it?"

"I don't know."

Andrea slumped onto a chair. There was a long silence. "Anyway. I pulled myself together enough to quit drinking. Once I started waiting tables it was easy; you see what it does to other people. But Roy's still gambling, huh?"

"I'm not sure. But if he is, he's seriously behind. I mean seriously."

"There's nothing I can do about it," she said.

"I know. I don't know why I'm here. I just wanted to talk about it."

"And you can't quite believe we're not together anymore."

Dooley looked at her for a while and then sighed. "Maybe."

"Sometimes I can't quite believe it myself. It all went so damn fast. Sean died, and then a year later we were divorced. *Bang*. There goes your world."

"Yeah. And when it's gone, it's gone."

She gave him a searching look. "What was it with you? What was your vice?"

He shrugged and said, "I ran away."

"And that helped?"

"A little. Nothing helps much. Except time."

"No." She looked at him for a while longer and then her eyes fell. "I have to go to work."

They got up. To have something to say, Dooley said, "Where do you work?"

"The bar at the Marriott, out by O'Hare. It's brainless and the tips are good. And I only have to fend off two or three propositions a night." She gave him a wry smile.

"Comes with the territory, I guess."

She scooped a ring of keys from the counter. "It's not so bad. Quitting time's the tricky part. The bartender's more than happy to make sure I get to my car without any trouble. Of course, he's starting to get ideas himself."

Dooley watched her pull on her jacket. "You ever thought about going back to teaching?"

"No." Her tone and her look told him it was a stupid question. As she paused in the doorway she said, with a clear eye and steady voice, "I can't bear to be around children."

"Any trouble?" said Vincent Bonifazio. "Any trouble at all?"

Spanos pulled away from the curb and headed south on Harlem, cruising. Traffic was light and the neon restaurant signs gave the street a festive air. It reminded Spanos of Christmas, lots of red and green. "It went OK," he said.

"You made sure?"

"I made sure. He could breathe through his skull if he was still breathing."

"No witnesses?"

"Nobody. There was nothing to hear, nothing to see. And the hardware's gone."

"Good work, Johnny."

"There's only one thing." Spanos had been bracing himself for this all evening, weighing the pros and cons of keeping quiet or fessing up. "He saw it coming and he tried to put up a fight."

"Fuck, you were supposed not to scare him. That's why we sent you."

"Yeah, well, he saw it coming. He got in a swing or two with a tire iron."

"Jesus, who'd a thought that little hebe had that much fight in him? You OK?"

"Yeah. But in the fight I dropped a notebook. And I didn't notice till it was too late to go back."

He had to stop at a light then, and he forced himself to look at Bonifazio. "A notebook," said the old man, his face a blank.

"Yeah. My notebook where I keep track of the loans."

"Well, shit. You don't write no names in there, do you?"

"Code names. Initials, shit like that. And numbers. Keep track of the vig, the payments, you know."

"So is your name in there?"

"No, come on, you think I'm an idiot? The only thing that worries me is if they start going through this thing and really putting two and two together. I mean, at first glance it's not going to tell nobody nothing. But if some smart son of a bitch sits down and sees what it is and starts asking around who owes what and that kind of thing—I mean, I could be vulnerable. I mean, they get a handwriting sample or something, I'm fucked. Not to mention fingerprints. They could put me at the scene."

The light changed and Spanos kept driving, waiting for the explosion. "Well shit, Johnny, that wasn't real smart," said Bonifazio.

"I know. But I think I might have a way to handle it."

"Oh yeah?"

"I got a cop."

"You got a cop? Shit, everybody's got a cop or two. I don't know how a guy in Vice is gonna help you here, though."

"No, this one's a homicide detective. Fuckin' fell into my lap. Came into Duke's a while back and started gambling, losing a lot. He's into me for fifteen grand and I've been playing him real easy. I've been saving him. I'm hoping he can help me out here."

"What, like get the book back?"

"I don't know. That's what I'm hoping. All I know is, he owes me a big fucking favor."

They drove for a while in silence. "Just be sure you handle the son of a bitch with care," said Bonifazio. "You always gotta think about wires, shit like that. Especially with a cop."

"I'll be careful," said Spanos. "But I think this guy's in too deep to make any trouble. I think he likes his job too much."

6

ROY WANTED TO TREAT DOOLEY TO DINNER. "MEXICAN?" SAID DOOLEY. "I just got back from there, for Christ's sake."

"So you can tell me how authentic it is," said Roy. The place was a hole in the wall on Belmont: half a dozen tables in a narrow room, stucco walls and paper Mexican flags strung everywhere, festive green and red. The owner and her daughters waited tables in gaily embroidered dresses. Dooley pronounced the mole sauce reasonably authentic.

"Only gringos ask for tacos in a restaurant down there," said Dooley. "But one thing's the same in both countries."

"What's that?"

"All the busboys are Mexican."

Roy grabbed the check. "You're a cheap date," he said. "And I bet I can get you to come home with me, too."

"Only if I get the bathroom first."

Roy laughed. "Deal. This is the best my social life's been in months."

"Grim, huh?"

"Hell, it's OK if you like hanging out with coppers. Women, that's another thing. We're talking drought. I mean, we're talking Death Valley."

"It ain't easy."

Roy shook his head. "When I first moved out, I was like hey, I'm footloose and fancy-free again, watch out ladies here I come. There were beautiful women everywhere I looked, and I knew twice as much as I did when I was twenty-one. But you know what?"

"What?"

"I found out, the ones that are easy to sleep with are just that, easy. And all the good ones are taken."

"Well, you got high standards."

Roy gave him a speculative look. "What about you? Down there. Eight years is a long time."

"Yeah. The first couple, I wasn't really interested. You lose someone like I lost Consuelo, your thoughts don't turn to other women right away."

"No, sure, I know."

Dooley shrugged. "After that, flings. Just flings. Somebody to go to bed with for a week, a couple of months. Nothing serious. I wasn't living a real stable lifestyle to begin with." Dooley remembered: Marta, Graciela, Teresa. A weekend in Guadalajara; what was her name?

Roy let him brood for a while and then said, "So how'd you get hooked up with this politico?"

"Contacts, like everything else. Once I got the lay of the land, got the language down a bit, Consuelo's old man put me on to a guy who ran a trucking line. He had problems with theft, some shady drivers using his trucks to run dope up across the border, all kinds of shit. I was able to do him some good. Had a couple of hairy moments, made a few enemies, got the word out he wasn't a pushover anymore. Word got around, I got other jobs. Eventually I hooked up with the Honorable Ernesto Cruz Zamudio, a senator for the PAN. That's one of the political parties. Being at least a nominal reformer and not connected with the local narco-tycoon, he had a certain amount of concern about getting shot. I managed to keep him alive. I even made a little money."

"Oh yeah?"

"Yeah. You wouldn't believe the deals these people are into. I think the guy was reasonably honest, but he sure had a lot of irons in the fire. That's Mexico. And after a while, if he trusts you and you run a few key errands for him, he cuts you in on a deal or two. Land, coffee beans, the odd container load of copper, whatever. You put up a little money, you make some. I came back with a bit of a nest egg."

"That's cool. What are you going to do with it?"

Dooley laughed, shook his head. "Damned if I know. I don't even know where I'm going to be next week."

Roy's pager went off. Roy swore and plucked it off his belt. Looking at the number, he frowned. "I gotta go call this guy," he said.

Roy paid while Dooley chatted up the waitress, impressing her with his Spanish.

"Hey, you come back at closing time, you score tonight, man," said Roy with a grin as they left.

"Not my type," said Dooley. He was in a strange mood tonight, confused. He missed Mexico, but he was glad to be home. For the first time in a long time he missed Consuelo, badly. "So who's beeping you?" he said.

Roy didn't answer till he was unlocking the car. "Maybe a break. I think somebody's ready to talk."

Roy started the car and swung out into traffic. "Which case we talking about?" said Dooley.

"We had a Spanish Cobra go down a couple of weeks ago. Nobody saw it except the girlfriend, and she was scared to death. We left a card with her and I think this is her."

"I thought you said it was a guy."

Roy flapped a hand. "She lives with her uncle or something. We were hoping he'd lean on her a bit, get her to open up. That's what I meant."

"Huh. Sounds like a handle-with-care."

"Yeah." Roy pulled to the curb at the El station, something cops can get away with, and went inside. Two minutes later he was back. "It's her, all right." He started the car. "Listen, you mind if I drop you off at my place? I think I'd better handle this by myself. She just might talk to me or Tommy, but I don't know about somebody she's never seen, you know?"

Dooley felt a sharp pang of jealousy. He was out of it, long gone, an outsider now. "Sure. You got beer at home?"

"I don't know. Want to stop and get some?"

"No, you better get going."

Dooley stood at the curb in front of Roy's building and watched Roy's taillights recede up the block. He had his car keys out before they went around the corner, asking himself if Roy had ever seen the Nova. He had never pointed it out to him, and he decided it was a good bet Roy wouldn't recognize it in the mirror. Dooley jogged to the car and fired it up. He peeled out of the parking space and hauled ass up toward where Roy had turned.

It wasn't just the confusion over whether it was a man or a woman calling. For two days they had talked like old partners about every case Roy was working on, and now suddenly Roy was playing it close to the vest. Maybe most of all it was that notebook up in Roy's place.

Dooley wheeled west, heading for Ashland, looking for the characteristic taillights of Roy's Grand Prix. If he missed which way Roy went on Ashland, it was all over. He had caught a break and the light at Ashland was red; as it went green Dooley drew in range to see the Grand Prix go left, turn signal flashing.

Dooley stayed a block or two back; Ashland was straight and wide and there wasn't much traffic. Roy was heading south, the direction you'd expect him to head if he was going to find a Puerto Rican girl whose boyfriend had been a Spanish Cobra, and Dooley thought for a moment that everything was all right and Roy was doing exactly what he had said he was doing.

Roy turned west on North Avenue, heading for Humboldt Park

and the PR gang badlands, and Dooley started to relax and think about other ways of spending the evening. He could hit Kathleen's again; something domestic was starting to sound real good. Scrabble, hearts, tell Bob and the kids some war stories. Work on the bottle of Jameson's a little.

Roy turned into the parking lot of a Pizza Hut at North and Western, and Dooley figured that was it; this was frontier territory, far enough east that no gang-bangers were likely to happen by and see something they shouldn't but not too far to make a scared girl travel. Dooley put on his right turn signal and slowed to turn onto Western, seeing Roy's car backing into a slot in the far corner of the lot as he passed. He made the turn and looked again as he went north, seeing Roy's headlights go off.

Dooley wasn't sure why he flicked on his turn signal again as he approached the first street north; it was not a conscious decision. He was halfway into the turn before he wondered what he was doing, and then the answer was that after all the man was his partner and things could go wrong and a little discreet backup was just good sense.

Or maybe, at that, it was just that little throb of suspicion.

Spanos backed into a parking space in the back corner of the lot where he could see whoever pulled in and whoever went past on either North or Western. He turned off the ignition and waited. He looked at the restaurant, which wasn't exactly breaking records; the lot was mostly empty. Spanos hated pizza; he hated cheap franchise places. He liked menus in leather covers, nice china, muted lighting, good service. Places like this reminded him of growing up, being young and stupid. He checked his watch and looked toward the street.

The cop didn't keep him waiting; Spanos generally found that people were pretty good about not making him wait. The cop's

Grand Prix came off North, cruised slowly toward him and parked one slot away. After a minute or so the big cop got out of his car and came ambling toward Spanos's Stratus. Spanos unlocked the door and the cop got in.

He didn't look any happier than usual but Spanos was used to people with an attitude; he spent his life dealing with attitudes of one sort or another. The cop gave him that look of just-suppressed hostility and said, "A Pizza Hut. Jesus, I thought you guys went in for places a little higher up the scale."

"Are you clean?"

"Fuck no, I'm not clean. I'm sitting here with you, ain't I?"

"I mean did anyone follow you."

"I know what you mean. Nobody followed me."

"You're careful about that, are you? I mean, I'd hate to think there could be a rumor going around about you and me."

"Don't worry about it. What do you want?"

Spanos got out a cigarette. The cop didn't smoke and Spanos enjoyed making him sit there and wait while he lit up. "I need a favor, Roy."

"Yeah, I figured. I didn't think you called me out here to sell me a car."

Spanos blew smoke at him. "What kind of access do you have to other guys' cases?"

"What do you mean?"

"I mean do you have access to evidence in cases being handled by other detectives?"

"Whoa, hang on a second."

"Don't panic."

"Listen, I'll do you some kinds of favors. I'll run a plate or whatever, but I'm not gonna fuck with evidence."

Spanos gave him a long look in the half-light coming across the parking lot from the restaurant. Spanos was not intimidated by policemen and had not been ever since his father had explained the facts of life to him, many years before. Policemen are just like you and me, Peter Spanos had told his son, except if they hit you they have to explain it to somebody. "How much money do you owe me?" Spanos said.

"A little over thirteen grand now."

"Plus the juice. Don't forget the juice."

"You'll get it."

"The way it's adding up? I doubt it. The juice on fifteen grand is three thousand a week."

The cop just blinked at him. "That's the way it's gonna be now, huh?"

"It doesn't have to be. Let's talk about options."

"OK. I can pay you off next week."

"Wow. You can raise sixty thousand dollars in a week?" It was a stare-down now, and Spanos always won those.

"You said at the start, don't worry about the juice."

"That was on the understanding that you helped me out once in a while."

When the cop looked out the windshield it was over. "There are limits to what I can do."

"OK, I understand that. What I need is pretty simple."

"I can't tamper with evidence."

"I don't need you to tamper with it. I just need for a small piece of it to disappear."

The cop laughed. "Oh, man. That's all you need, is it?"

"Look, you're a detective. Don't tell me you can't pull a few strings."

"Jesus."

"They store the evidence someplace, right? And you can get in there because you're a detective, right?"

"God, that would be . . . shit, you don't know what you're asking."

"Yes, I do. Listen, there was a guy got clipped the other day, up on Touhy Avenue."

"Christ, did you do that?"

"No, I didn't fucking do that. The guy was a friend of mine."

"Oh, I know. That means a lot in your line of work."

"Just listen. I ain't asking you to do anything that would fuck up the investigation. I wouldn't ask you to do that."

"No, of course not." The cop laughed.

"But the guy had a notebook on him. A little blue notebook. And what's in that notebook could fuck me up royal. That's what I need. I need you to get that notebook."

"What's in it?"

"Numbers. Names and numbers. All the fucking guy's records. This guy was Angelo Casalegno's accountant, right? And I'm connected to one of Casalegno's guys. Can you understand what I'm saying? It won't mean anything to you or anybody else. Unless they put it together with other things, break the code or whatever, and then I'm in deep shit, because I'm one of the code names in there. Me and a bunch of other guys. Now they don't need the fucking book to find out who whacked him. They'll find that out in a couple of days, and I could give them a name or two if you wanna know the truth. But man, I'd hate for them to get interested in that notebook."

He let the cop work on it, staring out the windshield. "That's a tough one," said the cop finally.

"Well, look. If you can't handle it, I understand. I'm sorry I wasted your time." Spanos reached for the key and turned on the ignition. "See you around, Roy."

The cop didn't move. After a few seconds he said, "What if I can't do it?"

"Well, then we start working out a payment plan, I'm afraid. Unless you really can raise sixty grand in a week."

"And what if I tell you to go fuck yourself?"

Spanos sighed. "You could do that, sure. Go ahead. But then your life gets a lot harder. Then I have to turn you over to a collector. And the collectors I work with, they don't have to follow rules. They'll be at your house, on your doorstep day and night, and they don't take no for an answer. And you're not going to be a position to complain to anybody because you're already dirty. You don't want to throw your career down the toilet and maybe go to jail. That how you want to do it?"

The engine idled; Spanos waited. Finally the cop said, "How do I recognize this notebook?"

Dooley had been lucky with alleys, finding one that ran into the fence around the Pizza Hut parking lot. A tangle of weeds and a single ambitious sapling grew along the fence. The leaves of the young tree made good cover for Dooley as he stood with his head just above the fence, twenty feet from Roy's car. The first thing he had seen was that Roy's car was empty, and he didn't like that. The custom was, you wanted to talk to someone, they came and sat in your car.

In a car near Roy's, Dooley could see two figures, and the one on the passenger side looked a lot like Roy. He had been hoping for a Puerto Rican girl in the driver's seat but this was a man. Dooley stood and looked at them, feeling things go sour. They were talking and the man in the driver's seat was watching the street, but neither of them seemed particularly alert to the alley behind them. Dooley had been a cop and he was used to looking at license plates, so he memorized the number on this one; they were dealer plates on a new-looking Dodge Stratus. He could just make out the logo of a well-known Dodge dealer in the suburbs. All he could see of the man at the wheel was a good head of hair and broad shoulders.

Dooley watched until Roy got out of the Stratus, which pulled out immediately and went west on North Avenue. He ducked down below the fence and listened as Roy went back to his car. He could have called to him, told him in a normal tone of voice that he'd seen everything. Instead he stood with his hands on his knees, stock-still, until Roy started the car. Then he watched the Grand Prix pull out and go back east.

Dooley thought for a second about trying to follow the Stratus, but he figured the guy had too much of a head start. Dooley didn't worry much about it; he'd seen enough.

7

DOOLEY LOOKED UP THE NUMBER OF THE DODGE DEALERSHIP OUT IN Elmhurst and picked up the phone. He identified himself as an Officer Francis Dooley from Central Auto Theft. "We had a call on an abandoned vehicle last night, sitting out in the middle of nowhere, near the railroad yards south of Grand Avenue. Turns out it's one of yours." Dooley read the plate number. "You missing one?"

"Shit, I don't think so." The salesman sounded like a ripe case of bronchitis. "Can you wait a minute?" Dooley waited at least five, leaning on the window frame with the phone to his ear, watching leaves fall, hearing asses being covered out in Elmhurst. "Ah, yeah, hello? That car is kind of like on loan to one of our salesmen right now. Has he reported it stolen?"

"Not as far as I know. Is he there?"

"No, see, he's a, he's a part-timer. He ain't here much. I mean he ain't here today, anyway. Do you have the car?"

"No, it wasn't there when we checked and we haven't gotten a call on it. As far as I know everything's kosher, but I thought I ought to check with you. I mean, cars do go missing from dealers."

"Ah, yeah, thanks. Jeez, I don't know what he woulda been doing over there."

"Who knows? Maybe he needed to take a leak and he was a long way from a bathroom. Look, why don't you just give him a call, make sure everything's OK?"

"Yeah, yeah, OK, I'll do that."

"And I'll need his name. Just for the record."

"Can you run a guy for me?" said Dooley.

He almost could hear Kevin frown over the phone. "What the hell are you up to?"

"I'm doing a favor for an old friend."

"Who would that be?"

"Nobody you know. It's this woman I met through Consuelo, part of that crowd. She's hanging out with a guy but she's starting to wonder about him. I told her I'd find out if he has a record."

"Jesus Christ. You haven't even been back a week, you know that?"

"I can't help it. People ask me for help, I say yes. She's worried, she thinks the guy may be a little crooked."

There was a brief silence. "I'll get back to you," said Kevin. "But listen."

"What?"

"You're not gonna do anything foolish, are you?"

"Gimme a break, Kevin," said Dooley. "What am I gonna do, shoot the guy?"

"Heat," said Vincent Bonifazio. "The heat's gonna be fucking unbelievable."

"No way around it." Spanos couldn't look at Bonifazio; he took another sip of vodka and concentrated on not backhanding the little greaser off the bar stool.

"See, that's why we gave it to you instead of one of Angelo's people. All his guys made sure to have alibis you couldn't break with a fucking sledgehammer. If you didn't go and leave your fucking note-book, they never woulda got it straightened out."

"They still won't. It'll be taken care of. Don't worry about it."

"You better be right, that's all I got to say. *Gimme another scotch here, will ya?* I'm telling you Johnny, we had it made until this asshole goes and gets himself indicted. Some genius. I fucking told Angelo, watch what this Jew does with your money. Now it's all gonna splash back on him."

"It's the risks of the game."

"Things have been quiet for a long time. They'll go apeshit now, with this."

"I know."

"Fucking Angelo. He couldn't be happy with what he had. Him and his fucking schemes. I told him, I says if it ain't green paper I can hold in my hand I don't want nothing to do with it."

"He wanted to make money."

"He was making money. What the hell, you know what Angelo was pulling down, just from the books, the games? Gambling and juice, that's all you fucking need in this world to get along. Spend the money to get what you need and keep some in a suitcase in case of emergencies. I told him, this bullshit with investment companies, off-shore banks, all the stuff this hebe was into, who the fuck needs it?"

"Let me just say, Vince, I understand what Angelo was thinking. You can see how the world's going, can't you?"

"The world's going fine."

"I mean, where's the big money?"

"Don't start with that."

"I'm just saying, where's the fucking money? Who's buying governments these days? It ain't us. There are Colombians rich enough to afford a fleet of 747s. The fucking Gangster Disciples have their own political party now, for Christ's sake."

"Don't get me started. Joe Batters had it right."

"Accardo's dead. And it ain't just the zips that's into drugs, and you know it."

"I don't give a fuck. Long as I'm here, we don't touch that fucking shit. Taking the tax, that's one thing. That's one thing we *will* do, I guarantee you, any motherfucker comes into these streets. Getting into it ourselves, that's another."

Spanos shook his head; trying to tell Italians which end was up was making him old. "This thing's about money, and that's where the money is now."

"You don't have enough money? How much do you need? Your kids don't have shoes? You don't have enough to eat? You can't afford the broads you want?"

"Vince." Spanos held up a hand. Bonifazio was giving him that wide-eyed pre-eruption look. "I got ambition, that's all. You wanna make a nice little living or you wanna put the Outfit back where it used to be?"

"The Outfit's fine."

"Right now the Outfit is a fucking myth."

"Bullshit."

"It's two dozen Italian guys trying to live up to a movie they saw once."

"You watch your mouth."

"Vince, I'm telling you the truth and you know it. Hell, you're not even collecting the tax where you should be. You know how many bookies are out there these days, making money at your expense?"

"I told you, anybody you find, you put the arm on 'em."

"I'm working on it. But we're still talking chickenshit. If you and Angelo and everyone else was serious about making money, you'd be talking with the Colombians or the Mexicans about supplies and the GDs about territory and you'd be looking for another guy like Herbie Blumberg to tell you where to put all the fucking money. The world's different now."

Bonifazio gave him a sour look. "You remember who brought you up," he said. "If it hadn't been that your old man was a friend of mine, you'd be pouring ouzo and saying *Opaa!* in some fucking joint down on Halsted Street."

"Vince. Do I earn OK for you?"

"You do OK."

"Have I ever crossed you? In any way?"

"Not yet. Don't start now."

"I just think I've earned the right to express an opinion, that's all. I'm just telling you what I see."

Bonifazio sucked down scotch and thumped the glass onto the bar. "All right, Johnny, I hear you. But you gotta think about the heat, too. You wanna get into that stuff, you'll have the fucking G in your face day and night. "

"I know that. I'm just saying there's possibilities there, there's money to be made."

"Let me tell you something. I ain't gonna do no more time. I don't care what, I ain't going back to jail. You wanna change things, you wait till I'm gone. I don't have that many years left. Till then I'm the fucking boss, you understand?"

"I got you, Vince."

"Just don't do nothing to piss me off. We got a good thing going."

Spanos clinked his glass against Bonifazio's, lips clamped shut. "Here's to it," he said.

Roy got in late, racking up overtime again. Dooley had had dinner at Kathleen's, told a few yarns, left before the bottle of Jameson's came down off the refrigerator. When Roy plunked his holstered 9mm down on the coffee table and sank onto the couch, Dooley was there with a beer to shove into his hand.

"Ah, bless you. I knew you'd come in handy."

"I got in another couple of six-packs and some microwave dinners."

"Thanks, man, I already ate. This'll do me." Roy took a deep pull on the bottle.

"Any fun today?"

"Nah. The usual bullshit. Guy raped his former girlfriend in his car, with her two-year-old in there with 'em."

"That'll be fun. Put the kid on the stand."

"Yeah. She probably knows all the right words."

Dooley wandered to the window, scanned the street. He was starting to get to know the neighbors by now, who had what car parked down there. Roy was in a foul mood and Dooley decided maybe it wasn't the time to bring up what he'd spent all day thinking about.

"What's the matter with you?" said Roy.

Fuck it, here goes, thought Dooley. He turned to face Roy. "I ain't gonna bullshit you," he said. "I'm worried about you."

Roy looked startled for three seconds and then his face settled into the old cocky defiant mode. "For what?"

Dooley paced, coming back across the polished wood floor, his beer dangling at his side, placing his feet carefully. "It wasn't like I had to snoop too hard," he said.

"What the fuck are you talking about?" said Roy, and looking at him Dooley could tell he knew.

"You owed some bookie a shitload of money. You paid most of it off, and I don't know where a cop gets that kind of money. But I can guess."

Roy stared for a moment, then turned his face away, eyes narrowing in disgust. Suddenly he was up off the couch, lurching away from Dooley. "Fuck, man, you been going through my stuff?"

"Yeah. And I didn't need a fine tooth comb either. You're not only a shitty gambler, you're careless too."

"Aw, fuck you!" The bottle came spinning out of Roy's hand, spewing beer, sailed a couple of feet wide of Dooley and crashed against the base of the wall under the windows. There was a gentle fizzing noise as beer leaked onto the floor. Roy was leaning against the frame of the door into the hallway. "Some friend," he said.

Dooley hadn't moved. "If I wasn't your friend," he said quietly, "Internal Affairs would know all about it by now. Nothing I found out has gone out of this room."

"I can't believe you went through my stuff, you prick."

"It ain't exactly hidden, Einstein."

"So shit. So I lost some money on some ball games. Big fuckin' deal."

"Roy, I saw the notebook."

"You fuckin' weasel."

"You lost big time. You were in a hole the size of the Grand Canyon and then you paid it off."

Seconds went by. "I borrowed some money from my dad. And I quit gambling. It's under control. It scared me and I got it under control." Roy sounded whipped now, exhausted.

Dooley gave it a few seconds' thought and said, "OK, I'll buy that. Now set my mind at ease, I'm begging you. When you drove out North Avenue last night and sat in John Spanos's car, tell me it was for an undercover operation. Tell me that's why you had to lie about it. Tell me, make me feel better."

Roy was staring at him, frozen. "You son of a bitch."

"OK, I'm a son of a bitch and a prick. Let's see, did I miss anything? Oh yeah, I'm a weasel too. I'm also your fucking partner—and let me tell you, partner, it looks pretty bad."

"What'd you do, follow me?"

"You made it easy."

Roy shook his head. He went down the hallway to the kitchen and came back with a new beer. "You shouldn't have followed me. It's none of your business." The fire had gone out of Roy; he just looked beat. He went back to the couch and flopped on it.

Dooley eased down onto the armchair. "It's none of my business if you're some asshole off the street. But you're my partner."

"I was."

Dooley sat and watched him drink. After a while he said, "OK, it's an operation, a sting. I can keep my mouth shut. Like I said, it doesn't go out of this room."

"You had to talk to somebody to find out it was Spanos. Who knows?"

"Kevin ran the plate for me. I told him some bullshit. Your name never came up."

Roy finished half the bottle, never looking at Dooley, before he said, "OK, it's private business. I owe him money."

"The fifteen grand?"

"Yeah."

"That's a hell of a lot of money. What's he take every week?"

"Nothing. No juice. I pay off the principal as I can."

Dooley sat and let that sink in. "That's worse, isn't it?"

"Why is it worse?"

"Because he's taking the juice in favors, isn't he?"

Roy finished his beer, set it down on the table, and lapsed back onto the cushions, his eyes closed. "Look, Frank. You been away a while. You're out of it. It's my life, my problem. I'm dealing with it."

"Doing favors for a fucking loan shark is not dealing with it."

"Look, it's bullshit. Once in a while he asks me to look at a file, run a plate, whatever. Insignificant bullshit."

"Insignificant illegal bullshit."

"All right, for Christ's sake! It was a mistake, I know that. Look, I stall the guy, I jerk him around a lot. What I give him don't mean shit. Christ, you don't think I'd ever give him any real help, do you?"

"How the fuck can you know what kind of help you're giving him? How do you know what he's using the stuff you give him for?"

Roy rubbed his face with both hands. "I'm paying him off. Once I get back even, he's fuckin' history. I told him that."

"I'm sure he's lying awake at night worrying about that. You think he's ever going to let you get even? You know how those Outfit guys are."

"What Outfit? Spanos is a small-time bullshit hustler."

"He's got arrests for gambling and extortion. But he never did time. You gotta know he's connected."

"To what? The fuckin' Outfit's finished. The old guys are all dead or in jail. You been away, you don't know."

"The Outfit's never gonna be finished. I don't care who's in jail, there's always gonna be new people coming up."

"Yeah. And what do they do? Do they shoot children? Do they rape college girls? Do they beat old ladies to death for their purses? No. They run places where assholes like me can lose their money. I'm sorry, I'm a homicide dick. I got other things to worry about than what John Spanos does for a living. Shit, you're the one who was always saying how stupid the vice laws are."

Dooley nodded at him, slowly. "Yeah. But they're still laws. And you're still sworn to uphold them."

Roy was up off the couch again and back down the hallway to the kitchen. Dooley waited for him to come back but he heard a chair scrape across the linoleum and he decided it wasn't going to happen. He could hear Roy picking the bottle up, setting it down on the table. Dooley got up from the chair and went to his pile of belongings in the corner of the living room. He unzipped the black canvas grip that was his only luggage and pulled out handfuls of underwear and socks. He dug with his fingernails and took up the cardboard false bottom of the bag. He laid it aside and started pulling out his nest egg.

Dooley counted some of it off and then went down the long hallway into the kitchen. He dumped the stacks of hundred-dollar bills on the table. Roy sat there looking at it, the beer bottle halfway to his mouth. Finally he looked up at Dooley.

Dooley said, "There's fifteen thousand dollars. Now you can pay off Spanos. If he decides all of a sudden you owe him the juice, I don't know what you're going to do."

Roy set the bottle down on the table. "Put it away," he said quietly. "I won't take your money."

"You're a hell of a lot better off owing it to me than to John Spanos."

"It's my problem. And it's your money."

They stood there and looked at it for a while and then Dooley said, "OK, what are your other options? You go on like you are, which as far as I can see means you go on with a hook in your mouth till you or John Spanos dies. Or you try something smarter."

"Like what?" Roy's eyes were still on the money but his gaze was far away.

"You go to somebody and you say here's what's going on, I fucked up but I'm ready to try and make it right. Wear a wire, whatever. You sting Spanos. You nail him."

Time went by; Roy's eyes flicked up at Dooley at last. "Pick up your money, man."

"If you change your mind it'll still be there. I got nothing to spend it on."

"Put it away. I'm sorry I said all that shit."

Dooley began raking the bundles together. "That's OK. You're entitled."

"I'll fix it."

"I hope so." Dooley paused in the doorway, clutching bundles of hundreds to his chest. "And look, I'm the last man on earth that's gonna get moralistic on you. Believe me, I'm in a position to tell you: the most valuable thing you have is your integrity as a cop. Of all the things I threw away, that's the one I miss the most."

8

"IT'S LIKE ANY BUSINESS ON EARTH. YOU WANT TO MOVE UP, YOU GOTTA pay your dues. You start at the bottom of the ladder. You prove you can bring in the money. Then, by the time you're my age, you should start to have a little respectability, a little more responsibility, some more money. You start out with the shit jobs, the hard jobs, and you move up to giving them out to other people. Someday if you're good you have a big fucking house out in River Forest and all you do is talk on the phone and enjoy what the money buys you."

Spanos could see Terry eating it up, hunched over the table so as to hear him above the noise of the jukebox. Sometimes the kid seemed about six years old. Spanos lit a cigarette and offered the pack to Terry, who shook his head. "That's right, I forgot you're a clean liver. That's good. Keep it that way. Don't ruin your fucking health like I did."

"I wanted to ask you something," said Terry.

"What's that?"

"I wanted to know if I could get in on a book."

Spanos had known this was coming; he stalled for a few seconds, blowing smoke. "You know what Vince would say."

"Yeah. But Vince doesn't have to know about it."

"He promised your old man."

"My old man's a hypocrite."

"He wants you to do better than him. He wants you to finish school, do something good."

"There's nothing I could do that would bring in the money like what you do, what my old man did. Look, I know the business, I got some contacts. I could bring in the people. Give me a fifty-fifty deal to start with, see how I do. That's all I'm asking."

Spanos tapped ash off his cigarette and studied the kid for a second or two. "You want to think about it," he said. "I see you getting in deeper, I just want to tell you, maybe you should think about what you're doing."

Terry looked at him across the table, looking amused, incredulous, like every kid that ever ignored advice from his elders. "What are you telling me this for?" he said. "You're the one that keeps calling me, taking me on jobs."

"Yeah." Spanos shrugged. "That's right. You kind of got into it by accident, helping Sal with the phones and all, and then you came along that time with me and Bobby and you handled yourself real good and I've used that . . . ability you have. All I'm saying is, now that you've had a taste of it, it's maybe time to think, is this the way I wanna go?"

Terry drank beer and shook his head once, venting a little exhalation of laughter. "Hey, why the fuck not? It beats pouring coffee all day."

"Yeah, well, your ma might not be too happy."

"Well, she ain't gonna stop me."

"Look, Terry. All's I'm trying to say is, you can quit now. If you want to, you can get the fuck out and go back to school. And there's a lot to be said for that. The deeper in you get, the harder it is to quit."

Terry gave him that keen look across the table, the look that made Spanos think this was a kid who could go places if he wanted to. "You seem to like it OK."

Spanos shrugged. With great clarity suddenly he remembered his own fork in the road, the phone call coming into the frat house in

Urbana, his sister Maria sobbing over the line. He remembered
driving back up Interstate 57 in the middle of the night, thinking
about his old man and making that choice he didn't even know he'd
made until months later. "It's a living. It's money. But there's a price.
Your old man's paying it right now."

"I know. But he's standing up. I go see him, he tells me it's not so
tough."

"Don't kid yourself. What else is a father gonna tell his boy? It's
tough."

"You never did time. If you're smart enough you can avoid it."

Spanos waved a hand, modestly. "You gotta be lucky, too. I had my
share of breaks."

There was a brief silent standoff. Two blondes in tight jeans walked
down the bar and Spanos and Terry watched them go. Terry finished
his beer and said, "I mean it, John. I'd be good. I could really bring
it home."

Spanos watched the women disappear into the rest room and took
a drag on his cigarette. "I'll think about it," he said.

Dooley couldn't believe how much they charged him for a beer. The
bar was dark, decorated in a firehouse motif with red ceiling tiles
and fake gas lamps in wall sconces, with piano music tinkling aim-
lessly from hidden speakers. From his stool at the end of the bar he
could see Andrea working, not having to hustle too much now that
things had thinned out. She was dressed in a short black skirt and a
white blouse with a crimson bow tie and she didn't look at all bad.
She hadn't caught sight of him yet.

When she did, looking up from a check at the opposite end of the
bar, she froze for a couple of seconds and Dooley really wasn't sure if
she was irritated to see him or just surprised. He raised his beer in

greeting and then felt stupid and set it back down. She gave him a little smile then but went away to tend to business.

A minute or so later she was at his shoulder, tray in hand. "You're out kind of late, aren't you?"

"And without adult supervision, too."

It wasn't much of a witticism and she didn't laugh. "I'm assuming it wasn't just our reputation for fine cocktails that brought you out here."

He smiled. "No." He opened his mouth, flapped a hand and said, "I thought maybe quitting time might go a little easier if I was around."

She stiffened, just perceptibly. "I'm a big girl. That wasn't a cry for help when I said that."

"And this isn't a come-on. Look, I came out here because Roy and I kind of got into it tonight and I wasn't ready to go to bed yet and I needed someone to talk to."

Her mouth tightened a little. "What'd you do, have a fight?"

"Let's say words were exchanged."

"Let me guess. You lectured him about his gambling."

"Something like that."

Andrea just looked at him for a second or two before shaking her head. "I told you. I can't do anything about anything Roy does anymore."

"I know that. You don't want to talk about Roy, we won't."

I've got her totally confused now, Dooley thought. She looked around the bar, blinked at him a couple of times, and said, "Let me close out." He watched as she walked away.

Last call had come and gone; there were two tables still occupied but Dooley was alone at the bar. "We're closed," said the bartender, coming toward Dooley. Dooley had paid up and drunk about half his beer. He shoved the glass away. "I'm waiting for Andrea," he said.

The bartender was a tall middle-aged man with heavy black brows. "Not unless she says so."

"Fine. Ask her."

The barkeeper gave him a sullen look as he cleared the glass. When Andrea brought the last check over to close out, Dooley watched as he muttered something to her. Andrea nodded without looking up but it didn't make the sullen look go away. The last customers shuffled toward the door. Andrea said good night to the bartender and came past Dooley, saying, "I'll get my coat."

Dooley put on his jacket. A big shambling man in a suit peeled off from the group that was leaving and intercepted Andrea. Dooley couldn't hear what he said, but he could see Andrea shaking her head. He leaned back, elbows on the bar, and watched as the man reached out and caught her arm. Andrea looked down at his hand and tugged her arm free. The man leaned over her, lips working, swaying just a little. The man reached for her again.

Andrea shot Dooley a look. His reflexes said here we go, but he stifled them. He looked back at Andrea without moving. The drunk had hold of her arm again. Andrea snapped her eyes back to the drunk and stuck her free index finger in his face. Dooley couldn't hear what she said, but the drunk let go. Andrea wheeled and walked on and the drunk just reeled for a few seconds before he turned and saw Dooley looking at him.

"T'fuck are you looking at?" he said.

"You tell me," said Dooley.

The drunk came straight at Dooley with the look of a man using all his resources just to focus. "You want to go outside?" he said in a low moist rumble. He was a good six-four but past his prime, well into an ill-tended middle age. He had a rug on his head that had cost a lot of money but was still just a rug. Behind Dooley the bartender was making distant cleaning up noises.

Dooley shook his head. "You want to start something, you start it right here, friend. Go on, I'll give you one free shot." Dooley hadn't moved his elbows off the bar behind him. He looked up into the watering eyes and waited for a move.

Whatever the drunk saw in Dooley's face, it gave him second thoughts. He looked past Dooley to the bartender and back again. "You stay out of my fuckin' way," the drunk said, and reeled away.

Andrea came back, zipping up her coat, in time to see the drunk clip the doorpost on his way out. When Dooley joined her she said, "Well. Did I pass?"

"You passed. What the hell did you say to him?"

"I told him if he didn't let go of me I was going to rip off his toupee and throw it across the room. You have to know what their weak spots are."

"That's good."

They left the bar. The drunk had rejoined his friends, who were making drunk noises in the lobby. Dooley and Andrea walked past them and made for the exit. "Just out of curiosity," said Andrea.

"Yeah?"

"What would it have taken to make you step in?"

Dooley considered. "About three more seconds."

Outside was the parking lot and very brisk night air. Overhead a jet was lumbering in on a landing path toward O'Hare, lights flashing. Andrea stopped on the sidewalk. "Well, what now?"

"I don't know. Is there someplace we could go and get a cup of coffee? An all-night pancake house or something?"

"You're asking the wrong person. I don't usually hang out in this neighborhood. If you can call it a neighborhood."

Dooley felt foolish and Andrea was giving him no help with that expectant look. "I don't know. I just wanted to talk."

Her look softened. "OK, my car or yours?"

"Well, I've got a radio in mine."

"I've got CDs."

"Let's go for yours, then."

With Wynton Marsalis blowing softly in the background, they sat and watched planes take off and land. "I'm sorry," said Dooley. "I visualized something different."

"This is all right. I got used to cheap dates with Roy."

"No, I mean coming back. This whole visit. I thought I'd find—I don't know, I guess I thought everybody would be happy. Down there in Mexico I had an image of this big happy family that I could come back to."

"And instead we're all miserable. Sorry we let you down."

She was determined to make it hard for him, Dooley thought. "I guess what I mean is, I thought all the grief was behind me and I could come back and just soak up some happiness and stability. And instead I find you've got grief, too. And that doesn't seem fair. I thought I used up all the bad luck for all of us. And of course the first thing I want to do is fix everything, make it right so I can have that pretty picture I wanted down in Mexico."

"But that's not going to happen."

"No. I never said it was rational. I'm just explaining why I drove out here tonight. I guess I just want you to tell me we can get it back somehow. All the good times."

"We can't. All that's gone."

There was no answer to that, and they just sat and listened to the music for a while. Planes landed and took off; a drunk went wheeling out of the parking lot with a squeal of tires. Dooley put his hand on the door handle. "I'm sorry, Andrea. I don't know what the fuck I'm doing here."

She reached for his free hand. "It's all right." She gave his hand a squeeze.

"I'm lost. Maybe I should have stayed in Mexico."

"Don't give up on it yet."

Dooley squeezed back. "We'll see. I gotta get Roy straightened out."

She let go of his hand. "You want to tell me about it?"

"Not now. I know, his troubles aren't yours anymore. Look, I'll let you get home. Here I am hassling you like one of those drunks."

Andrea reached for the ignition key. "You want to have lunch tomorrow?"

Dooley was so surprised he just blinked at her. "Sure."

Andrea started the car. "I can recognize a cry for help when I hear one."

9

DOOLEY WAS WORKING ON HIS SECOND CUP OF COFFEE, LEAFING absently through the *Tribune* he'd brought in from the box on the corner, when the doorbell rang. He went up front and pressed the button to buzz open the door downstairs, and then opened the apartment door to listen to two sets of feet coming up the stairs.

He smiled when Bill McPeak came into sight on the landing. McPeak hadn't changed at all; he was still a wiry gray-haired bantam in a suit, the best dresser in the old Area Six and one of the best dicks. Behind him was a copper Dooley didn't recognize, a younger, larger and meaner-looking specimen with a mustache.

"Frank, good to see you." McPeak offered his hand but his smile was perfunctory, and suddenly Dooley's stomach was in free fall, because he could see this wasn't a social visit. "Roy treating you right?" said McPeak.

"Can't complain."

"This is Dave Tracy, my partner." McPeak flapped a hand at the young guy. "You can call him Dick—everybody else does."

"How you doin'?" Dooley shook a hand that felt like a boxing glove. "Make yourselves at home. Sorry about the mess. I just can't get Roy to do any housework, the lazy slut." Here we go, he was thinking. He went for the armchair, hoping his knees didn't give out before he got there.

McPeak sat on the couch, delicately hitching up his trouser legs. His partner took the other end. "Welcome home," said McPeak.

"Thanks. It's good to be back."

"Mexico, huh?"

"That's right." Manslaughter, Dooley thought. Plead guilty to manslaughter and see what kind of a mood the judge is in. He took a sip of coffee to cover a rush of stark terror.

"How was it down there?" said McPeak.

"It was interesting. Real interesting."

McPeak sat nodding vacantly. His partner was looking at Dooley with a totally blank expression. The silence went on three or four seconds but Dooley wasn't going to give them any help. McPeak said, "I'm sorry, Frank, but I have to ask you some questions."

"Go ahead." Dooley barely got the words out.

"It's about the day you left Chicago, eight years ago."

Dooley stiffened on the chair and his look went up to the far corner of the ceiling. He took in a deep breath, remembering in a flash that Roy had told him Roddy McShea had the Century Mall case. "That was a long time ago," he said.

"I know. But I'm sure you remember that day."

"Sure."

"I'm sorry, Frank, but I gotta ask. I want you to tell me what you did that day. Times and places. As much as you can remember."

Dooley closed his eyes briefly, trying to get back on an even keel. "I'll have to think."

"Take your time."

"Well, I had a flight out of O'Hare sometime in the early afternoon. I don't remember when, exactly."

"Two-forty."

"You checked, huh? That sounds right. I think I got out to the airport around one."

"What'd you do in the morning?"

"Packed."

"Leaving it a little late, weren't you?"

"I didn't take much stuff."

"Where'd you have lunch that day?"

"I skipped lunch."

"How'd you get out to the airport?"

"I took a taxi."

"I don't suppose you remember the number or the driver's name after eight years."

"You suppose right."

"So you got in the taxi around what, noon, twelve-thirty?"

"Something like that."

"What'd you do, call for it?"

"No. I picked it up on the street. On Western Avenue. Western and Bryn Mawr. Right by Rosehill Cemetery."

"You'd been in the cemetery?"

"Yeah. That's where my wife's buried."

McPeak nodded and said nothing. His partner shot him a brief look. McPeak stopped nodding and said, "How long would you say you were at the cemetery?"

"A couple of hours."

"Two hours?"

"About that."

"Did anyone see you there? Did you talk to anyone?"

Dooley closed his eyes again. It let him look as if he were trying to remember, and it excused him from looking at McPeak after the lie he had just told him. "Christ, that was eight years ago. My impression is that I saw some other people there, but no, I didn't talk to anybody." Shut up, Dooley told himself. Answer the questions and shut up.

"So you got to the cemetery around what, ten o'clock?"

"Something like that."

"How'd you get there?"

"Another taxi. I'd sold my car by then."

"And you went out and flagged down a second taxi around noon."

"As best I can remember, yeah."

"And you went directly to O'Hare and got on your plane."

"That's right."

McPeak nodded. He and Dick Tracy exchanged a look and then McPeak stood up abruptly. "OK, Frank. Like I say, I had to ask."

"That's it?"

"That's it." He moved toward the door, his partner following.

Dooley stood up. "You've got the file, huh?"

"I've got it."

Keep your mouth shut, Dooley could hear his inner voice screaming. He ignored it and said, "Well, as far as I'm concerned, whoever killed that son of a bitch did us all a favor."

"I can't say I disagree with you," said McPeak. "Good to have you back."

Dooley listened as they walked down the stairs. McPeak trod with the firm step of a man whose ass is now covered. Dooley stayed leaning in the open doorway for a long time, sparring with a conscience that was gaining strength as the fight dragged into the late rounds.

"Fuck this god damn machine." Roy Ferguson tore the botched report from the typewriter and flung it half crumpled at a wastebasket. He rooted in a drawer for a new form.

"You feel all right?" said Tommy Crane.

"I feel like shit," said Roy. "I ain't been right for days."

"Take a day off."

Roy fed the new form into the typewriter. "Nah. What am I gonna do, sit home and watch *Oprah*?"

"Well, if you feel bad, shit. The criminal justice system isn't gonna grind to a halt if you miss a couple of days."

"I'm OK. Listen, did you finish the Felony 101?"

"Yeah, it's right here."

"Then why don't you go ahead and get something to eat?"

"Hell, I'll wait for you."

"No, man. Go get something to eat. I'm not hungry."

Crane shrugged and stood up. "You sure you don't want me to bring you something?"

"No. Don't worry about it."

"Christ, you *are* sick."

When Crane had left, Roy stood up and went to the door of the Watch Commander's office, listening for voices coming from inside. He felt like a kid in school again, angling for a moment alone with a girl so he could ask her out. The door was open but the office was empty. Roy went in and sat on a vacant chair. He rubbed his eyes, let out a sigh, and waited.

Greg Douglas came through the door in shirtsleeves, looking harried and purposeful. "You look like you been called into the principal's office," he said, slapping a handful of papers onto the desk. "What'd you do, go off school grounds?"

"I gotta talk to you."

Something in Roy's tone or perhaps his look froze his boss for a second. "What's the problem?"

"The problem is, I'm an asshole."

A couple of beats went by and Douglas said, "You want to amplify that a little?"

Work it right and I can eat free for life, thought Dooley, pushing west on Peterson past Korean restaurants, medical offices, strip malls. Free eats and a free bed, how long can I stretch this little vacation? He was close to Kevin's house and he thought about Sunday coming up, how good it would be to sit on the couch in Kevin's basement just like old times, with beer and junk food to hand, watching the Bears, swearing at them. Where were they this week? He had read it in the paper but couldn't remember. He had stopped paying attention to the Bears eight years ago along with everything else.

The curtains were open at Andrea's house this time, and she answered the bell in a few seconds. Today her hair was pulled back in a ponytail, revealing the trim lines of her neck and jaw, and she looked scrubbed and cared-for in a cable-knit sweater and faded jeans. What had looked like the ravages of time a couple of days before looked like character today. "You like pesto?" she said. "I should have asked. Not everybody does."

"I like everything. I'm the easiest man in the world to feed." Dooley started to throw his jacket on the couch but then saw her reaching for it and smiled, sheepish. "It's been a while since I was in civilized company."

She had laid the table in the dining room, where a large window gave onto a backyard with a maple tree, an overgrown garden and a lot of weedy grass. "The yard looks like hell, I know," said Andrea. "It hasn't been a real priority with me."

"It's green," said Dooley. "Looks like heaven to me, after Mexico."

She had a Chianti to go with the pasta and a salad that had cleared the vegetable bins at the Jewel. Dooley had an Irishman's taste for wine; he could drink it when he had to. He watched Andrea bustling from the kitchen to the table and back again, sweating out the gaps in the small talk. Last night the invitation had sounded as natural as a good-night; now that he was here it felt too much like a date.

He told her all about Mexico; she was the first person he'd talked to who really seemed interested. "Didn't you have culture shock?" she said. "I went to Mexico once, on vacation. I had a good time, but it scared me, too. I couldn't talk to people, I couldn't make sense of half of what was going on around me. I really learned what the word *foreign* meant. I wanted to kiss the ground when I got back to O'Hare."

Dooley mused. "You weren't connected. I was plugged in from the start, with Consuelo's folks down there. Human roles are universal—dad, mom, brothers-in-law. The landlord, the guy at the newsstand, the boss. Those roles are a lot stronger than language differences and what kind of food people eat. Eight years can go by fast when you're into the life of a place. After a while that's all it was—just life. I forgot it was a foreign country. Most of the time, anyway. Sometimes it does hit you. And then you think about coming home."

He stared out the window for a while. The wine had given him a comfortable buzz and the silence didn't feel like a gap anymore. Finally Andrea said, "Made any decisions yet?"

Dooley shook his head. "As long as I can work the free lunches I don't have to."

She smiled at him over the rim of her wineglass and said, "How the hell did a nice Irish boy like you get hooked up with a Mexican anyway?"

"I met her down at UIC. Remember when I went back for the master's? I was gonna get the degree, move up the ladder, be a top cop or something. God knows what I was thinking. All I ever got out of it was this gorgeous Mexican girl I met in econ class."

Andrea set down the glass and her eyes went away out the window. "She *was* gorgeous."

"And she didn't hit you over the head with her identity. She was like, here I am, I was born in Mexico but I grew up on 18th Street and I'm comfortable with that. I'm more Mexican than half these Chicano nation blowhards but I've read the *Federalist Papers* too. I liked that. She even won over the family, eventually."

"What, they didn't like her?"

"They liked her OK. And they were perfectly decent to everybody at the wedding. But she wasn't Irish."

"That was a good wedding. We had fun."

"Yeah. When my family was tying itself in knots trying to be nice to her, you and Roy actually talked to her. That counted for a lot."

"I'll never forget the first time you brought her over to our place. Roy and I were rolling our eyes behind your back. You two had it bad."

"Yeah, we did." Dooley remembered. "That was a long time ago."

When the silence got a little heavy, Andrea went into the kitchen and got some coffee started. Dooley sat and listened to the noises she made and eventually roused himself to clear the table. When the coffee was made they sat at the kitchen table to drink it.

"So what happened to the master's degree?" Andrea said.

Dooley shrugged. "One, I made detective and decided I liked it. Roy had a lot to do with that. He was a great partner, a hell of a teacher. And the other thing was my brother. He had the street cop's contempt for the type of cop that waves degrees at people. For him, the only education you needed you got out on the street."

"So you let him talk you out of going for the degree?"

"He didn't have to talk me out of it. I just quit. It was a hell of a lot of work anyway." She just blinked at him and he knew she was waiting for the real reason. "Plus, Kevin's approval is important to me. That's why I've done everything I've done since I was about thirteen years old."

"You're kidding."

"No." Dooley set down his coffee cup and ran a hand through his beard. "You gotta understand, I had a couple of tough acts to follow. First there was our old man, a tough Irish cop from the old school. Michael Dooley, the famous Michael Dooley. A good cop and an honest one, and you didn't always assume that about a cop. We'd go down to the Emerald Society on St. Patrick's Day, and all the other cops would come up to us and tell us what a hell of a man our father was, what a great cop. A legend. And then there was Kevin. First he goes and joins the Marines and goes off to Vietnam and wins a Navy Cross. That's one step below a Congressional Medal of Honor. He was in the papers and everything, Kevin in his dress blues looking like God Himself. Then he gets back here and goes on the department and he's the old man all over again. Meanwhile, I'm the one with asthma who's being groomed to be a priest. Franny."

"That's what they called you?"

"I made 'em stop. Kathleen still calls me that sometimes. My mother always called me Francis. Everyone else I made go to Frank pretty early on. The priest thing, that lasted till about puberty."

"That'll do it, I guess."

"It did it for me. Since then, it's been pretty much, can I possibly live up to my old man and my brother?"

"Oh, my. The impossible goal."

"That's what Consuelo always said. And I would always say, thanks for the vote of confidence."

"And you're still trying?"

"Well, I think I blew it pretty thoroughly when I ran off to Mexico. Now I'm just picking up the pieces."

They worked on the coffee for a while. After a silence Andrea said, "I never understood why the guy walked."

"Fruit of the poisoned tree."

"What?"

"Any evidence resulting from an unjustified action is going to be thrown out. That's what they call it, the fruit of the poisoned tree. He was arrested for disorderly conduct in the hallway of his building, drunk on his ass. And he thought the officers who were arresting him had come to get him for killing Consuelo. So he babbled something like 'I never meant to hurt her.' The officers realized he fit the description and they got a little too eager. They went into his place without consent and found Consuelo's underwear. When Dickens sobered up, he shut up and asked for a lawyer. They charged him on the basis of his statement and the physical evidence. But the public defender got the search suppressed because they never read him his rights. Without the evidence, the State had no case. He walked."

"But that's ridiculous."

"That's the system. You have to work with it."

"No wonder you—" She stopped cold.

"No wonder I went off the deep end," said Dooley. He stared out at the trees, the ragged grass. "I found her. I came home late and found her in the bedroom. I remember standing there with my hand on the doorknob, seeing light under the door, thinking she was still awake, waiting up for me. I remember that very clearly as my last happy moment, on the other side of this enormous divide. I pushed the door open and everything changed."

"God," said Andrea softly.

"I had enough of the homicide cop there not to mess up the scene. I called it in and went and sat in the living room and looked out the window and waited for somebody to get there. Shock is a very useful thing in a situation like that. I don't have a real clear memory of what went through my mind. Except I remember thinking, somebody's going to pay."

Andrea said nothing for a while, and when Dooley looked at her she was staring out the window too, frowning faintly. She said, "I have the same thing with Sean, remembering that last moment before everything came crashing down. I waved to him. He was standing in waist-deep water, just splashing around with his cousins, and he looked at me, a hundred feet away, and waved. I waved back and he was smiling and the sun was shining on the water and I remember it as the most beautiful moment of my life, that last contact with my son. Five minutes later we noticed he wasn't in sight."

That pretty much killed the conversation. Andrea poured more coffee. "So tell me about Roy," she said finally.

Dooley told her. "I think he'll do the right thing," said Dooley. "He's a good cop."

Andrea stared at him with those big gray eyes. "Maybe that's why he wasn't such a good husband."

"It's a damn hard combination to pull off," said Dooley.

10

"STAY THE FUCK AWAY FROM INTERNAL AFFAIRS," SAID DOUGLAS.
"Those assholes will ruin your life. Besides, you haven't done anything wrong yet."

"No," said Roy, thinking of a couple of license plates he'd run.
"Not yet." Through the window of the office he could see his col-
leagues at work, typing, talking into telephones, drinking coffee.
More than anything in the world he wanted to be out there with
them instead of in here on the hot seat. He could see Tommy Crane
across the room hacking at the keyboard, stealing glances in the
direction of the closed door.

Bill Matic, the Commander of Area Three, shook his head, drag-
ging on a cigarette that had burned down to finger-singeing length.
"Still," he said. "Gotta cover our ass. You been consorting with
known criminals, making illegal bets. Gotta get a CR number and
hope for the best. If you really haven't done anything they could go
easy on you."

Desolate, Roy nodded. "You don't think we can just go out and
bust the son of a bitch for attempted bribery, huh?"

Matic shook his head. "Hell, no. They'll turn it right around on
you. Some mob mouthpiece gets up and holds a press conference
and the whole fucking world will know about your problem. 'This
supposed officer of the law ran up fifteen thousand dollars in gambling debts.' That what you wanna see on the news at ten o'clock?"

"So which way do we go?"

Matic shrugged, blew smoke. "We might be able to work something. We could try and flip the son of a bitch."

Douglas nodded. "Get him to hang himself."

Roy blinked at them for a moment. "Wire me up, huh?"

Matic stubbed out the cigarette. "That's it. You go back and stall, make him talk. I wanna know more about this notebook."

"Yeah, what's with that?" said Douglas. "The files don't say a god damn thing about any notebook."

"Beats the shit out of me," said Roy. "He was worried about it, though. He said the guy had to have it on him."

"OK. There you go. You talk to him, you get him to spell out why he needs this notebook so damn bad."

Roy nodded slowly through the pause. "First thing he's gonna ask when I call him is do I have it? He's not gonna waste time meeting with me if I don't."

Matic shrugged. "So you tell him you have it."

"And what do I do when I have to hand it over?"

"We can fake up a notebook, for Christ's sake. We buy a little blue notebook and write some bullshit in it. He'll say it's the wrong one but you tell him you did your best, that's the only notebook the guy had on him. That's how you get him talking—have him describe it in more detail, tell you more about what's in it."

Roy nodded some more; he wished he could stop nodding but things had taken on a certain amount of momentum and all he could do was agree. "OK."

"We're gonna have to get a consent to overhear. We'll go through the Feds. That'll be easier."

"You'll have to make a statement, Roy."

"OK."

"We'll go to OC on this. They do this all the time."

"And they've got the toys."

"Oh, yeah. We'll get you the latest toys, Roy."

"We can do that?"

"Hell yes, we can do that. I got good contacts in OC. We'll have to notify I.A.D. but I don't see any problem, really."

Roy sat and watched his superiors taking big chunks of his career, his life maybe, into their hands. Somewhere below his stomach was a place that ran cold at the thought of going back to talk to John Spanos with a wire on.

Plans made and clocks ticking, Matic and Douglas stood up. "Well, Roy," said Matic, "I can't say what you did was real smart, but you got balls to come to us with it."

"Yeah," said Douglas. "You did the right thing."

"I fucked up bad," said Roy, rising slowly to his feet. He felt hot and a little unsteady on his pins.

"We'll make it right," said Matic, slapping him on the arm. "We'll nail this piece of shit. And you'll come out lookin' like a fuckin' genius."

Roy shook his head; he felt like a dunce. He stiffened a little as Douglas opened the door to the office, sensing all the pairs of eyes that were snapping toward the sound. He saw Tommy Crane looking at him as he came back out into the room; suddenly and with a force that surprised him he wished that instead of Crane waiting for him with that carefully neutral look it was Frank Dooley sitting there smiling his fuck-it-all smile.

Mary's Irish stew: another thing Dooley had forgotten about but now wondered how he'd gone eight years without. Chunks of lamb, carrots and onions, peas and potatoes, gravy to banish hunger forever. Dooley was full but he wanted more. "When was the last time you ate?" said Kevin in wonderment.

Dooley shoved his bowl away with an effort of will. "Something this good, years. I mean it. Mary, they should give you a Nobel Prize."

"I think I may have an extra side of beef in the basement," she said, rising to clear the empty serving dish. "If you're still hungry." Dooley laughed. Colleen and Rose were smiling at him; God, he had pretty nieces. Dooley was feeling good about the world tonight.

"So what the hell are you going to do with yourself?" said Kevin, leaning back in patriarch mode, folding his napkin.

"Time to talk about my future, huh?"

"Well, you're a big boy now."

"Yeah, I guess I am." Dooley could see everyone was hanging on his answer suddenly, and his high spirits went *pop* like a balloon as he pictured them all talking about him when he wasn't around. Was Uncle Frank always like this, Dad? He could hear Kevin grousing about the food bill. "I don't know what I'm gonna do," he said, looking Kevin in the eye. "I'm waiting for inspiration. You want me to throw some money into the grocery fund, I'll be happy to."

Kevin waved off the idea with a disgusted look. "Hell with that. I'm just asking. I'm just wondering. You planning on staying in town?"

Dooley shrugged. He took a drink of beer and placed the bottle carefully on its coaster. "I'm telling you the truth when I say I don't know. I mean I honestly haven't given it a minute's thought. I told myself I'd take a little vacation before I made any decisions. Maybe my idea of *little* is too generous, I don't know."

"'Cause if you're back to stay, I could probably get you a job."

Dooley shrugged. "Wow. Reality rears its ugly head."

"An ex-cop is always gonna be able to find something in the security field. I got a few contacts here and there."

"There's a thought. I could be a rent-a-cop. Sport one of those attractive brown uniforms."

"Nah, I mean with a corporation or something. It's a big field. Remember Joe Clancy? He's in charge of security over at First National, downtown. Got a bunch of people under him, a big office, the whole thing. It's serious business. I could give him a call."

"I don't know. It's something to think about."

Mary returned from the kitchen, sat down and said, "My cousin Jack Walsh has a real estate agency down in Beverly. He's been after me to get a license—he says if you can pass the tests and have the gift of blarney you can make a lot of money."

"The blarney I can probably handle. The tests, I don't know."

"You could come and teach Spanish at Saint Scholastica," put in Rose, breathlessly. You speak it a lot better than this *hopeless* dweeb they have teaching us now."

"They'd want credentials," said Dooley. "And the words I know, they won't want me teaching to innocent young Catholic girls."

Silence reigned. Mary smiled and said, "Let's all gang up on Frank, why don't we?"

"I was just wondering what his plans were," said Kevin, in a faintly plaintive tone.

Dooley stared down the table at him, thoughtful. He was thinking of Roy, of Andrea, of problems personal and financial. "I don't have any plans," he said. "Give me till the end of the month."

"There's no time limit," said Kevin. The way he said it, with the inscrutable and unassailable air of authority he had inherited from their father, made it oddly clear that there was.

"Who wants dessert?" said Mary.

Somebody had wanted to gentrify the neighborhood, looking across the expressway at the ugly concrete sprawl of the university. They had turned a decrepit six-story warehouse on Van Buren into six stories of lofts and waited for the espresso shops and used bookstores to fill in the gaps between the university and Greek Town. They had sold all the lofts, but the cafés and bookstores were slow in coming. One of the lofts had been bought by a bond trader looking for an investment; when his natural urge to gamble fell on the fertile soil of the

Greek Town bars he began to frequent, he quickly found himself owing more money than he had thought possible to John Spanos. Recognizing a poorly hedged position and giving up on the gentrification, he had moved out of the loft but left the keys with Spanos by way of settling the debt.

It was Spanos's favorite venue. The developer had done a wonderful job on the lofts; this one had an ample bar, discreet lighting and low-slung comfortable furniture and a stunning view eastward to the sparkling nighttime skyline of the Loop. Spanos provided the cards, the dealer, the bank, the booze, a bartender and two silent watchful thugs for security. The gambling went on at what had been the dining room table, leaving the spacious living area for drinking, bemoaning fate and impressing women.

Women were never a prominent feature of the scene, as gamblers tend to have time for only one vice at a time, but there were occasional hangers-on, mostly women in tow behind men who couldn't resist showing off the latest acquisition, be it automotive, sartorial or sexual.

Spanos controlled admission, seats at the table, credit. He smoked and sipped seltzer water and ruled with a nod or a raised finger, yes or no beyond appeal. He ran a tight ship and a game that was widely reputed to be clean. The best measure of his entrepreneurial skill and the mechanical skill of his dealers was the fact that it was not.

Tonight Spanos was tempted to slip something high-octane into his seltzer water. There were too many potential headaches tonight, with both Time Bomb Joe Delvecchio and Angelo Casalegno himself gambling in the dining room. Time Bomb Joe had earned the nickname not for any skill he had with explosives but for his violent and completely unpredictable temper. When Joe Delvecchio lost too much or was kept waiting too long or didn't quite like the strength of his drink, he had a way of blowing up in your face. Spanos would have loved to ban him from the game, but Delvecchio was too high up in Tommy Salerno's crew; you didn't do that.

Casalegno had sent an emissary earlier in the day to say he was coming. Spanos had wondered why; when Angelo Casalegno went visiting there was always a reason. On top of all his other anxieties, this one was giving him a bad case of in-flight stomach. Casalegno had showed up with three outriders, the usual aging toughs with sour looks and expensive shoes. For once Spanos was glad to have women there; there were three of them, all of them decent-looking, grouped in quiet and disciplined boredom around a coffee table in front of the east window with the view. Casalegno had spotted them and spent two minutes in clumsy septuagenarian lechery before proceeding to the table, where he had been for the past twenty minutes. Spanos had had a quiet word with Sammy Piccolo, his dealer, alerting him to the need for Angelo Casalegno to avoid losing too much. So far Casalegno looked and sounded happy.

Out in the living room, his attendants had moved in on the women and a party atmosphere was beginning to take hold; only a single disappointed gambler was there to spoil the mood, slumped back in an armchair with a glass clutched in his hand, contemplating his losses with a look of inner concentration.

Spanos had gone to the bar for more water when there was a scraping of chairs in the dining area. Spanos suppressed a faint feeling of alarm and went in to see Casalegno on his feet, folding a roll of bills away into a pocket. Sammy was leaning back on his chair, looking like a pilot who has just landed a crippled 747. Joe Delvecchio was smoking furiously, tapping the edge of a blue chip nervously on the table. "John," said Casalegno, extending a hand. "Gotta run."

Spanos hid his relief. "You just got here."

"Busy night, places to go." Casalegno had white hair, a lot of loose skin under his jaw, and enormous glasses; he looked like a near-sighted frog. "Thanks for the game. I did OK."

"Glad to hear it."

One of Casalegno's men handed him a glass full of scotch and ice. "Hell of a nice place. Jesus Christ, would you look at that view? How'd you get a hold of this place?"

"Friend of a friend, you know the kind of thing."

"I like it." Casalegno clamped onto Spanos's arm with his free hand. "Listen up." Heads turned. "I got a toast for my good friend Johnny Spanos here." He raised his glass. "To the man that runs the best god damn card game in town. And one very bad dude. We'll make him an honorary Italian, huh, Tony? Huh, Joe? Here's to ya." Casalegno drank while others groped for their glasses.

Spanos grinned in discomfort. He understood now. This was the blessing, the touch of royalty, such as it was in an Outfit where all the genuine royalty was dead or in jail; this was the whole reason for Casalegno's visit. This was what ten minutes' work in a North Side alley had gotten him: status. Spanos raised his glass and clinked against the old man's. "Thanks for the kind words."

Casalegno took his leave of the women, lingering over the youngest, a frizzy-headed brunette with legs that went all the way up and disappeared under a short and very tight blue skirt. "Stacy, you got a wonderful pair of limbs there. Good-bye, ladies."

The gambling had resumed by the time Casalegno slipped out with his people. Spanos went and stood at the window for a moment, looking at the city and feeling his stomach calm down. When he went in to watch the game he had the impression people looked up at him with just a touch of something that hadn't been there before. Spanos had no idea how much they knew of the reason for his favor with Casalegno; not much, he hoped. But he could tell that word was starting to get around.

At three the party began to break up. Men came shambling out of the dining area, smelling of smoke and liquor. The bartender poured a couple of nightcaps. Spanos went in to confer with Sammy, make a quick estimate of the take. "Pretty good night," said Sammy softly, squaring the edges of a stack of bills.

Out in the living room somebody was shouting. *"Nobody asked your fucking opinion, bitch!"* Spanos and Sammy traded one tense look.

"I been waiting all night for him to blow," said Sammy.

"Son of a bitch," said Spanos, pushing away from the table.

When Spanos got to the living room Delvecchio had Stacy by the hair, fingers entwined in the frizzy brown locks. Her face was twisted in pain and she was half bent over, trying to ease the strain on her scalp. *"When I want your wise-ass comments I'll ask for 'em!"* Delvecchio screamed in her ear.

"I was just trying to be sympathetic," said Stacy in a panicked squeal, eyes squeezed shut. "Let go of my *hair*."

Spanos's two guys were looking at him, waiting for a word; they were there to maintain order but this was a heavy guy and this was his woman. Only a couple of gamblers were left; Nick Pappachristides was leaning on the bar with a drink in his hand, peering at the scene as if he couldn't quite figure out what was going on; next to him a woman was watching in horror.

"You got a big fucking mouth!" shouted Delvecchio, bending the girl nearly double. Spanos crossed the room in six quick steps.

"Let go of her," he said.

Delvecchio looked up at him in surprise. "Stay the fuck out of this," he said. He was a middle-aged rake with heavy black eyebrows, a man aging gracelessly. He gave Stacy's head a shake and she sank to her knees.

"I said let go of her." Spanos had talked Time Bomb Joe down from the heights of his rage on more than one occasion, but it was a process that required time, patience and skill. Tonight he didn't feel like making the effort. "Get your fingers out of her hair or I'll break 'em off."

Delvecchio couldn't believe what he was hearing; people didn't talk to him this way. For a moment his face lit up with the joy of the impending fight; Delvecchio was long accustomed to winning because they were always rigged in his favor. Then steps sounded softly behind Spanos and Delvecchio's eyes flicked over his shoulder, and suddenly Spanos could see Joe Delvecchio remembering Angelo Casalegno's visit, remembering who he was dealing with now. "Let go of her," Spanos said again.

Delvecchio looked at him, chin raised, all the venom focused on him now. The light was still there in his eyes but it was going. "Hot shit," he said, and let go of the girl's hair. She sagged and stifled a sob, and Delvecchio rose to his full height. "You think you're hot shit now, huh?"

"Get out of my fucking house and don't come back," said Spanos. "Until you learn how to treat people."

Delvecchio jabbed a finger at him. "You," he said. "You wanna be careful from now on. I'm telling you." He took a step, looked down at the girl. "You, *putana*. You can't even suck a prick right. You're worthless." Delvecchio spat, incompetently, sending a little spray of saliva onto her. Then he stalked away. "Where's my fucking coat?"

George threw the coat at him and saw him out like a zookeeper herding a rhino. Within two minutes everyone had vanished except the employees and Stacy, who was sitting on the couch sniffling and rubbing her scalp, knees demurely together. Spanos brought her a glass of seltzer water. "Thank you," she said. "I don't know what I did wrong."

"You took up with him," said Spanos, sitting across from her.

"He was nice at first."

"He's got a temper. You don't need that."

Stacy looked at him, huge brown eyes still moist, brimming with gratitude and helplessness. "I don't know how I'm going to get home now."

"I'll take you." Spanos reached out and patted one perfect knee.

"Hang on a minute." He got up and went and had a quiet word with Sammy. He took the briefcase Sammy handed him and went back into the living room. Denny the bartender was busily gathering glasses; he and the younger muscle would clean up and close the place down. George was standing by the door, expressionless. Spanos went and got his coat and Stacy's. "Where do you live?"

"Barrington. It's a long way."

"Don't worry about it."

George led the way to the elevator. Stacy tottered a bit on her high heels, wrapped in a fur. In the elevator Spanos smiled at her. "You Italian, Stacy?"

She sniffed, smiled and said, "No. Actually I'm half Irish and half Polish."

"Well, you wanna stay away from those Italian guys from now on, I guess." He traded a look with George and they both laughed.

"My mother warned me," said Stacy.

"Listen to your mother," said Spanos.

The street was deserted; the muted roar from the expressway filled the night. George walked ahead of them toward Spanos's car, scanning shadows, hands in his jacket pockets. Spanos didn't expect any trouble but this was what he paid George for. At the car he thanked George and tossed the briefcase on the backseat. Pulling away from the curb, he shot a look at Stacy's profile. "Feeling OK?"

"Yeah. I don't know how to thank you."

"No thanks needed." Spanos steered down Jackson toward the entrance ramp to the Kennedy. He reached for Stacy's hand in her lap, felt it close around his. "Like you say, Barrington's a long way off. Wanna come home with me tonight?"

She only hesitated for a second. "Sure. I'd like that."

Spanos breezed over the bridge above the expressway, heading east. "I got a place on Lake Shore Drive."

"Oh, really? God, I bet it's nice."

Spanos was thinking about the last thing Delvecchio had said to the girl; now he was going to find out if it was true.

This, thought John Spanos, is power.

Roy had a bar he liked, a little neighborhood tap on Southport a few blocks from his place. Nobody had bothered to redecorate the place since about the time Truman was losing to Dewey, and it looked as if most of the people hunched over the bar had been there to be taken in by the headline. It was not too dark and not too smoky and not too geriatric but just enough of each to keep out anybody who was likely to disturb the peace by having too much fun. "I guess I'm getting old," said Roy. "I'm starting to feel at home in places like this." They were at the end of the bar where it curved to the wall, facing the door. The bar was something to lean on in an uncertain world, a massive length of dark polished wood glowing with the sheen of thousands of nights' worth of spilled shots.

"I'm surprised they let you drink here," Dooley said.

"I'm on probation. Another two years and I get jukebox privileges."

"They know you're a cop?"

"Not so far. I'm hoping to keep it that way. I like it here. Nothing ever happens." Roy was playing with his change on the bar, stacking it and spreading it out again with a look of ferocious concentration. "I quit going to the other place."

"What place?"

"The place where I gambled. Place called Duke's, out on Irving Park. I don't even remember why I started going there. Somebody took me, I can't even remember who. After Sean died I did a lot of stupid shit for a while, hanging out with a bunch of lowlifes from the old neighborhood. Anyway, I started gambling a lot, hanging out with these jerks."

"You fell in with bad companions, huh?"

"Oldest story in the book, me and Pinocchio. I'm lucky I didn't turn into a fuckin' jackass. Although I guess maybe I did."

"Shit, we've all been there."

Roy took a drink of beer. "I hated to go home. I couldn't face Andrea. And it got so I couldn't face people at Flanigan's either. I couldn't take the sympathy, you know?"

"I know. That look on their faces. You want to tell them, Look, I'm not gonna cry, so could we just get on with things?"

"Yeah. Out there at Duke's, nobody gave a shit. I guess that's what I needed. Sit someplace and drink, forget all about everything. Put a few bucks down on a game, just for the hell of it. And then you make a big score when the Bears pull one out of their ass and you can't wait to get some money down on the next one."

Dooley drank and said, "They're running this operation—what, right there over the bar?"

Roy shook his head. "The small-time stuff, informal friendly bets. But after I'd bet a few times with the bartender, a sawbuck here or there, he says if I'm interested in bigger action he can give me a phone number. And all my buddies are going, 'Yeah, you can really make some money if you call this guy.' Assholes. They'd make a thousand one week, drop two thousand the next. But I picked up the phone."

"And that was Spanos?"

"No. Not yet. That was just a wire room. I mean, I'm sure it was *his* wire room, but I never saw him. There were a couple of guys who would come around to the bar to pay up if you won, call you if you lost, set up a time to collect. I always dealt with them. Spanos didn't start coming around until I was losing big. He could smell the juice, see."

"Uh-huh."

"Seemed like a hell of a nice guy at first. Real personable."

"I'm sure."

"Didn't say a fucking word about money for weeks. We got to know each other, he'd buy me a beer, shoot the shit, just a guy in a bar. He was real interested in what I did. I'd tell him about cases, he'd ask all kinds of questions. I thought he was a wanna-be. You know, I thought he just liked cops. Even when I figured out he was running the book, I didn't care." Roy looked at Dooley and shook his head. "All my instincts, everything I ever learned, went out the fuckin' window when I walked into that place."

They were silent for a while. Dooley said, "Give yourself a break. It was a rough time."

Roy shrugged. "When I was starting to get in serious trouble with the money, Spanos finally says hey, you got a problem, maybe we can work something out. By that time I was so desperate I said sure. You develop an incredible capacity for lying to yourself. You tell yourself you can weasel out of this one. And then he gives you fifteen thousand bucks in a paper bag, says don't worry about no juice, just get square with the book and you can take your time, come up with the principal when you can. Man, it's a great scam. It's his fuckin' book but he gets to be the savior. I woke up in a cold sweat in the middle of the night and realized what I'd done. I haven't made a bet since. That's the only thing I can say for myself."

Dooley let half a minute or so go by. On the jukebox Johnny Mathis was trying to nail down just where the violins wanted him to be. "So you went and fessed up, huh?"

"Yeah. They're gonna do their best to keep it out of Internal Affairs. No boy of theirs is gonna get in trouble."

"Well, that's good. They're on your side anyway."

"Yeah. As long as they can make some hay out of it. They're gonna wire me up."

Dooley twirled his beer glass on a coaster. "That ought to be interesting."

"Yeah." Roy drank some more.

"You feel I pushed you into this?" said Dooley.

Roy gave him a crooked smile. "Sure I do. But I guess it was time." Dooley opened his mouth but nothing came out. Roy picked up his glass and clinked it against Dooley's. "You don't have to say nothing. You were right. It's stand-up time."

Dooley inclined his head to one side, an admission of doubt. "You nervous?"

Roy shook his head once, narrowed his eyes, stared far away down the bar. "Hell, I don't know. I was never scared to go talk to him before, when I was breaking every rule in the fucking book. Now I guess it's stage fright."

"They'll give you good backup, right?"

"That's what they say."

"What's he gonna do, anyway? He's not gonna touch a cop."

"That's what I keep telling myself. All I gotta do is be a little smart about getting him to talk. That's the hard part, not tipping him off but getting him to put his foot in his mouth."

"Well, you're not going to entrap him. He's already made you an illegal proposition."

"But I gotta get it on tape. And more. I gotta get him to say something that can be used against him. That could be the hard part. But no, I ain't worried about getting hurt. Shit, what's he gonna do?"

They sat in silence while the jukebox turned over and Sinatra came out swinging. "There you go," said Dooley. "Theme music. A famous mobbed-up celebrity."

"They're everywhere."

"You want me to come with you?" said Dooley, after a pause. "Watch your back?"

Roy didn't reply for a long time, long enough for the bartender to hobble down and offer them refills. When the old man took their glasses away, Roy said, "No. I think these guys from OC got it all scoped out. And they probably won't want any wild cards showing up. But hey." Roy slapped Dooley gently on the shoulder, let his hand rest there for a second. "I know you would, man. And I can't think of anybody who'd do it any better."

"You let me know," said Dooley. "Anything I can do, you let me know."

11

"SOMEBODY CALLED FOR YOU," SAID LAURIE AS SPANOS CAME INTO the deli. "Coffee?"

"Yeah, thanks. He leave a message?"

"He just said to tell you Roy called."

"Thanks. Hey, make that to go, could you? I gotta run do something. If Vince asks, I'll be back in a few minutes."

Spanos took his coffee out to the Stratus and drove up Harlem to his favorite pay phone, next to a muffler shop. This one was a rare and precious thing in a world spoiled by antiracketeering measures; it would still take incoming calls. He dialed the detective's pager number, punched in the number of the pay phone, and then went and sat in the car and drank coffee until the phone rang, just under five minutes later. Spanos got out of the car and picked it up. "Yeah."

"Spanos?"

"Yeah. You got it?"

"I got it. It wasn't no fuckin' picnic, either. I had to go down to 26th and California—"

"I don't wanna hear about it. When can you get it to me?"

"Well, what about tonight?"

"OK, tonight."

"Where?"

Spanos thought for a second or two. "You know the mall at Irving and Narragansett? There's a Jewel there, a bunch of other things."

"Yeah."

"Eleven o'clock. Park somewhere in the middle of the lot and wait for me." Spanos slammed the receiver down and walked back to his car.

Back at the deli, Terry was behind the counter now, making sandwiches. There were two customers standing there watching him. Laurie was nowhere in sight. Spanos sat on a stool at the window and waited until the customers had taken their food to a table. Then he went and ordered another cup of coffee. "I need you tonight," he said quietly. "Ten o'clock."

Terry put the cup in front of him. "OK. Where we going?"

"We're going to have some fun with a dirty cop," said Spanos.

Roy Ferguson sat in the conference room next to the Commander's office and tried to muster up some confidence in the expertise of his betters. Matic was sitting at the head of the table with the look of a party host worried about whether the guests are having fun, while the Intelligence honchos with their black cases full of electronic toys ran the show.

"It's a fully functional pen," said the balding Intelligence sergeant. "He asks for your autograph, you can sign it with this. No more recorders strapped to your chest, stuffed down the boot, whatever. Just put the thing in your shirt pocket and don't worry about it."

Roy turned the heavy pen in his hands. "OK. It'll pick everything up? I don't have to sit funny so he's talking to my chest or anything?"

"It'll pick up whatever he says. You could even let him play the radio if you want. The important thing is to keep the receivers within two hundred yards. If it goes like you said it always does, there's no problem. The one in the trunk of your car will do the trick. But we'll have one in another car nearby just in case we go mobile."

Roy nodded, slipping the pen into his pocket. "Where you gonna be?"

"We'll have visual surveillance on the roof of the banquet hall across Irving. There'll be a camera with a night scope on it. We'll get the whole thing on film. Unless he decides to go for a drive. We'll have four cars. One in each direction of egress. I don't care which way you go, we'll be right with you. We'll have a car up toward Wright College on Narragansett, one on Irving over by Saint Pascal's, one down by the cemetery south on Narragansett, and one over toward Oak Park to the west. You start moving, we'll be able to run parallels, keep right on top of you. We got the tracker onto his car this afternoon while he was having lunch. He's got a Can-Trac 360 stuck to his oil pan right now. We've been tracking him since about two o'clock."

Roy nodded. "I gotta say, I hope it's going to be real boring for you."

The Intelligence sergeant shrugged. "It usually is." He looked at Matic. "You call over to Five?"

"They know all about it. Sixteenth district patrol will stay out of the area."

"OK, I guess we're set then." He turned back to Roy. "You got the notebook?"

Roy tapped his pocket. "Yeah."

"You got any questions?"

Roy looked around the table, at the faces intent on him. The question on his lips was *Why me?* but he already knew the answer. "I guess not," he said.

"Remember, you want him to do the talking. You want him to tell you exactly why he needs the book. You're playing a role but I can't write you a script. That's where your ingenuity comes in. Make him talk to you."

Nodding slowly, a chill spreading outward from his stomach, Roy pushed away from the table. "Ingenuity," he said. "I guess we'll see how much I have."

Spanos had just come back from the toilet when Terry walked into the bar. The kid came down the room with that little bit of a slouch, a don't-fuck-with-me look. He eased in at the bar beside Spanos and said over the noise of the jukebox, "Looks pretty clear. He's sitting out there in the middle of nowhere and nobody drove in after him. There's a few people going in and out of the Jewel, but that's it."

Spanos nodded, chewing on a toothpick. "OK. I'll go talk to him. You cruise, look for anything that looks like a car full of cops. You see anything, come by and honk."

"You got it."

After Terry left, Spanos sat at the bar a while longer, thinking. He really didn't expect any trouble, but you never knew. He had bumped the stakes up a little higher now by asking Ferguson to tamper with evidence, and you never knew how people would react. He had gone out on a limb a little bit here, and if he had any serious doubts about it, it was best to just get in the car and go home.

Except Spanos prided himself on reading people, and he wouldn't put Roy Ferguson down as somebody who was likely to have a sudden crisis of conscience. Ferguson was the type of guy who wanted as little trouble as possible.

And to just go home now meant possibly not getting that notebook. If there was even a chance it was recoverable, he had to take it. Spanos got little feverish chills when he thought about that notebook.

He left the bar and got in the Stratus. He drove the four blocks to the mall and went in the entrance off Irving Park. The parking lot was huge, six acres of asphalt serving a twenty-four-hour Jewel food store and a dozen other shops. There were maybe thirty cars scattered in the lot, mostly near the Jewel. Spanos drove slowly along the perimeter of the lot until he spotted the detective's Grand Prix, on the fringes of the food store cluster. He circled around and parked directly behind him, one rank over, a couple of empty slots from the nearest vehicle. He flicked his brights once, seeing the detective's head move in the sudden illumination, and then cut the lights and the ignition.

Ferguson got out of his car and came back to the Stratus, walking slowly. He got in and said, "I been waiting for forty minutes."

"What else you got to do tonight?"

"All right, look." The detective pulled a notebook from his shirt pocket and Spanos held his breath; he hadn't realized until this moment just how much the thing had tied him in knots. "Here's your book," Ferguson said.

Spanos snatched it and held it eagerly to the dim light from the windows of the distant grocery store. It wasn't quite right but he didn't fully realize it until he opened it up and saw the totally unfamiliar ranks of figures on the first page. He froze, flipped over another page, and then went rigid with anger. He threw the book back at Ferguson. "That's not it, dumb-fuck. That's the wrong notebook."

Ferguson picked it up off his lap. "That's the only one they found on the guy."

"Fuck. That ain't it."

Ferguson shrugged. "That's what was there. There's no other book mentioned in the files. This was in his pocket."

"How about on the ground? It might have fallen out or something."

"It would be in the files, on the evidence report. This is it for notebooks. I got what you asked me for."

"You didn't get shit. You're trying to pull something."

"I ain't pulling nothing. You asked for a blue notebook, I got you a blue notebook. I went way out on a fucking limb for you. I had to go down to ERPS and risk my fucking career for you."

"You faked it up yourself, asshole. You went and bought a note-book and wrote in it and thought you could put it over on me."

"Ah, bullshit." The detective was starting to get steamed now, pointing at him. "Look, I did what you told me to. You told me to get the guy's notebook and I did it. Now, you want it or not? If it's the wrong one, I gotta go put the damn thing back."

"Jesus." Spanos wanted to put his fist through the guy's face but he was getting nowhere. He had to do some fast thinking here. Logic, he told himself. The Greeks invented logic, his old man used to say. So think. There were two possibilities. One, the guy was telling the truth, in which case where was his fucking notebook? Two, he was lying, he'd faked up this notebook. In which case, what?

"Look," said Ferguson. "Maybe you don't really need this book. Maybe it can't hurt you as much as you think it can."

"Shut up." Spanos stared out the windshield, thinking. Why would he do up a fake? Because he was too fucking chicken to go down to wherever he had to go and get the real notebook. This was his way of trying to weasel out of the whole thing.

"So give me a better description," said Ferguson. "Tell me what to look for."

Or, thought Spanos, he had worked up the fake and the bullshit story because he had the real one and didn't want to give it up. No. In that case there was no reason for a fake; if he had it and didn't want to give it up, he'd let him know, he'd use the damn thing. He didn't have it, he couldn't.

"Look, why don't you level with me?" said Ferguson. "Who does the damn thing really belong to?"

He knows, thought Spanos, turning his head to look at him. He knows all about it. "I told you," he said.

"Yeah, you told me. Look, you want me to get it back, you can't lie to me." The detective wasn't pissed off any more; he was talking in a calm quiet tone and looking as if he was back on top. "I don't think it's what's in the notebook that's worrying you. I think it's how it got wherever it is."

Spanos opened his mouth but said nothing; if there was ever a time to shut the fuck up, this was it. He felt suddenly that his mind was working at the speed of light; he had a handle on things. "You're full of shit," he said. "You didn't go get the notebook because you're too fucking scared. You got one more chance. Bring me the right notebook or I'll put the dogs on you. Now get out of my fucking car."

Roy pulled the fat pen out of his shirt pocket and tossed it on the desk. "You heard it," he said. "Zero."

The sergeant from Intelligence picked up the pen. "I don't know about that." He slipped the pen inside his jacket.

"I was too obvious," said Roy. "I was trying to get him to spell it out and it didn't sound right to him."

Matic shook his head. "There was nothing wrong with what you said."

The Intelligence guy said, "I don't think I'd have led him like that, suggested it was his notebook."

"Christ, I was trying to get him to say something. I was trying to get a reaction. You told me to get him talking."

"I know, it's tough. And it's you there in the car with him, not us. I'm not gonna Monday-morning-quarterback you."

Matic said, "The more I think about it, the more I think Roy's right. It's his, he dropped it or something. That's why he told you it was on the ground. But where the hell is it? They sure didn't find it at the scene. We double-checked."

There were three or four seconds of silence. "What happens now?" said Roy. He wanted to go home, find Dooley, drink some beer.

"I think now you tell him it's all over," said Matic. "You did your best, you didn't find it. What's he gonna do? He won't bother you anymore." He looked at the OC guys across the desk.

"Could be." The sergeant shrugged. "Still, I'd like to do this again, keep you wired for a while. I think he'll be back."

"Terrific."

"Look, basically we got nothing tonight. We got nothing we can use, and we don't have the god damn notebook. We don't even know for sure what he wants it for, what's in it. We need more. If he approaches you again, we'll do it again and see what he has to say for himself. If he's worried enough, he'll tell us something we can use."

A few looks were exchanged. Roy shook his head once, a gesture of profound doubt.

"I know," said the sergeant. "It's no fun. But then you kind of brought it on yourself, didn't you?"

"I ain't arguing that," said Roy.

"I didn't see nobody," said Terry.

Spanos had parked behind Terry's Corvette and waited for the kid to come back and stoop at the window. "Nah, well, you wouldn't, necessarily. They're good at what they do."

Terry leaned on the car, looking down at him with a blank stare. "So what now?"

"So we didn't get busted. Now you can go home. I'll see you around."

Terry shrugged. "Let me know if you need me."

"Yeah, I will, thanks a lot. Listen, you be at the deli tomorrow? I'll come by and I'll have something for you. You been a big help." Spanos watched the kid walk back to the car and get in. He lit a cigarette and watched the Corvette pull away. His mind was still working a mile a minute.

Spanos smoked and tried to think his way through things. The most likely scenario, he had decided, was that Ferguson hadn't even tried to get the notebook, had just run up the fake and the bullshit story, a story so bad it was pathetic. But right at the end he had gotten the right idea about the notebook, and that worried Spanos a lot. He remembered that look on the cop's face, the look of a man thinking he had rediscovered some leverage. Spanos smoked the cigarette down to the last inch and threw it out the window. With the notebook still out there somewhere and a cop with ideas, Spanos was starting to find the world a bleak and comfortless place.

12

Spanos sucked down coffee, looking over the balcony rail at the lake, spreading gray and sullen to the horizon, an endless sheet of steel under a sky of heavy wet wool. Eighteen stories below him cars jockeyed for advantage along the double ribbon of Lake Shore Drive, their roar drifting up to him through the mist. Spanos tossed the dregs of his coffee out over the rail, watching the brown dollop dissipate into nothing, just enough to make a bald man frown and run a Kleenex over his head somewhere down there. There were nights when he stood out here and pissed off the balcony, the gesture of a man who'd wound up living on Lake Shore Drive despite all the dire predictions.

Spanos came in off the balcony, trembling a little as a chill passed through him. He was going to need a lot of coffee to get him through the day. He had drifted off to sleep before dawn and then come awake with the first light, full of purpose and with all cylinders clicking. He went into the kitchen and set his empty mug in the sink and then leaned on the counter and took a deep breath, trying to quiet his stomach. He was a little amazed and a little frightened of what he was going to do today.

"The thing is, there is no notebook," said Roy.

"There's gotta be one," said Dooley. "He's worried about something." He sucked in some coffee. It was too early for him to be up, still not quite light out.

"Yeah, but we don't have it, I mean. Nothing that fits Spanos's description. There's all kinds of papers and computer disks and all that, but nothing like what Spanos described. They searched Blumberg's office, his home, everything. Got nothing. Of course, I don't think Blumberg ever had it. I think Spanos dropped it at the scene, or thinks he did, and that's why he's worried. He knows I didn't buy that about it belonging to Blumberg, who the fuck's he trying to kid? But we can't find the god damn thing."

"And you can't tell him that because then he knows he's off the hook."

"Yeah. So I gotta keep wearing the wire until he says something we can use, which I don't think he's gonna."

Dooley shook his head. "That puts you in a rough spot, man. As long as he thinks you can hurt him, no telling what he'll do."

"Nah. I can't hurt him, and he's gotta know it. He's gonna figure, if I had the notebook I'd either give it to him, if I was crooked, or I'd use it to nail him, if I wasn't. And if I was gonna use it to nail him, there wouldn't be any reason to come up with a fake one. I'd just nail him. I think he figures I just didn't want to risk getting it and came up with that horseshit fake. So he's gonna pressure me again. And I'm gonna have to try to get him to talk again." Roy pushed away from the table, a faint ironic smile on his face, a man reaping what he had sown. Dooley followed him into the living room, cup in hand, and watched him strap on the gun and the cuffs. He felt like a little kid again, watching his father get ready to go off in the morning.

"I hope you got all that figured right," he said.

Roy shrugged. "He's not gonna hit a cop, whatever happens, right? They don't do that." Hand on the doorknob, Roy flashed him that big handsome smile. "They got rules to follow, remember?"

"So they say," said Dooley.

* * *

117

It had to be a solo effort, Spanos knew; he'd thought hard about using Terry but this one was going to be such dynamite he didn't want to involve anyone who might cough up his name. He found his cutout in Uptown, where he knew there was an inexhaustible stock of the type of person he needed: rootless, secretive and willing to do anything for money. In a Broadway diner crackling with grease and rumbling from El trains passing overhead he sat at the counter and picked his mark, a malnourished kid with spiky yellow hair and a pierced nose who sat in a window booth smoking and nursing a cup of coffee, watching the street. Spanos thought the kid looked just reliably alert but sufficiently desperate. He slid into the booth. "You wanna make a quick clean fifty bucks?" he said.

The kid had made deals like this before, though probably not at eleven o'clock in the morning. He smoked and looked at Spanos and made his evaluations. Finally he said, "You got a car?"

"You don't have to get in a car," said Spanos. "All you have to do is make a phone call."

Kids like this were good at showing nothing in their faces; the kid smoked some more and said, "Who do I have to talk to?"

"A cop," said Spanos. "You have to get a message to a cop."

Spanos drove east on Chicago Avenue, looking in the mirror. As far as he had been able to tell, nobody had been watching him since the last spasm of FBI-CPD cooperation in the spring, but it wouldn't do to get careless, today of all days. He drove till he found a secondhand clothes store. He went in and bought a navy pea jacket, a pair of black leather gloves and a blue ski mask. "Getting ready for the cold weather, huh?" said the tottering old woman who took his money, her voice quavering and breaking.

"I got a feeling it's gonna come down hard this year," said Spanos. He got back in the car and went around the block, still looking for a tail. When he was sure there wasn't one, he pointed the car south. He drove down Sacramento and things began to get ugly; there were vacant lots and boarded-up windows and idle dark-skinned males clustered on street corners. Spanos didn't much like driving around this type of neighborhood, but business was business. He crossed the Ike, looking east along the wide expressway to the distant Loop towers poking up into low clouds, and then he was getting close.

He made a turn or two. There were blocks here that were still living blocks, with intact houses, some nice cars parked along the street, little black girls on the sidewalk doing amazing things with jump ropes, but the commercial blocks looked bad; this wasn't a hotbed of economic activity. Bunkerlike food stores with big bright signs advertising Lotto games, liquor stores, storefront churches with hand-lettered signs. Spanos pulled up in front of a storefront with the burglar grate still pulled across the window. A sign said B&B BARBER SHOP. He got out of the car. He drew a look or two, but a white man in a nice car wasn't all that unusual here; he could have been a landlord, a city inspector, a cop. The window of the shop had been almost completely obscured with big color head shots of models smiling into the camera, black guys pleased about the strange things somebody had done to their hair. Spanos pushed the door open. Inside there were three barber chairs and no barbers; it looked like the customers had taken the place over. There were four of them and he had their complete attention. They were large and black and clothed in ways that created a variety of options for concealing firearms. The looks he was getting said he'd better have a damn good reason for being there.

"Morning," said Spanos. Nobody responded; Spanos would have gotten the same stony looks if he'd said something in Greek. "Jumbo's expecting me."

"He better be," said one of the men, sliding slowly off one of the barber chairs and tossing a copy of *Players* onto the seat. He had on expensive sneakers and a black warm-up suit with the jacket unzipped, revealing a purple fishnet undershirt stretched over a massive chest.

Spanos smiled. "You can tell him Johnny's here." He looked around at the other three men, all of them in the same relaxed pose, maybe a leg up over the arm of the chair, but with that sullen intent look that said remember, your right to stand there is only provisional.

"I'll see if he's here," said the man in black. He went through a door, taking his time. Walking across a room is a fucking art form with these guys, Spanos thought. He turned around and went to stand at the door looking out, hands in his pockets. Small talk, he had a feeling, was going to be out of the question.

"Hey, Johnny," said a voice behind him. Spanos turned and saw Jumbo coming out of the back room. Jumbo was called that because he just made five-four in his high-heeled alligator boots, but he walked like a bigger man; Jumbo was confident of his stature. He wore a Sox cap on a shaved head and a ring with a stone the size of a small walnut on his left hand. He had bright black eyes in a chocolate-colored face that at some point had been laid wide open below the left eye, leaving an impressive scar. He was pulling on a black leather jacket that would retail for five hundred dollars, but Spanos knew that people like Jumbo seldom bothered with retail. Jumbo stuck out his hand and Spanos shook it; there was never any soul-shake nonsense with Jumbo. "'S'up, man?" said Jumbo.

"Not much. Business as usual."

"Your car out here?"

"Yeah."

"Let's go for a little ride. Back in five," he tossed over his shoulder as he opened the street door. They got into Spanos's car. "Nice piece a metal."

"Yeah. I got a guy out there that owes me some favors, so I get the pick of the lot. It's just about time to try something new, though. They got one of the new Vipers that looks pretty good."

"Take her up to the corner and then right, come back down the alley," Jumbo said. Spanos put the car in gear. "You still hangin' out with the Italians, huh?"

"Still eating lotsa spaghetti, yeah."

The black man laughed. "Well, you must be doin' OK."

"OK. Just OK."

Jumbo gave him a brief look. "I guess things can't be goin' too good, seein' what you're here for."

"Hey, this is for somebody else. You kidding me? I got no idea what's going down. I get told to do things, I do 'em. All I do is drop the thing off somewhere, keep my fuckin' head down, read about it in the papers like everyone else."

"Well, I appreciate the business."

Spanos turned the corner. "Someday, there'll be real business. I can't say when."

"Them fuckers ain't never gonna deal with no niggers."

Easing into the mouth of the alley, Spanos said, "Some of them already are. When that day comes, when somebody sees the light— then you and me. Then we really do business. The kind of business we couldn't fucking dream about back when we were peddling dime bags of dope to frat houses in Urbana."

The black man gave a skeptical grunt of laughter. "Well, you let me know, man. Pull over here."

Spanos parked and watched as the black man got out and went to the padlocked door of a slightly swaybacked frame garage with boarded-up windows. He selected a key out of a jangling cluster at his belt and opened the lock. He shoved the sagging door open and disappeared inside. When he came back out he was carrying a dark green Marshall Field's shopping bag, which he set on the ground while he relocked the door. Then he picked up the bag and got back in the car.

Spanos looked in the bag and saw the two short barrels and the sawed-down grip wrapped with electrical tape and the four loose

Double O Buck shells at the bottom of the bag. "I'm assuming two are gonna do the trick," said Jumbo. "But I threw in a couple extra. You don't wanna have to reload this thing, but you never know."

Spanos set the bag on the backseat and reached inside his jacket for the roll of bills. "If it gets to that point, somebody's in deep shit," he said.

"I got somebody here that claims to know about Margaret Egan," said Roy, looking at the message slip in his hand. He looked up and gave Tommy Crane a look that Crane had learned to recognize: the eager look, the hunter look.

"Damn," said Crane. "*There's* a blast from the past."

Roy went on giving him that look for a moment. "Chuck took the call, says it sounded like a kid, a teenager. I'm trying to remember, did we talk to any teenagers?"

"We talked to a million people. Christ, that was a year ago."

Roy laid down the paper. "He said he had one of my cards. I'm trying to remember who all I left cards with."

"What does he want?"

"He wants to meet me tonight, at some joint on Irving Park. The message says 'Can tell you who killed Margaret Egan.'"

"Jesus."

"Yeah. Although who the fuck knows? Everybody had a theory on that one."

"Still, a year later. That doesn't happen much."

"No. I think we gotta go see this kid."

Crane said nothing. He shoved papers around the desk until Roy looked at him and said, "All right?"

"Yeah."

"What's the matter?"

"Nothing. We gotta go, we gotta go."

"Shit. Your little girl's in the play tonight, isn't she?"

"Hey, I missed it last year, I can miss it again. She'll get over it."

A moment went by. "It's probably a long shot," said Roy. "I'll run out there, see if this kid shows up."

Crane shrugged. "I'll come with you if you want."

"No," said Roy, pushing away from the desk. "You got a family waiting for you at home. All I got's Dooley, and he can wait."

When it got to the point of stealing a car, Spanos had his first real case of cold feet. He was breaking every rule there was. And for what?

He went through it again, sitting on the bench watching the cars cruise through the park in the lowering dusk. Is it necessary? The answer to that was hell yes, if Roy Ferguson was planning to use the notebook against him. The real problem would be if he had already gone to somebody about it. In that case Spanos was just fucked, already. But Spanos didn't think Ferguson had; he just didn't see it, not the Roy Ferguson he'd brought along over the past year or so. As long as the cop was thinking of the notebook in terms of leverage, he wouldn't tell anybody. If Spanos was dealing with a dirty cop, then there was a fairly simple solution.

Is it feasible? That was the tough one. Pulling the trigger was the easy part. Making absolutely sure nothing splashed back was the hard part. That was why it had to be a solo job, because on this one he was on his own; he knew that nobody in the Outfit was ever going to go to bat for him on a cop killing.

Spanos looked at his watch. It was time to move and he had his mark picked out. He stood up and pulled the ski mask out of the pocket of the pea jacket. He put it on like a regular stocking cap; he would pull it down to obscure his face when he got closer. He picked up the Marshall Field's bag and started to walk toward the red Ford Escort parked at the edge of the asphalt, above the rocks. When it got right down to it, he decided, the reason he was going to kill the cop was because in his business you couldn't just let somebody say no. That was it, the bottom line. Nobody says no. You let people say no to you, pretty soon you're out of business. He looked down onto the rocks at the water's edge and saw the two lovers who had gotten out of the Escort.

And maybe, Spanos thought, pulling the mask over his face and reaching into the bag, he didn't need any reason beyond this feeling, right here and now, this racing pulse and lighter-than-air stomach. This is power, he thought. He jumped down onto the rocks. "I want your car keys," he said, leveling the sawed-off shotgun at a very surprised young man. "Now."

Hermenegildo saw the man through the window, out on the sidewalk, and thought he was just passing by. In the hours that followed he would be haunted by the thought that if he had paid attention to the face he could have given a description. As it was, he looked away, back at the gyro sandwich he was putting together on the counter, and when the door burst open, the man pulling the ski mask down over his face now, it was too late.

Nobody move!" the man shouted and nobody did; the black lady standing at the counter gave a little squeal of alarm as the man pulled the shotgun out of the shopping bag. He swept the room with it, freezing everybody, and then bracketed it on Hermenegildo, who went cold and thought immediately and desperately of Yolanda and the children in the third-floor apartment two blocks away. "Clean it out, Paco. Everything in the register goes in the bag. Now!"

All I wanted was a sandwich, LaKeesha had time to think, clutching at the counter as her knees nearly gave way. I'm going to get shot because I wanted a gyro sandwich and there will be nobody to take care of my mother. Oh dear Jesus take care of Mama; I have been a bad daughter but I tried. The man was moving fast, jumping halfway down the room, sweeping the stubby little gun this way and that, covering the people in the booths along the wall and the people at the counter and the two behind it and then turning and jumping back toward her again. She made eye contact with the man through the ski mask and a little whimpering sound came up out of her; from hard experience LaKeesha knew that if you looked them in the eye they got vicious because they were ashamed. But this man was not interested in LaKeesha; he swung the gun toward the poor Mexican boy who stood there with her gyro still in his hands. The man was shouting and LaKeesha started praying dear Jesus again and the Mexican boy reached for the cash register and started punching at the keys.

Nikolaos saw the whole thing in advance, the whole tragedy laid out before him the instant the man in the ski mask came through the door shouting. He even looked at the cop, sitting there in the booth with his basket of fries and the radio sitting on the table in front of him, and thought, what are you going to do, officer? Nikolaos had frozen with the knife in his hands and a half-chopped onion on the cutting board and he didn't even dare set down the knife; all he could do was stand there and hope nobody did anything. He wanted to call down to Hermenegildo to relax, do what the man says, but the kid had understood and had already gotten the register drawer open. He started digging out bills as fast as his greasy fingers could get a purchase on them and dunking them in the bag.

"Everybody sit tight now," said the man, turning to sweep the room with the gun again, shouting in that slightly hoarse voice that Nikolaos would never forget. And Nikolaos saw the whole thing happen, saw the man in the ski mask fix for a second on the cop and realize he was looking at a cop and he saw the cop realize that the man had realized it and Nikolaos knew bad things were going to happen. He was fooled for a second when the man in the ski mask turned back to Hermenegildo and said one word, "Hurry," but then he saw the cop start to move and he wanted to shout *no* and he saw the man in the ski mask start to turn again, as if he had eyes in the back of his head or maybe just knew the cop would try it, and then he was bringing the gun around and Nikolaos closed his eyes.

Roy started thinking about Sean the second he recognized Spanos's voice. "Everybody sit tight now," Spanos said, looking right at him, and Roy sat tight and everything became clear and it was just a question of getting the jump, because he had no doubt whatsoever who it was under that mask and why he was here. Wish me luck, Shawnie, he thought, seeing Spanos turn back to the counter. "Hurry," said Spanos, and Roy knew that was for him as well. It was going to be a bitch with no elbow room and Roy only had time to unto the snap on the holster at his hip before Spanos was turning again. Roy pushed hard with his feet and got halfway up, the automatic hitting the edge of the table as he brought it up a little too late and he knew exactly what hit him; he saw the fucking gun go off.

There wasn't much time then, but as he died falling back against the wall, somebody screaming, Spanos jumping forward for a second shot, Roy wanted to tell everyone in the place it was all right.

I'm going to see my boy, he wanted to tell them.

13

IT CAME ON THE NEWS WHEN DOOLEY WAS OVER AT KATHLEEN'S, IN the kitchen teasing Maureen about boyfriends, nursing a beer. Bob had the TV on in the living room and Dooley heard him say, "A cop got shot," his voice raised just a bit, knowing this was of immediate and urgent interest to everyone in his household.

Channel 7 had a shot of the Uptown gyro joint, blue Mars lights reflected in the big windows, a blonde with wind-whipped hair talking into a mike in the foreground. "At this time the police are not saying how seriously the officer was wounded," she said. Everybody had crowded into the living room to watch, remembering other bad moments through the years, waiting to hear a name. Kathleen went and dialed Kevin's house; all over the city cops' wives and sisters and parents and children were picking up the phone.

The name came fifteen minutes later when Kevin called back. Kathleen answered the phone in the kitchen and gasped and said "Oh dear God no." Who? thought Dooley, thinking of everybody he grew up with, everybody in the world except Roy until Kathleen looked at him, wide-eyed and pale, the receiver pressed to her chest. "It's Roy Ferguson."

Dooley took the phone from her. "How is he?"

"He's gone," said Kevin. "They shot him with a sawed-off."

Dooley made a noise, just an outrush of breath with no articulation, and sagged onto a kitchen chair, stretching the phone cord to the limit. "Ahhh, Jesus."

"He tried to draw on the guy and he shot him. That's what they're saying."

"Aw, fuck. No. Roy, Jesus Christ." Dooley wanted to tear the phone out of the wall.

"It was quick. He was dead when they got there."

Dooley sat with his eyes squeezed shut. He drew breath and said, "Whadda they got?"

"Not a fucking thing. The guy ran. They think he had a car in the alley. They got everybody in the Area out there canvassing."

"They get a description at least?"

"Yeah. White male in a ski mask. Lotsa luck."

"They know what Roy was doing there?"

"I don't know. I just got the basics from Ted over at the Area. You wanna come over, we'll sit up for a while and see what comes out."

Dooley let out a long breath. "Maybe later. How late you gonna be up?"

"You kidding? Tonight? You think I'm gonna sleep?"

"I'll be over. I gotta do something first."

Dooley hung up and went for his jacket. Bob had his arm around Kathleen on the living room couch; Patrick was staring into space, chewing a nail. Maureen was standing near the door, hands covering her mouth in a gesture of shock, very pale, tears gathering at the corners of pretty blue eyes that were fixed on him. Dooley wrestled into his jacket and reached out and put his hands on her shoulders. He kissed her on the forehead. "Don't ever marry a cop, Maureen."

Spanos could see he had made himself an enemy, but he didn't care. He took another drink of wine and looked at Terry across the table. Laurie was making noises in the kitchen, rattling plates and slamming drawers. Terry gave Spanos a thin smile. Spanos raised his glass in a toast. I fucking did it, he thought.

Terry had been there waiting, right where Spanos had said to be when he ditched the stolen Escort in the parking lot of a strip mall on Irving. The Marshall Field's shopping bag with the shotgun and the ski mask and the gloves inside had gone into a trash can as Spanos crossed the lot to the Corvette; the pea jacket had gone into a different can near Montrose Harbor when Terry dropped Spanos two hundred yards from his car, parked on the road by the soccer fields. There was nothing to be traced to him. He had killed a cop in front of witnesses, but the witnesses were his strength; they would all swear it was a holdup gone wrong. As for Terry, he thought it was a debt collection, Spanos being careful because he'd had to get a little rough. All he knew was that Spanos had gotten into his car in a parking lot on Irving Park and stuffed a handful of cash into his coat pocket, saying Happy Birthday.

Laurie had been surprised to see Spanos show up at the dreary little apartment above the deli but hadn't put up a fuss about feeding him along with her son; the shock and the anger had come when Terry had explained that if anybody ever asked, they had been there since six-thirty. "My husband's not enough for you, huh?" she had said to Spanos, desolated. "You can't leave my son alone?"

Spanos had shrugged and said, "He's a big boy." She had turned on her heel and left then. Spanos and Terry finished the wine in silence, listening as she stormed around the kitchen. Spanos had drunk quite a bit; he had needed to, to come down off that rocketing high. I fucking did it, he thought. He kept feeling the buck of the shotgun, seeing the surprised look on Roy Ferguson's face as the impact of the load slammed him back against the wall. Spanos was glad he had shot Roy in the chest; with a shotgun it was just as sure and he had, after all, liked Roy. Until the last second he had intended to aim for the head, but he had found he couldn't; he didn't want to see that. He had remembered Roy telling him he usually didn't wear a vest even though he was supposed to. They could hold an open-coffin funeral now.

Spanos drained the bottle into Terry's glass. In a low voice he said, "Don't rehearse her too much. It's OK if she's not sure about the time. Just make sure she says we were here for supper."

"OK." Terry jerked his chin in the direction of the kitchen. "She'll come around. She knows what to do. She ain't happy, but she'll do what she has to."

Because she loves her son, thought Spanos.

WMAQ had it on the radio as Dooley sped out the Kennedy toward O'Hare, nothing more than the TV had had at ten. Dooley wondered if Andrea would have seen it on the TV at the cocktail lounge but remembered that they hadn't given a name. When he got there she was waiting on a table in the corner; he went and stood at the waitress station at the bar, grinding his teeth.

"You need something?" said the bartender, none too friendly.

"Andrea's got an emergency," said Dooley, watching her walk back with an empty tray. She spotted him and must have read his bearing; when she got to the bar the first thing she said was, "What happened?"

"Roy's dead." Dooley watched her stiffen, close her eyes, sway a little. She set the tray on the bar. "He got shot in a robbery attempt. About two hours ago."

She steadied herself on the bar and looked at him; he couldn't quite place what he saw in her eyes when the first shock cleared. He thought it looked a little like reproach. "You want me to take you somewhere?" he said.

Andrea took a very deep breath and let it out and stood looking at the floor, her hands still on the bar. Finally she looked up and said, "I want to go to my parents' house."

"Can you drive?"

"Of course I can drive. No, wait. Maybe you better take me." She looked at the bartender and said, "I'm sorry, Bill. I have to leave."

Bill had heard enough not to put up a fuss. In the car Dooley told Andrea everything he knew about it; she sat in silence. Her parents lived in Mount Prospect and she had to direct him through unfamiliar streets. He pulled up in front of the house and put the car in park. "You want me to come by tomorrow, take you back to your car?"

"My dad'll take care of it." Andrea sat with her arms folded, looking at him in the feeble light. She looked as if someone had sucked all the life out of her. "Well, that's it," she said. "Full circle. It's all gone now." Dooley looked out the windshield; there was nothing whatever to say and he was starting to realize that this was the wrong place to come to for commiseration. She reached for his hand. "I'm sorry, Frank. You're probably grieving more than I am." She squeezed his hand. "I'm sorry," she said in a whisper.

Dooley laid his forehead on his other hand, still resting on the steering wheel. He closed his eyes until he heard the first soft plosions of weeping. Then her head was on his shoulder and she was sobbing and his arm was around her and they just sat that way until she grew quiet.

She sat up after a few minutes and wiped her eyes on her sleeve. "I have to go home and be taken care of for a while," she said. Swiftly she was out of the car, not giving him the option of walking her to the door. He watched her run up the walk and lean on the doorbell and stand waiting with her head down. When the door opened and she slipped inside, Dooley put the car in gear and rolled away into the night.

Kevin had put a bottle of whiskey and two glasses on the bar in the basement but neither he nor Dooley was drinking. It was past midnight and the house was quiet. "I don't think Roy's that stupid," said Dooley.

Kevin had to be at work in four hours but he hadn't even yawned. "Who knows what happened? Everything I've heard was second or third hand."

"He wouldn't have just tried to do a Clint Eastwood on the guy. Roy wouldn't have drawn unless he had the jump, a sure thing. We used to talk about this shit."

"And nobody knows how they're gonna react until they're in it. He was a cop. He could have thought there was a danger the guy'd start shooting. And maybe he wasn't as fast as he thought he was."

Dooley shook his head, stubborn. "I don't know. Something ain't right." Dooley gave in and poured himself a couple of inches of whiskey. "Who's got it, you know?"

Kevin shook his head. "Go over there tomorrow and talk to 'em."

Dooley let the liquor burn a trail down his throat into his belly. "You know Roy was in trouble with some Outfit shylock?"

Kevin looked up at him. "No. I didn't know that."

"But he was standing up to the guy. And now this. That makes me real fucking suspicious."

Kevin frowned at the idea for a while. "Man, that would surprise me a lot, one of them hitting a cop. But make sure you tell them over at the Area."

"They know. He put on a wire and went to talk to the guy the other night."

"No shit."

"Yeah. You see where my thoughts are heading?"

"I see."

Dooley tossed off the last of the whiskey in his glass and said, "Somebody's gonna pay."

Kevin looked at him across the bar for a few seconds, with that gaze that Dooley could never stand for long. "I don't have to tell you," said Kevin. "I'm sure you won't do anything . . . hasty."

"No." Dooley set his glass on the bar and slid it across to clink against the bottle. "You don't have to tell me."

14

SPANOS STOOD ON THE BALCONY WAITING FOR THE POLICE TO COME. He hadn't slept more than a couple of hours, feverishly and in brief dozes, seeing Roy Ferguson dying over and over again. At six he had given up and come out to the balcony in his bathrobe and an overcoat and stood there, watching the sun come up over the lake and waiting for the cops. The sun made the horizon faintly orange but faded as it got higher; it was a pale sun that didn't have the wattage to make it through the clouds.

When he got too cold he came in and made some coffee. He waited some more and then went to get dressed; when he was dressed he kicked around the apartment having a second cup of coffee. He turned on the TV and looked at shows he'd never seen before because he was always asleep in the morning. Finally he turned off the TV and went into the bedroom and lay down and thought about everything, breaking into a sweat.

The police were taking their time but he knew they would be there, sooner or later.

Matic had never really known Dooley; Dooley could tell he wasn't entirely comfortable with him being there but he wasn't going to kick him out as long as he didn't rock the boat. It was Area Three now, not Six, but nothing much had changed; Dooley had spent thousands of hours in this room. He sat on the corner of a desk and listened to Matic.

"We asked the Mexican kid if there was any chance he could spot him in a lineup. He said there was no way. He didn't really notice the guy until he came in the door, and then he already had the mask on."

Somebody said, "Shit." A handful of detectives were clustered around Matic. Tracy and McPeak were there; Roddy McShea, Hal Marks, three or four Dooley didn't recognize. Work was going undone, but it wasn't every day a detective got killed. The atmosphere at Belmont and Western was thick and electric, lowering clouds just waiting for the first thunderclap. Dooley hadn't said a word.

"Any kind of consensus among the witnesses?" said Marks. "I mean, what'd it look like?"

Matic shook his head, wearily. "You kidding? We're lucky they agree they saw somebody get killed. The owner thinks the guy just recognized he was looking at a cop, from the radio on the table. A lady that was in there said she thought the guy heard him going for his gun. Those were the two statements we got that weren't totally useless."

"Roy was supposed to be meeting an informant, right?" said McPeak.

"Supposedly."

"Well then, are you thinking what I'm thinking?"

"We're all thinking that. We're working on the phone call. But we gotta keep in mind, it could just be a stickup, happened before the informant got there."

"Why the fuck was he alone? Where was Tommy?"

"Roy told him to go home, he'd take it. Tommy feels like hell."

"Christ, I hope so."

Somebody said, "What's the street saying?"

"The street ain't saying shit. Nobody knows a thing. But it's early."

There was a silence. Marks drained his coffee and shuffled away. Somebody started typing. Matic made for the door to the Watch Commander's office as the cluster broke up. Dooley slid off the desk and went after him. When he got to the door of the office he saw Douglas behind his desk, phone to his ear, and Matic sinking onto a chair. Dooley rapped on the open door and came in, nodding at Matic. "Can I talk to you?"

"Sure." Matic was fishing a cigarette out of his shirt pocket. Douglas murmured something into the phone and hung up.

Dooley said, "I'm hoping John Spanos is at the forefront of your mind right now."

Matic lit his cigarette and traded looks with Douglas. "Close the door," he said. He watched Dooley do it and said, "What'd Roy tell you?"

"Everything. Enough to know it was Spanos that set him up and shot him last night."

Matic smoked and peered at him. "You know that, do you?"

"It's a hell of a good first guess."

Matic nodded. "Yeah. But it's still a guess."

"OK, sure, it's a guess. The witness who said Roy went for his gun. Was she sure about that?"

"She said she saw him move, out of the corner of her eye. He moved, the gunman turned around and shot him. Roy's gun was on the floor when we got there."

"So he drew on him."

"Looks like it."

Dooley took a deep breath and let it out. "See, that proves it for me. He would never have drawn on the guy unless he was sure, one hundred percent, that the other guy intended to pull the trigger. Are you kidding? In a crowded restaurant? Roy was no cowboy. We talked about this kind of thing. Let the fucking Marines do the shooting, he used to say, I'm a homicide dick. He would have waited till the guy got out the door and then called it in, maybe gone after him. If Roy drew his piece, it means he knew the other guy was there to shoot him."

"Why him? Maybe he thought the guy looked unstable and he had to try and get the jump. Or maybe he just panicked."

"Bullshit. Not Roy."

"So how would he know the guy was there to shoot him?"

"The voice. He recognized John Spanos's voice."

Matic worked on it while he worked on the cigarette. "Maybe. Everything's a maybe right now. You're not telling me anything I haven't thought about already."

Dooley could see the look and hear the tone; he wasn't in the club anymore. "I'm not here to complicate your life. I'm here to do what I can. Hell, I'm in the middle of it. I was the one who got Roy to come to you."

Matic shrugged. "OK, what do you want me to say?"

"Just talk tactics with me, make me feel better. Who's got this?"

"Hoffman and Combs."

"Do they know about the thing with Spanos?"

For a second Dooley thought Matic was going to shut him off, but the flicker of irritation on the older man's face faded. "They know what they need to know. You're not the only one this has occurred to. Everybody from the judge who approved the wire right on down the line is thinking the same thing. But right now we've got not one fucking thing that says Spanos was involved last night."

"OK, I believe you. You'll look at any alibi Spanos may have with a fucking microscope, I'm sure."

Matic traded another look with Douglas and Dooley could see he'd reached his limit here today. Matic said, "Hey, Dooley. I know you used to work here. That doesn't make you smarter than the people that still work here. OK?"

Dooley stood and looked at them and saw everything clearly: the Spanos angle was maybe just a bit of a sensitive topic, since sooner or later somebody was bound to suggest that the proper way to handle Roy Ferguson's problem might have been to put it meekly in the hands of the I.A.D. "OK," said Dooley. "I'm not trying to step on your toes. You know what you're doing."

Dooley drove east, toward the lake. He passed the Mexican place where he and Roy had had dinner, and the first real wave of grief hit him. When he got to the lake he parked near Belmont Harbor and started walking. He wound up standing on the rocks just out of reach of the angry tossing lake, looking south to the skyline and wondering if life was always going to be like this. Maybe it was him; maybe he carried some virus with him. He was immune himself but he was a carrier; he brought violent death wherever he roamed. He sat down with his head between his hands and cried a little.

After a while he stood up and walked back through the park toward his car. Leaves were falling and he could feel winter coming, a big slouching beast out of the north. A great fucking time to come home, he thought. He drove back west along Belmont, starting to get pissed off.

They found Spanos at the Plaka on Halsted, where he'd gone for an early dinner. Spanos liked the Plaka because it was quiet, a little upscale, a little muted and understated, a cut above the rowdier places up the row. He'd just started to think maybe the cops were going to let him dangle for a while when the two detectives came into the place. Spanos spotted them right away. He didn't know these two but they would have talked to somebody who knew him and started cruising his regular spots. "John Spanos?" said the older one, a short graying man with a long sharp nose.

"Yeah. Who are you?"

"Detective Hoffman, Area Three Violent Crimes. This is Detective Combs."

Spanos looked at the younger man, a lean dark specimen with the completely humorless look of the cop in business mode. "OK, fellas. It's a pleasure to meet you. What can I do for you?"

"We're going to have to ask you to come with us, Mr. Spanos."

Spanos stared at them, fork in the air. "What the fuck for?"

"You are being detained for questioning in the investigation of a homicide."

"A homicide? You're jerking my chain."

"I don't kid people, Mr. Spanos."

"Whoa, hang on a second. You mean I'm under arrest?"

"That's correct."

"What am I charged with?"

"You're not charged with anything yet. But we do need to talk with you."

"Look, can I at least finish my dinner here?"

"Sure. We'll wait." Hoffman pulled out a chair.

Spanos watched as they both sat down. So far nobody seemed to have taken much notice of them; Spanos thought he detected some heightened attention from a neighboring table but there was no general stir as yet. He looked at his plate and said, "Funny, I think I'm losing my appetite."

"That's a common reaction," said Hoffman. To Spanos he looked like the kind of cop who had illusions about the distance between them, not Spanos's favorite kind of cop.

"Aren't I supposed to get a warning? I think there was something about a fellow named Miranda a few years back."

"I haven't asked you any questions yet."

Spanos sighed and shoved his plate away. "I didn't mean to do it, officer. She backed into the knife by accident."

"OK, wiseass. You have the right to remain silent. . . ."

"She was a worthless hag and I needed the money. I didn't know the gat was loaded."

"Shut the fuck up and listen." The younger detective had a snarl that cut through the hum of the restaurant like lightning through clouds. There was a hush in the place now and Spanos could see Nick the owner rigid in his dark blue suit, dying a thousand deaths. Spanos laid down his fork, took a healthy mouthful of Roditis and folded his hands.

"All right, officer. You were saying?"

The older dick was smiling a little now. "You have the right to shut the fuck up," he said. "Am I making myself perfectly clear?"

"OK, you want to save us the work, I appreciate that. Nobody likes a nice short interview more than I do. Now I can go home and watch some TV, see how Dennis Franz does it. Just for fun, though, I'm gonna ask you again. Where did you have dinner last night?" The dick didn't really look as if he expected an answer.

"You don't have to answer that," said Sciortino patiently. The lawyer was the picture of legal rectitude in a gray suit and a matching toupee; his briefcase lay on the table in front of him but he hadn't even opened it.

"My lawyer says I don't have to answer that," said Spanos. The detective's eyebrows rose in mock surprise and he pushed away from the table, shaking his head. Spanos took another drink of water.

"I'll tell you one thing," said the younger dick, leaning back on his chair. "You sure as hell got my attention. You just about guaranteed we'll be in your face till hell freezes over. Whereas if you didn't do anything, all you gotta do is give us an alibi. Give us something we can check out." Spanos shrugged. He was tired but he was starting to feel things ease a bit in his stomach; he was starting to think he was over the hump.

Sciortino shot his cuffs and let out a sigh. "My client doesn't need an alibi," he said. "You haven't charged him with a crime. You're not

going to, either. You have no evidence whatsoever that he was connected to this killing, which by the way he deplores, as he was a friend
of the officer's. I can't see any possible reason for you to continue to
hold him."

The detectives had been playing these games for a long time;
Sciortino could have been talking to the wall. The older dick stood
up wearily and said, "I'm going to continue to hold him because the
law says I can. For another..." He checked his watch. "Goodness. I can
hold him for another seventy hours or so." He smiled at Spanos.
"Make yourself comfortable. We'll be back."

Sciortino gave Spanos a shrug. "They're just blowing smoke. It'll
go maybe twenty-four, max, because the longer they hold you without
charging you the worse they look, and I guarantee people will know
about it."

"That's OK." Spanos watched the dicks leave. "They got a job to do."

His voice a shade lower, the lawyer said, "There's gonna be a lot of
heat on this. A cop goes down, the rest of 'em get a little agitated."

Spanos nodded. He knew there were dozens of cops out in the city
right now, trying desperately to find something to nail him with before
they had to let him go. He ran cold for an instant but then told himself again he'd been too careful; there was nothing for them to find.
He could feel Sciortino looking at him, wondering. "I didn't do it,
Jim," he said.

"I'm glad to hear you say that," said the lawyer, and Spanos could
see he meant it.

Dooley had finally slept and the world had a morning-after feel to it,
a feeling of irrevocable difference. In the squad room Roddy McShea
was at a desk, pounding typewriter keys. He looked up as Dooley
approached. "They had to let him go," he said.

"No shit." Dooley was not surprised, but it still hurt.

"They're still in there doing the postmortem, if you want to throw in your two cents' worth."

"Thanks, man." Dooley found Hoffman, Combs, and Douglas in Matic's office. When he rapped on the open door the looks he got were not welcoming, but Dooley didn't wait to be invited. "Couldn't hold him, huh?" he said, settling in with a shoulder against the door frame and his arms crossed.

Matic gave him a look but chose not to make an issue of it. "We didn't expect to, necessarily."

"He had an alibi, I'm sure."

Hoffman laughed without humor, a grim sound. "We didn't even get that far. He just stood on his constitutional rights as a citizen of this great nation."

"And you didn't come up with anything?"

"We ran down his activities and associates, as many as we could. Apparently he had dinner that night with another wise guy's wife and son. They were a bit vague about the time, and I wouldn't call it a hard-and-fast alibi. But even if it isn't, we got nothing else on him. We got warrants for his apartment, all his hangouts. Nothing. On the other front, we think we found the car that was used but nobody saw a driver and the people it was stolen from can't identify the thief. No sign of a gun yet. We got shit, in a word."

Dooley said, "So what happens next?"

"What do you think happens? We continue to work the homicide in a professional manner." Matic was digging for another cigarette.

"Can you bust him for the loan sharking and the bookmaking?"

"Sure," said Hoffman. "Close the fucker down, get in his face a bit. Pressure him."

"Or better yet, not him," said Dooley. "Everybody else. Make him a liability to the rest of the crew. Let 'em know things stay shut down till they give him up."

Matic shook his head. "I don't know. You're talking about a major operation there. We'd need to get OC with us, and maybe some help from the G. I don't see it happening right now. Things are quiet on that front; resources are going elsewhere."

"What? You can't get people behind you to go after this guy? After he hits a cop?"

"We don't even know Spanos killed him, OK? What we have is a strong presumption and no evidence at all."

"Man, presumptions don't get much stronger."

"And they'll still only carry you so far." Matic sounded weary, drained. "Besides, I gotta work with the harsh realities. Like for instance, a nice line-of-duty killing is a lot better for public relations than a dirty cop getting whacked by a mobster. So we're not gonna get any support for a big OC operation on this."

"Dirty or not, Roy was a good cop."

Matic looked him in the eye and said, "I know that. Who the hell do you think you're talking to? You think I'm not gonna do whatever it takes? You think I want to see the first unsolved cop killing in the thirty years I've been here? Let me tell you something, hotshot. While you've been off on your Mexican vacation, the rest of us have continued to work homicides in this town. We know what we're doing. And let me tell you, Roy was at least as important to us as he was to you."

Dooley stared, then nodded. "OK." He knew it was over, and he turned and left. Out in the squad room McShea looked up from the typewriter, haggard from hours of paperwork, and said, "So what do you think, Dooley?"

Dooley just looked at him for a few seconds. "I think somebody just got away with something."

15

THERE WAS A FUNERAL. DOOLEY WASN'T KEEN ON FUNERALS; THERE
had been a spate of them in his life at a certain period—his father,
his mother, Consuelo, all within two years—which had put him per-
manently off the concept. This one was going to be particularly
rough. Dooley would have given a lot to be one of the pallbearers,
standing tall in the uniform, carrying his partner to the grave, but he
had thrown all that away.

As it was he tagged along with Kevin in a hastily bought sport
jacket, feeling lost in the crowd that jammed the old neighborhood
church, staring up at the luminous stained glass windows while the
priest droned, wishing a lot of things had been different.

He spotted Andrea with Roy's parents, taking hugs and condo-
lences as the crowd milled after the service. He had wondered what
her status here would be, but nobody seemed to think she didn't
belong with the family; Roy's sister murmured something in her ear
with a hand on her shoulder. Roy's parents looked dazed but Andrea
was calm and detached, nodding here, squeezing a hand there, her
gaze going far away when she disengaged. She looked careworn but
had a quiet beauty in a midnight blue dress with her hair falling free.
As Dooley approached she gave him a totally blank look.

He reached out to hug her but felt suddenly it was a bit forced; she
made a minimal response and he gave her a quick couple of pats on
the back and drew away. "How you doing?" he said.

A little toss of the head. "OK." Her gray eyes were very large.

Dooley opened his mouth again but nothing came out. He wanted to take her away out of there and go someplace and pour out his heart, but that wasn't on the program today. "I'll give you a call," he said finally. She smiled, just a quick compression of the lips, and said "OK" again, and then her attention was elsewhere, somebody else leaning in for a word or two. Dooley moved on.

He caught up with Kevin on the steps of the church. There was a lot of blue in the crowd and a couple of camera crews jockeying for position around the fringes. Kevin was standing with Matic and a couple of other heavyweights in gold-banded caps. Dooley nodded briefly at Matic and the other brass and put a hand on his brother's arm. "I'll see you back at the house later."

"Aren't you coming to the cemetery?"

"Nah. I'd just as soon skip it."

Kevin raised an eyebrow, an old familiar look. "How you gonna get home?"

"I got a ride. See ya." Dooley took off, feeling that old skeptical look of Kevin's on his back, wondering why at forty-four years of age he still couldn't just tell his big brother the truth, that he was dying inside and would rather walk until his feet blistered than stay and pretend to be part of something he had thrown away.

"John Spanos." Dooley could tell word had gotten around just from the way D'Amico reacted; he stopped chewing for a second and then he smiled a little after he swallowed.

"What do you want to know about John Spanos for?"

It hadn't taken Dooley as long as he'd feared to run Mike D'Amico to earth. D'Amico worked at Eleventh and State now, and a couple of calls had gotten Dooley through. D'Amico had been a sergeant out on the West Side when Dooley was just starting out in a squad car. D'Amico had grown up poor but honest on Taylor Street and he hated the mob; nobody had been surprised when he wound up in Organized Crime. Now, not too far from retirement, he ran the OC Intelligence unit and was mostly off the streets. "At least the wife's happy," he had said.

Now D'Amico was waiting for an answer, washing down his lunch with coffee in the Loop diner where he'd come to meet Dooley. "I worked with Roy Ferguson," said Dooley. "I got a personal interest."

D'Amico shrugged. "What do you want to know about him?"

"I want to know who he is. I want to know what he is. Is he a made guy?"

D'Amico leaned back on his chair, frowning, the expert organizing his thoughts. "Well, no, he's not a made guy, because he's not Italian. The made guys are the bosses, the crew chiefs, and they can only be Italian. But you don't have to be made to be an Outfit guy. If you bring home the bacon, they don't care who you are. You can be Greek like Spanos, Jewish, you name it. There have always been Outfit guys who weren't Italian. They didn't get made, but they enjoyed a lot of the privileges. One thing is, being made means you can't be whacked without it being sanctioned. It's admission to a protected society. But here's the thing—if you're a moneymaker, nobody's gonna mess with you. And Spanos is a moneymaker."

"What's he do? Where's the money come from?"

"Well, he's one of Vincent Bonifazio's guys. They're the descendants of the old Taylor Street crew that all moved out to Elmwood Park and those places. They've got some wire rooms, they got money on the street, the usual stuff. And video poker. That's the big thing now. They got machines all over. Spanos has some bookies working for him, he collects juice, he probably still runs some card games in Greek Town where he started out. That's where he got to know those Taylor Street boys."

Dooley nodded slowly, looking out the window onto Michigan Avenue. "You ever nailed him for anything?"

"No. Spanos has never done time. He's been arrested once or twice, I think, for gambling, but that's just a night in jail and something to brag about back at the bar."

Dooley nodded slowly. "Do you think he's capable of killing Roy Ferguson?"

D'Amico gave it some thought, sorting things on his plate with his fork. "You know, he's not the one I would have picked to do something like this. He doesn't have that kind of reputation." D'Amico took another bite and chewed for a while. He swallowed, laid down the fork and said, "There are guys, you know they're mobsters because they're basically thugs. They like to beat people up, they like to hurt people. They're mobsters because the mob finds them useful. The mob is based on the threat of violence and you need violent people to give it credibility. And then there are other guys who're smarter. You know they're basically crooks, but they're smarter, they're in it more for the money. Those are the guys that wind up with their own crews and the big houses in Florida. They're a lot less likely to go off half cocked and shoot a cop. And I would have said John Spanos was one of those guys. He's smart and he doesn't have a reputation for violence. He even, I think, has a couple of years of college, which in that crowd makes him Albert Einstein. I don't think he was supposed to wind up being a wise guy."

"What do you mean?"

"I knew his old man. Steve Spanos was a fence. He had a discount store down on Jackson just off Halsted, or maybe it was Van Buren, I'm not sure, and he used to—Christ, he used to sell anything anybody would bring in down there. He was a gambler, too. Ran some card games there in Greek Town. He was a crook but he wasn't really a bad guy. And he wanted his kids to do better. John went off to Urbana, I think, was supposed to get his degree and do something legitimate, but then Steve got whacked."

"Aha. What happened?"

"Well, we never knew for sure. What you usually get whacked for is one of two things—you get greedy and start holding out, or they think you're gonna talk. They take care of you in a hurry then. They found Steve Spanos in the trunk of his car with a few turns of good stiff wire around his neck."

Dooley nodded. "And so what happened with John?"

D'Amico shrugged. "He dropped out of school, came back, went into the rackets. I guess he thought he had to carry on the family business. It's too bad, because he could have made something of himself."

Dooley had eaten all he was going to eat. He shoved his plate away and drank some coffee. "If Spanos did shoot Roy, would he have had to get it sanctioned?"

"In theory."

"And if he didn't get the OK, what would the reaction be?"

"Depends on how much heat comes down. They're not going to mess with him unless he's a real liability. Like I said, Spanos has some stature. Even if there is a lot of heat, if he could convince them he had a good reason, he might ride it out. Or if he could convince them he didn't do it. It still looks like a stickup to a lot of people."

Dooley looked out the window across South Michigan Avenue into the park. It had cleared a bit but there was a cold wind blowing scraps of cloud across the sky over the lake and trash along the sidewalks. "Yeah. It looks a lot like that."

Dooley let himself in the back door of Roy's place and walked slowly up the hall, his footsteps going *thump-thump* on the hardwood floor, echoing a little in the empty apartment. All the way up at the front he could see branches tossing in the wind, shedding the last few leaves. Nothing had changed but everything had changed; this was a dead man's place now and Roy was never coming back to flop on the couch and flick on the TV, empty a couple of beer bottles and fall asleep dreaming of his lost little boy. Dooley had waited a month before he had been able to go back and clear out the apartment where Consuelo had died; four days was a new record for him. He stood in the living room for just a moment, thinking how little of his friend there really was here, before he turned and went back down the hall to Roy's bedroom.

He'd never been in here, and he was a little afraid of what he'd find, but if what he needed existed at all, it would be in this room. He started with the dresser drawers, finding only the briefs, socks, T-shirts and jeans of a man who had never been much of a clotheshorse; in the bottom drawer under the sweaters he found three skin magazines. He wasn't surprised but it made him sad; it embarrassed him. Dooley went and stuck them deep in the trash can in the kitchen, thinking that here at least was something he could spare a mother or a sister. He went back into the bedroom and opened the closet door.

There were three suits, a sport jacket or two, a dozen or so shirts, ties flung haphazardly across the bar. The floor was littered with shoes that might have sorted themselves into pairs if anyone had bothered with them. There was a shelf just above eye level that held a few boxes and a tightly rolled sleeping bag.

Dooley found the Smith & Wesson .38 Police Special in a Payless shoe box. He'd known it would be here; everybody had gone to the 9mm auto but they hadn't thrown away their revolvers. The cylinder was empty but there were six rounds in a speed-loader lying beside the gun. Dooley set the box on the bed and took out the revolver and hefted it. It felt good in his hand but there was no place to put his index finger because of the trigger lock that Roy had left in place, rendering the gun useless to anyone without a key. Maybe I could beat John Spanos to death with it, thought Dooley.

He pondered briefly, looking around the room, deciding that Roy would never have left a key to the lock lying around where anybody in Dooley's position could find it. The key would be on his key chain along with the keys to his house and his car and anything else he didn't want people messing with. If they weren't evidence, the keys would now presumably be with Roy's parents. And that was just about that, thought Dooley. He put the gun back in the box and returned it to the shelf. He backed out of the closet, looked around the room, and stood still, hands on his hips, not ready to give up.

Fifteen years before, Dooley had taken a little .25 automatic off a tavern brawler who had murmured in his ear as he put the cuffs on, claiming a sergeant at Grand and Central as an uncle and pleading with Dooley to keep the gun as a token of his esteem and let him plead guilty to the assault with a pool cue. The gun hadn't entered into things and Dooley had gone along, slipping the .25 into his jacket pocket and keeping it in his closet for seven years until he had brought it out to use it on Leroy Dickens. Guns had a way of crossing a cop's path, and Dooley thought there was a chance there might be one more on the premises.

Dooley knew his way around old Chicago three-flats, and it took him only five minutes to find the second gun. This was the illegal one, and Roy had hidden it under a loose flap of linoleum that covered a hole in the sheet metal floor of the cabinet under the kitchen sink. He had wrapped it in a plastic bag and sealed it with duct tape, and when Dooley stripped off the covering it lay black and lethal in his hand, an honest-to-God Walther PPK, an antique. It was a solid, heavy piece with the stopping power to put a mobster on the floor with any kind of decent hit. Dooley pulled out the magazine and sure enough it was full, six rounds full. He shoved it home and worked the slide, moving a round into the chamber. The action was smooth and the safety flicked off and on again with a comforting *click*. Somebody had taken care of this piece. Maybe this had been Roy's ace in the hole, his plan for getting John Spanos out of his life if he ever got tired enough.

That would be appropriate, thought Dooley. He slipped the gun into his jacket pocket, just like before.

On the phone Andrea sounded less than thrilled; Dooley put it down to the general gloom of the circumstances. The important thing was she said yes. She had a couple of hours before she had to go to work and no, she didn't have anything planned. He picked her up and drove east, along Devon. She looked good, hair pulled back, made up already for work, a nice-looking clear-eyed woman in a gray wool sweater, maybe a little melancholy. Conversation was sporadic at first, Dooley tossing out observations about this and that, things he had missed, things that had changed. Along the South Asian strip of Devon, sari shops and halal meat markets on either side, she started pointing out restaurants, the Viceroy of India, Mehran. Dooley didn't think much of Indian food but he said sure, we'll go there sometime. His spirits rose, going places with a friend in the car, making plans.

He swung north to Pratt and took it all the way to the lake. Where the street ended just shy of the beach he squeezed the Nova in a bit too close to a fire hydrant and they walked across fifty yards of park out onto the breakwater. The sky was clogged with ragged dirty clouds but the wind was working hard to clear it; the sun came through at intervals, warming the dead colors of the cityscape and dappling the restless lake. Walking out toward the light tower at the end of the long breakwater they passed a couple of old and patient fishermen, but nobody else was out. Eight miles south they could see the downtown skyline, a cutout of angular shapes.

"This is what makes the city," said Dooley. "The lake. Without the lake we're just an overgrown Indianapolis or something." They had reached the end of the line, screened from land by the tower. Dooley leaned on the restraining cables, his back to the water.

"It's beautiful." She put her hands on the wire next to him, looking out toward the horizon. "I sometimes think about moving closer, giving up the house and getting an apartment over here."

"This neighborhood right around here was going down the tubes when I was around last."

"Oh, I don't know. I haven't gotten to that point yet, thinking about neighborhoods. I just get these feelings sometimes: maybe it's time for a change. But I never do anything. The word *inertia* was invented for me."

There were gulls along the shore, swooping, plunging, making noise. "A change of scene can help," said Dooley. "But it's just cosmetics. Sooner or later you gotta deal with the basics."

They were silent for a while, looking in different directions, buffeted by the wind. When Dooley turned his head she did too, and they looked at each other for a long moment. "He won't get away with it," Dooley said.

"Who?" Andrea shook her head, a look of irritation passing over her face.

"The guy that killed Roy. He won't skate this time."

He wasn't sure what that look was; he wasn't sure what he'd expected. "That's good," she said.

"Roy was my partner. It's an obligation."

Andrea was staring down into the water, the melancholy taking over again. "You're not personally responsible," she said.

"Look." Dooley could tell he had said something wrong. "I don't know what you feel about Roy right now. I can't imagine. But me, I'm hurting. Roy was my partner and my best friend. He taught me everything I know about being a detective, and he taught me a hell of a lot about being a man." Dooley had to stop; he could feel himself starting to tear up, the throat clutching. He took a breath, looking out over the water, and said, "So I'm telling you because he was your husband. I'm promising you. The guy will not get away with it. That's all. He won't get away with it." Dooley wanted to tell her, to tell her exactly what he was going to do, but he had enough cop left in him to know he'd already said plenty.

When he looked at her she was just staring at nothing, somewhere out over the waves. "That's fine," she said, almost inaudibly.

Dooley hadn't expected her to turn cartwheels but he'd wanted something more than this; he didn't know what. Time went by and she shook herself, coming back from somewhere distant. "I'm cold," she said.

"Let's go get some coffee."

"That'd be good."

He put a hand on her arm as she moved, stopping her. "Did you wind up hating him?"

Andrea seemed to give it some thought, looking him right in the eye; finally she said, "No, I never hated Roy. Never. But you get to a point where you just can't put it back together. It's gone."

Dooley nodded and let go of her arm. "I'm sorry. Maybe you don't want to hear all this."

She closed her eyes briefly. "It hurts, that's all. I mean, I lost him already once. And now . . ." She shrugged and started to walk back toward shore. "It's tough to lose somebody twice."

Dooley had picked a bar at random; he wanted someplace where nobody knew him. This one was on Clark Street south of Foster, a dark little neighborhood place like a thousand others in the city, with a bar to lean on and a jukebox with a little of everything and somebody to pour the whiskey. Dooley didn't want to talk to anybody and nobody wanted to talk to him.

The Walther was stuck in his belt at the small of his back, under the jacket, a nudge in the spine to remind him of pressing business. He was glad it was there. Despite the bourbon, his good judgment kept butting into the conversation.

The Outfit gets what it wants for one reason, thought Dooley: people know Outfit guys would just as soon kill you as shake your hand. And most people are not prepared to fight back. They are not skilled at violence and they are not ruthless. Outfit guys are not necessarily skilled either, but ruthless—they wrote the book on that.

Dooley knew there was a simple way to bring John Spanos to justice. He could just shoot him. Dooley had become sufficiently ruthless and even reasonably skilled, and he knew there would not be any problems of conscience. The only problem was practical: he was already vulnerable. He had already gone careening around the landscape leaving bodies, and there was a limit to how long a man could get away with that.

Two swallows into the first bourbon Dooley had given a few seconds' thought to the question of justice. Proof? He had no proof John Spanos had killed Roy Ferguson, but there was that strong presumption. Dooley had laughed a little, drawing a look from the bartender, a loner in a bar laughing into his whiskey. Nobody was better placed than Dooley himself to confirm the validity of strong presumptions.

Kill him, thought Dooley. Tell him why, give him three or four seconds to be sorry, then put out the lights. He saw Leroy Dickens dying again, slumping over with that resigned look on his face.

And jump the next flight out? Here we go again. Dooley drained his second drink and thumped the glass down on the bar. Despite his best efforts to weaken his judgment and wash out his inhibitions with the best Kentucky had to offer, something had laid a great big hand on his chest and said hold it. Dooley had pulled off one premeditated killing in his life and that was going to be enough. The costs were too high.

Which didn't mean, Dooley thought as he slid off the stool, that he was going to let John Spanos get away with anything.

Not in the least.

16

DOOLEY WORKED ON HIS BEARD IN ROY'S BATHROOM, USING ROY'S scissors and electric razor. He hadn't shaved in two years but it was time for a new look. The thing now was the mustache and goatee, the trim and rakish goatee just darkening the chin. Dooley shaved his throat and cheeks and trimmed up what was left and decided it was good; he looked like every asshole he saw with his baseball cap on backward. He looked like Basil Rathbone.

He found an old Sox cap in Roy's closet. He was damned if he was going to wear it backward, but it went with the old flannel shirt he pulled out of the closet. Roy had been bigger than he was, but with the sleeves rolled up, worn jacket-style over a T-shirt, it wouldn't matter. Dooley had dressed fairly neatly down in Mexico, and it had taken him a while to get back into Chicago casual. He needed some more jeans.

The flannel shirt would cover the Walther even if he took his jacket off; another good reason for the look.

"They caught Sammy with a fucking trunkful of cell phones. Confiscated the whole lot of 'em. You know how much those things cost?" Vincent Bonifazio was indignant, spilling coffee as he gestured. "And if it hadn't been for Chuckie's guy downtown they would have scooped him too. He got the call just in time to flush everything and get the fuck out. Hadda leave a bunch of stuff behind. He was more pissed off about his god damn microwave than he was about almost getting busted. Now he's gotta start all over again. And Jimmy D, they don't even come for him but he gets nervous and packs everything up, the fucking computer's on the backseat of his car and he's getting me out of bed asking what the fuck should he do. Suddenly I got more headaches than I can deal with. Angelo's pissed off too. And it's because of you."

Spanos sat impassive at the head of the table. He traded a look with Pete Bianco, who hadn't said a word while Bonifazio raved. When he was sure Bonifazio was through he spoke. "It's a tempest in a teacup, Vince."

"What the fuck does that mean? I got people sitting in jail and I gotta raise bail and pay fucking lawyers. What the fuck, it's a tempest in a fucking teacup?"

"It's two or three guys in CPD Vice with a bug up their ass. They didn't go to the Feds, they didn't even get the sheriff in on it. They hit half a dozen places inside the city, and that's not even where the action is. It's a nuisance raid."

"And they didn't touch you."

"OK, they didn't touch me."

"And the reason is, they think you killed that fucking detective."

"Well, the question is, what do *you* think? Are you gonna let them work this scam on you?"

Bonifazio came halfway around the table, the strange light blue eyes fixed on Spanos. "Boy, Johnny, I'd love to believe it's a scam. I'd love to believe you. But you gotta admit, it looks real fucking suspicious."

"I didn't kill him, Vince. I'm not that stupid." Spanos gave the stare right back; now that he was lying not to stay out of jail but possibly to stay alive, he knew the only thing to hang onto was complete all-out brazenness.

"No, I don't think you are," said Bonifazio. "You're not stupid. But here's what's bugging me." He reversed direction, paced back up the room. "You could have done it and you could be counting on the fact that it was stupid to make me think you didn't do it."

"Jesus, Vince." Spanos shook his head, exhaling loudly. "You're working too hard."

Bonifazio spun around. "Look me in the eye and tell me I'm wrong."

"You're wrong, Vince, you're way off base. OK?" Calm now, Spanos told himself, don't let the dumb-ass guinea with his evil-eye stare get to you. "Listen, Vince. Suppose you're right. Just for the sake of argument. OK? Just supposing here."

"You did kill him, didn't you?"

"For Christ's sake, will you listen to me? Even if I did it, does this hurt us, what happened last night? Pete, what percentage of our assets got confiscated, what percentage of our people got arrested?"

"What percentage?" Pete Bianco looked stunned, as if somebody had asked him what the capital of Kazakhstan was. "How the . . . I don't know, I'll have to figure it out."

"I'll tell you. Less than ten percent. We've still got six major books running full steam, bringing in over a hundred thousand a week. They haven't scratched the fucking surface."

"This could be just the start," said Bonifazio.

"It ain't the start of nothing. They do this kind of thing once a year, just to justify their fucking salaries. Remember last year, before Christmas? We went through the same shit. We bailed a few guys out, found some new rooms, got up and running again. Hell, they didn't put a dent in us, and they won't, as long as all those assholes out there wanna get their hundred bucks down on fucking Notre Dame. There's too many of them."

Bonifazio sat down, drank coffee, stared at him. "So what's your point?"

"My point is this. I've already talked to the cops and they don't have a thing, not a fucking thing. They can think I killed that detective until the day they die, but if they had anything, I'd be in Cook County Jail right now. And the more they think I did it, the more they spread it around, the better that is for us, because I got away with it. And then the word is out again, like it used to be: you don't mess with the Outfit. Not even a cop can mess with the Outfit. And that makes us stronger, Vince."

There was a silence. Bonifazio finished his coffee, tapped the empty cup on the tabletop, looked at Bianco. He looked back at Spanos and said, "Fuckin'-A, Johnny. You may just be the smartest god damn Greek I ever met."

Duke's was a bar like a dozen Dooley had known: a place where you went to watch a ball game, shoot pool, talk about women, kid your friends and once in a while take a swing at your enemies. It was a man's bar and a young man's bar at that; it was loud and bright and decorated for durability. The jukebox had a lot of Aerosmith and Guns N' Roses and the rest room had condom machines covered in obscene graffiti. Dooley had gone through a phase of hanging out in bars like this, years ago. Friday night at the bar: get wasted and wind up in a fight. If you were twenty-two and indestructible this was your kind of place.

Dooley had guessed a Tuesday night would be a little better for a man who was twice that age and had no illusions left. He sat at the bar working on his second beer and more or less watching a hockey game on the TV high on the wall. The crowd was thinner and a little older than it would be on the weekend; he could see Roy fitting in here. The bartender wasn't working too hard and he tended to camp near the cash register with a couple of pals, older men with hard liquor in their glasses. To Dooley's left was a trio he could see as Roy's asshole buddies: three of a kind, late thirties or early forties, heading downhill with a load of alcohol on board. Chicago working class tough guys, just starting to hit that wall.

Dooley had been listening; the alpha male of this little herd had a mustache and deep pockets, a careless way with the pile of bills in front of him and a careless tone with the bartender. They were watching the hockey but not too closely; what they were here for was the talk. After some meandering they had hit a rich vein, the legendary incompetence of the Bears. The mustache was the expert, the man who had all the stories.

"Remember that time, like 'seventy-one or -two maybe, Douglass is quarterbacking, down in Saint Louis? He steps up under center, starts calling the signals, doesn't like what he sees. He steps back all of a sudden, turns to the ref and calls time out. The center thinks it's the snap count. He hikes the fuckin' ball, it goes straight up in the air, a jump ball. The play starts 'cause the ref never called time, the Cardinal defensive end comes in and catches the god damn ball on the fly, goes for a TD. Bam. The Bears are down seven-zip and the game's just started. Douglass is going out of his mind screaming at the ref, but the play stands."

"You're fuckin' kidding me."

"No. God help me. Saw it with my own eyes."

Much shaking of heads, some incredulous laughter, everyone thinking hard, wanting to top this one. Dooley turned on the stool, facing them. "I saw that one," he said. "It wasn't Douglass. It was Jack Concannon."

Mustache gave him a look: who the fuck are you? "No it wasn't. It was Bobby Douglass."

"It was Jack Concannon, and the guy that caught the ball wasn't the end. It was Larry Stallings, the outside linebacker."

"Says who?"

Dooley reached into his shirt pocket. "Says a hundred bucks." He tossed the bill on the bar. He smiled, cool as could be, and took a drink of beer. "Jack Concannon."

Mustache looked at the bill and back at Dooley. Dooley could see him coming to the rapid decision that he wasn't a hundred bucks' worth sure; his pals were giving him that look, waiting for him to brush this fly away. Instead he stalled. "What are you, the fucking sports encyclopedia?"

Dooley shook his head. "Just a fan. But I remember stuff. I watch a game, I remember it. It just sticks in my head. And I remember that one. That was in 'sixty-nine, by the way, the year they lost all but one of 'em." Dooley smiled again, conciliatory, and reached for the hundred. "Forget it. It ain't worth a hundred. I'll bet you the next round. A round of drinks says it was Jack Concannon." He tucked the bill away, still smiling.

Mustache hadn't smiled yet. "Put your money back on the bar." Backing down meant losing face, and Mustache would never do that. "I'll bet you. We'll ask Jack." He nodded toward the bartender's group sitting near the register.

Dooley took a look over his shoulder. "Why should I take Jack's word for it?"

One of Mustache's friends piped up. "Jack knows everything. What he don't know about the Bears ain't worth knowing."

Dooley shook his head, smiling. He pulled out the bill and tossed it back on the bar. "I'm assuming Jack is an honest man?"

"Hey. You don't walk in here, somebody we never seen before, and start insulting people," said Mustache.

"Who's insulting anyone? Do I get to see your money?"

Mustache almost balked at the last second; Dooley could see calculations happening fast behind the tough-guy look. Finally he dug in a pocket or two and came up with five twenties.

His friend called down the bar. "Hey, Jack."

Jack had white hair and a collapsing face; too much booze and too many Bear games had made Jack an old man. He turned his head slowly and said, "What."

"We need a referee here. We got a bet going. About the Bears."

Jack blinked at them. "What is it?"

Mustache said, "Remember that play a long time ago where the Bears' quarterback called time out and the center hiked the ball straight up in the air? And the defense caught it and ran for a touchdown?"

"Sure. Down in Saint Louis."

"Yeah. Who was the quarterback? This guy says it was—"

"Hang on." Dooley raised a hand. "Don't lead him. Just ask him who the quarterback was."

Mustache gave him a murderous look but said nothing. Before anyone could rephrase anything, Jack called out in his rasping voice, "Jack Concannon. And the linebacker that caught the ball was Stallings. Strangest god damn play I ever saw."

In the uncomfortable silence that followed, Dooley turned slowly and swept the two hundred dollars toward him. He took his time straightening and folding the bills. Mustache said, "Well fuck you, Jack. Thanks a lot."

"You made the bet, dumb-ass."

Dooley called to the bartender. "Give everybody a refill on me, will you?" He flicked a thumb at Mustache. "And while you're at it, give my friends here a shot of your best bourbon too. Maybe some of that Maker's Mark up there." He turned to Mustache and said, "You want a chance to win it back?"

"Don't do me any favors."

"Call it a no-hard-feelings gesture. No further risk to you. I'll put your hundred back on the bar and we'll flip for it. You supply the coin. You win, you get your hundred back."

Mustache looked at him long and hard through a pull on his beer; he looked at him while the bartender brought new beers and poured out the shots. Finally he said, "Keep it." The look on his face said keep it but keep out of my way.

Dooley raised his hands, the have-it-your-way sign. "OK. You're a straight-up guy, I appreciate that. Listen." Dooley shot a look over his shoulder, slid off his stool, took two steps, closing the gap between them. Just loud enough to be heard over the music, looking into three half-hostile faces, he said, "I'm serious about winning it back. If you ever want to do some real betting, get some action down on a game or two, I can get you better odds than anybody else in town."

A couple of looks were exchanged and Mustache said, "Who the fuck are you?"

Dooley stuck out his hand. "Frank Dooley, pleased to meet you."

Mustache gave his hand a look but didn't move. "I don't mean your name. I mean, who the fuck *are* you?"

Dooley shrugged. "I just got back in town, been away for a few years. Made some money down south of the border, I'm just looking to spread a little of it around. I got together with an old partner of mine. We can give you odds on a ball game; we can get a card game going."

Mustache laughed into his beer. His friends traded a look and shook their heads. "I don't bet with anybody I don't know," said Mustache.

"Well, you broke that rule just now," said Dooley. "But hey, I understand your caution. Forget I said anything. Look, lemme give you back your hundred bucks. I fuckin' sandbagged you there. I feel bad about it."

"Keep the god damn money, will ya? I took the bet."

"OK. Shit, all right. Hey, let's do this. I'll consider this one hundred bucks from you to be credit. You got one hundred bucks of credit with me if you want to get a little action down on the Bears sometime or whatever. Fair enough? I don't usually let guys run a tab, but for you I'll make an exception 'cause of the way I hit you with the Jack Concannon thing, which wasn't really fair because I got this freak mind that retains shit like that. I shoulda kept my fuckin' mouth shut."

"Yeah," said Mustache. "I kinda wish you had."

"All right, OK. Look, I'll be around. Maybe on Saturday. I ain't gonna bother nobody, but you think about it. If you want to get a little bet down on some football, remember what I said. You got credit now with me."

Mustache shrugged and reached for the shot Dooley had bought him. "Yeah, OK. That's mighty white of you." Body language said the conversation was over, and his pals were already crowding Dooley out, hips shifting, backs turning.

"Take care," said Dooley. "I'll talk to you soon."

How to win friends and influence people, thought Dooley, driving north on Harlem. The worst part of this whole thing was that he was going to have to go back and hang out in a bar full of assholes again. For as long as it took.

Which shouldn't be too long, he thought. He had just made maybe the clumsiest approach in the history of illegal gambling, but he didn't give a damn; all he wanted was attention. He wanted John Spanos to come calling, and this was the quickest way he could think of.

"Who the hell would want to live out here?" said Spanos, looking out a window. All he could see was highways and gas stations.

"What's wrong with it? My mother lives out here," said Lou Messina.

Spanos shrugged. "What's she do for fun?"

"She's too old to have fun. She's got a kitchen and a TV. What the fuck?"

"What the hell kind of neighborhood can you have in a place like this? You go straight to your car and drive the hell out of here, that's what you do."

"Right. Which is why it's the perfect place for us. You think the neighbors give a shit what goes on up here?"

Spanos shrugged again and turned away from the window. The apartment depressed him; it was a fairly new building but there were already water stains on the gray carpeting and holes punched in the drywall. In place of furniture there were empty pizza cartons lying on the floor. This was a dead space in the exurbs, a nondescript apartment complex trapped between expressways. "You have to sign a lease?" he said.

"No lease. Month to month. The landlord's some kind of camel jockey. He don't give a shit, long as he gets his money."

Spanos nodded. Low voices were coming from the next room; somebody was taking bets already. "OK. Looks good, Lou. Fast work."

"Hey, all you need's a phone or two."

"Yeah. Who's got keys?"

"Me and Frankie. You want one? I can make a copy."

Spanos nodded, heading for the door. "Yeah. Get it to me tomorrow or something."

Messina faded into the next room. Bobby Marino came out of the bathroom zipping up his pants. "Hey, Johnny."

"What?"

"Got something for you." Marino shot a look at Messina's back, dug in his shirt pocket.

"What's that?"

"I found this in the car." Marino held out a small blue notebook.

Spanos froze. He stretched out his hand and took the notebook. "What car?"

In a low raspy whisper Marino said, "You know, the car we drove.

That day. This was on the floor. It musta fell out when you jumped in. When I ditched the car I found it on the floor."

Spanos opened his notebook and skimmed a page or two, not focusing. He remembered jumping into the car, his nerve giving out. He remembered looking at his torn pocket. He remembered pulling the trigger, caving in Roy Ferguson's chest.

He took in a single sharp breath and let it out. "Why the fuck didn't you give me this before?"

Shrugging, Marino said, "I haven't seen you since. You need it that bad?"

Spanos shook his head, still leafing through the notebook, just to have something to do with his hands. "Nah. That's OK, thanks. Good thing you spotted it."

"Well, shit. You never ditch a car without making sure it's clean." Marino waddled away.

Spanos closed the notebook and put it in his pocket, trying to decide how he felt. He shook his head and made for the door.

Regret was something John Spanos had trained himself to suppress. It only took him a moment to step on the brief pang he felt at the thought that he had killed Roy Ferguson for nothing. What bothered him was the inefficiency. All that risk for nothing, he thought, going down the stairs.

17

THE SECOND TIME DOOLEY SHOWED UP IN DUKE'S THE JOINT WAS jumping. It was Saturday night and there was a college football game on six or eight different TV screens and the din was considerable. The crowd was rowdy and a lot younger, entirely white and heavy on testosterone. There were a few women, young, hardy and ostentatiously nubile. The pool tables and the video games were getting a workout and two bartenders were breaking a sweat as well. Dooley squeezed in at the bar and managed to flag one of them down.

He drank his beer with his back to the bar and scanned the crowd, looking for somebody he'd seen before. Working-class city people on a Saturday night: tans that had been earned on a construction site and hadn't faded yet; big hair and loud voices and bills stuffed in jeans pockets. Dooley had been watching people professionally for twenty years, and after ten minutes he had sorted out the picture: who was flirting, who was feuding, who would make a pass at whom before the night was out, who would come to blows. And who had money on the game.

He spotted Mustache moving through the crowd toward the bar and raised his glass; Mustache raised his chin in response and pushed on. Dooley turned his back on the crowd and waited. He waited long enough to get a good start on a second beer and see three touchdowns on the TV, Florida State running all over some SEC doormat. When he felt the hand on his shoulder it had been thirty-five minutes by his watch. He turned and said, "Hey, what's up?"

"How ya doin'?" Mustache looked as if the words had cost him an arm and a leg. "I wasn't sure you'd come back."

"I said I would, didn't I? What's new?"

"Not much. Just came in to rent a little beer." Dooley had never seen anybody put less into a joke; Mustache looked as if he were reading lines with a gun held to his head.

"Boy, that's the truth, ain't it? Recycling in action." Dooley raised his glass in salute.

Mustache drank, looking at the TV, and said, "Hey, listen. I got some guys who are interested in what you were talking about the other night."

"No shit? They got a little money to put where their mouth is, huh?"

"Yeah. We were wondering if it was too late to get something down on the NFL tomorrow."

"Hell, no. It ain't too late till the kickoff goes up."

"Yeah, well, you got a line? You got something to show us?"

"I can call my partner for the up-to-the second line. Your friends here?"

"Yeah." Mustache looked up and down the bar. "You wanna come in the back? I mean, we can't do it out in plain sight, right?"

"Lead the way, man." Dooley grabbed his beer off the bar.

He let the larger man run interference; he followed him back past the rest rooms, down a hallway decorated with beer-company posters of past Chicago teams, the Sox in ugly black uniforms, peeling off the wall. There was a door at the end of the hall on the right and Mustache pushed it about halfway open and stood back out of the way. "Here you go."

Dooley was flying by the seat of the pants; right up until this moment he truly hadn't given too much thought to what was going to happen once he looked John Spanos in the eye. All he knew now was that as setups went this one was about as thin as they came. He shifted his beer to his left hand, keeping the empty smile on his face but starting to get the rush now. He put his hand on the door and shoved hard. The door whipped open another forty-five degrees or so and hit something; Dooley came into the room fast, registering stacks of boxes and the man sitting on a chair opposite him, looking for what had stopped the door. When the door came back at him even faster, he was already out of the way and the door missed him as it slammed shut. A kid in a red Hawks jacket stood there with his arms extended, eyes going wide and pressure building, pissed off in an instant. He was a good-looking kid with black hair and a bit of stubble on his chin, a big broad-shouldered kid who would pack a wallop. Dooley gave him a look from head to toe and said, "You missed."

"Hey, *fuck* you."

"Hang in there. When you grow up I'll give you pointers."

Dooley was ready for anything but when the kid's eyes went to the man on the chair he knew it wasn't going to get rough quite yet. The man on the chair smiled, putting a lot of contempt into it. He was sitting with one leg crossed over the other, one elbow up on a pile of boxes, leaning back looking comfortable. "You need to learn some fucking manners," he said. His voice was deep and slightly hoarse.

"I don't waste manners on assholes."

A very long second ticked off the clock. "You know what? I think I'll let him hit you for that."

"I'm not talking about him," said Dooley.

That brought everything to a standstill; the script had gone out the window and everything was up for grabs. The man on the chair was about Dooley's age but had thirty or forty pounds on him, some in a broad chest but a lot at the waistline pushing at the green silk shirt under the top-of-the-line brown leather jacket. He had Mediterranean coloring with an oval face that came to a point at a chin that had been clean shaven that morning but looked as if it could light a match. The face had a brutish handsomeness that certain kinds of women like, and its owner evidently spent a good deal more money than Dooley did on his hair to keep it dark and flawlessly brushed back from a widow's peak. Dooley had seen a million of these guys. They got all the girls early on but by fifty they were blimps. This was a man who was depending on money rather than virtue to preserve his looks. He had dark eyes that showed all the warmth of the bottom of a well. "You must be talking about me, then," he said slowly.

"If you're John Spanos, I am."

The eyes narrowed. "OK, you're talking about me. Who the fuck are you?"

"I'm Frank Dooley and I'm here to make you pay."

"Is that so?"

"Can I kill him?" the kid said.

"Not quite yet," said Spanos. "We gotta find out what this *asshole's* talking about."

Dooley smiled, riding the crest of the adrenaline wave, ready for anything. "I'm talking about justice," he said.

A look of incredulous mirth appeared on the man's face. "What?"

"Court is now in session," Dooley said. "The prisoner stands accused of murder in the first degree."

Spanos's face went totally blank. He raised a hand and pointed at Dooley, not too emphatic, just a reminder of who was boss. "You got a big fuckin' mouth for a man in *my* house," he said.

"The prisoner will remain silent until adressed."

"Hey, jag-off," said the kid. Dooley was ready because he figured the muscle couldn't possibly stand by and take this; the kid was reaching for his shoulder when Dooley pitched the beer into his face. That gave him a second but the kid was a lot bigger than he was and Dooley knew he would lose if it went too many rounds. Still going on instinct, he just ducked and charged, planting a shoulder in the middle of the red jacket and getting legs and arms into the shove that knocked the kid backward over a stack of boxes onto his ass. The sound of Dooley's glass breaking on the floor was lost in the crash of the bottles inside the boxes. "Order in the fucking court, asshole," Dooley said.

The kid was going ballistic kicking at boxes; Spanos had put both feet on the floor. "Whoa!" he yelled. The kid stopped kicking but his eyes were on Dooley, and they were lit up. "Watch the fucking bottles," said Spanos. To Dooley he said, "You don't have any beer left. What are you gonna do now?"

On one knee, the kid fished a bottle out of the rubble and smashed it on the floor, brown glass flying everywhere. He held it by the neck and said, "I got a beer for you."

Dooley pointed an index at his chest. "Son, you come at me with that, I'm gonna shoot you dead and that's a promise."

They weren't used to resistance and they sure weren't used to the stakes being raised so suddenly; Dooley hoped the words were enough because even if he could wrestle the Walther out of the back of his waistband in time it would lead to all kinds of complications. He turned back to Spanos and said, "You killed a police officer named Roy Ferguson."

Two seconds went by and Spanos said, "I don't know what the fuck you're talking about."

"Wrong answer. If you were innocent, you'd know exactly what I'm talking about and you'd deny it. The court finds you guilty."

"The *court?*"

"That's what this is. The honorable Frank Dooley presiding in a bench trial. You got anything to say for yourself before sentencing?"

Spanos gawked at him and then looked at the kid, who was clearing the space between him and Dooley with his feet, still holding the bottle. Dooley could see them both, thinking, bluff, or no bluff? Spanos looked at him and said, "You're out of your fucking mind."

Dooley swelled out his chest, rose to his full five-ten and pointed at Spanos. "And you're out of time. You are hereby sentenced to live in perpetual uncertainty until such time as I can execute your worthless ass without getting caught. I'm gonna kill you, Spanos, sooner or later. The only way to avoid it is to turn yourself in to the CPD and make a full confession. You got that option right now. You want to come with me?"

Spanos shook his head, a sane man shocked by madness. He stared for another few seconds and then started to laugh. "You got nothin'," he said. "Nothin'. That's why you're in here foaming at the mouth."

"You're right, John. Legally I got nothing. But I'm just like you now. I don't give a fuck for legality. And that's why you've had your last good night's sleep." Dooley turned, freezing the kid with a look, and reached for the doorknob. He whipped the door open, slamming it against the wall, and stalked out.

He passed Mustache in the hall. The big man squeezed against the wall, giving him room.

Dooley was at the Marriott out by O'Hare before he quite knew what he was doing. It wasn't that far, and under the lingering effects of adrenaline he had broken all the speed limits along the way by a fair margin. As he pulled into the lot he realized he hadn't even considered whether Andrea would want to see him; all he knew was he wanted to talk to her.

He sat in the car for a while, coming down, wondering what he was doing there. He sure as hell wasn't going to tell Andrea about John Spanos, not yet. He wasn't going to tell her about putting the punk kid on his ass, though he would have loved to tell somebody about it. He would have loved to tell Roy about it, but that wasn't going to happen. For a moment Dooley was paralyzed with grief.

He sat in the car until the adrenaline was gone and all he felt was a great loneliness. He sat there a while longer afraid of the look on Andrea's face when he walked in, and finally he got out of the car.

She wasn't busy and she saw him right away when he took his spot at the end of the bar, but she took her time coming over. "You again," she said.

"Hey. Looks like you're having an easy night."

"Now, maybe. I had to fight off a platoon of conventioneers earlier."

"Any casualties?"

"A couple of egos. You must have gotten my message."

"What message?"

"I called Roy's and left a message on the machine."

"I haven't looked at it in a couple of days. What was the message?"

"Just a friendly hello. I thought things were a little chilly when we parted the last time."

"I thought so too. I couldn't quite figure out why."

Andrea swept the room with a professional gaze and came back to Dooley. "Keep working on it."

Dooley blinked at her, helpless. "Help me out here."

"I'm sorry. I don't mean to be a sphinx. Forget it, let's start over."

"I'm sorry, I guess I read things wrong. I had the impression for a while you didn't mind seeing me."

She stared and her face softened a bit. "It's not that I mind. You want to know the truth?"

Dooley waited a beat; did he? "Sure."

"I'm standing here looking at you, and it's like someone is standing between us."

Dooley nodded. "You mean Roy."

"Yeah."

He frowned; he had to get this right. "I'm not trying to hit on you.

I'm not bird-dogging here. I can see how you might think that. I get back in town and find out you're divorced and suddenly I'm on your doorstep all the time. But that's not it."

Andrea looked at him, not giving anything away. A party had come in and were settling around a table. "Excuse me," she said, and left. Dooley watched her work. He drank beer and waited for her to come back, and eventually she did. "I don't think you quite follow me," she said, sliding onto a bar stool.

"No, I guess not. Can you clue me in?"

"I never got the impression you were hitting on me."

Dooley nodded at his beer for a while. "OK. I'm not."

"So maybe you could clue *me* in a little. I mean, when guys wait for me to get off work at night, it's generally to hit on me."

Dooley was starting to smolder a little, losing patience with the games women played, but he gave it some thought and said, "I'm not sure why I keep coming after you, except of all the people I've talked to since I got back in town, you're the only one I get the feeling is really listening."

He risked a look at her then and saw her nod, once, and give him the ghost of a smile. "OK. Thank you."

"So what's with Roy, standing here between us? You think he wouldn't approve?"

She shook her head. "I don't think he'd mind at all."

"Well, you think we can get the son of a bitch to move out of the way?"

"Probably."

"You thought I came out here tonight just to talk about him some more."

"It crossed my mind."

"It seems to me we did manage to talk about a few things other than Roy."

"Yes, we did."

"Maybe we could keep going in that direction."

"Sure. Maybe we could even move on to happier things."

"I bet we could. Can I take you out to lunch tomorrow? It's my turn."

Andrea smiled again, like she meant it this time. "Yeah, that would be good."

18

DOOLEY HAD LOST TOUCH WITH THE WORLD OF CHICAGO RESTAU-
rants; some of his favorite places seemed to have gone under while he
was out of town. There were a million restaurants downtown, but he
didn't want to drive all over the city just for lunch. He called Kathleen.
"What's a nice place around here to take somebody to lunch?"

He'd caught her by surprise, he could tell. "A nice lunch? I don't
know. There's Byron and Hal's, there on Devon, in Lincolnwood.
That's where Judy and I go on our Thelma and Louise days. Who's
the lucky girl?"

"Nobody you know," Dooley said, not wanting to get the rumor
mill going. "An old friend. Thanks."

"You be good, Francis Dooley."

"It's lunch, for Christ's sake." In the car driving to Andrea's,
Dooley remembered things he'd heard about Byron and Hal's: there
had been talk it was a gambler's hangout. The rumor was years old
but Dooley decided he couldn't take chances showing his face in certain circles in his current situation.

They wound up at an Olive Mountain at Touhy and McCormick,
Andrea's suggestion. "I'm not particular," she said. It was fine with
Dooley, who liked Italian food OK and figured the Outfit probably
hadn't infiltrated the big restaurant chains, not yet anyway.

"So what do you want to be when you grow up?" Dooley said over
the rim of his Chianti, the wine getting to be a habit.

"You saying I'm not grown up?" Andrea looked good today in a light green turtleneck with her hair in a ponytail; she looked better every time he saw her.

"I'm just guessing you don't plan to spend the rest of your life as a cocktail waitress."

"I don't know. There are worse fates. I get to sleep in and I don't have to bring work home."

She did it deadpan and Dooley couldn't quite decide if she was serious. "OK," he said. "Me, I'm kind of between careers. I've done the cop thing long enough. I'm starting to think about the possibility of having a normal life."

"What's normal?"

"I don't know. Business or something. Make a little money. Figure out what people want and provide it for them."

"My dad ran his own business for years. Selling electrical equipment. He was always fretting about the bottom line but he wound up doing OK. It gave him gray hair and a great big house in the suburbs."

"That's starting to sound OK to me. You get tired of confrontation after a while. That's all a cop's life is. You get used to it but it gets old."

"Some people thrive on it." She said it with a distant look that told Dooley who she was thinking about.

"Sure. You can get addicted to it. And some people are naturally good at it. Me, I had to learn it. Not like my old man or Kevin. I was a timid kid, scared of my own shadow. I got pushed around, I let people take shots at me. Kevin had to teach me the facts of life. When I was about twelve, he took me aside one day and said, 'Look. You can stand up for yourself. Half the battle is being able to take a shot and keep swinging. And the other half is pure attitude, showing people you're not afraid to take that shot.' Kevin taught me the attitude."

She shook her head, looking sad. "You ever miss your innocence?"

Dooley laughed. "I never thought about it. I got tired of being a victim, I'll tell you that."

"So did Sean. And Roy took him aside and taught him the attitude. I knew he had to do it, but it made me cry." She poked at her salad. "Sorry, we were going to talk about happier things."

Dooley gave it a few seconds. "So, what are you going to do?"

She fixed him with a look and said, "Do I have to decide today?"

Dooley blinked at her. "I'm sorry, Andrea. I've forgotten how to make small talk." He was starting to think about exit strategies; this one was going to rival the *Titanic.*

She softened a little and said, "Me too. I didn't mean to snap at you. I don't know what I'm going to do. I feel like I've been asleep for about four years. I'm just waking up."

"I know what you mean. I woke up in Mexico City one day, staking out a warehouse full of stolen goods, thinking, How the hell did I get here?"

"At least you were in Mexico. I'm still living on LeMai Avenue, in a house full of ghosts."

"Maybe it's time to get that apartment over by the lake."

"Yeah," said Andrea, looking thoughtful. "Maybe. Over there by Loyola. I could afford to go back to school, too, with what I've saved. I could be a thirty-eight-year-old coed."

"The eighteen-year-olds won't stand a chance. Those young guys will be trooping after you."

She gave him such a peculiar look that Dooley knew he'd gone over the line; he'd even surprised himself. He grinned to make light of it. "You don't look thirty-eight," he said. "You look ten years younger."

"That's very gallant of you, but I have a mirror at home."

"You look nice," Dooley said, the foolish grin gone. "That's all I meant."

Andrea gave him a long grave look. "Thanks."

Dooley had his mouth open to tell her that wasn't a come-on, but he thought better of it. "What would you study?"

"Whatever I felt like." Andrea laid down her fork. "I'm just starting to realize, I can do anything I damn please."

"How does it feel?"

"It feels good," she said, with a look of wonder dawning in her wide gray eyes.

Somebody had been to Roy's place to start packing. The bookshelves were cleared and the bed in Roy's room had been stripped. Whoever it was hadn't had the heart to finish; half-filled boxes lay here and there on the living room floor. At the funeral Dooley had let Roy's father know he was in the apartment and gotten his permission to stay to the end of the month. It made a good deadline, two weeks away.

Dooley grabbed his bag out of the corner and flopped on the couch.

He rummaged until he found the address book. Dooley had been a cop, and cops don't throw away information. Dooley had brought every address and phone number he'd accumulated in eight years of Mexican intrigue back in a little red leather book. He flipped through the pages until he found *F*.

Dooley had to sit and stare at the phone a bit before he dialed, rehearsing. His Spanish was already getting rusty and he had to grope for a word or two; added to that, he wasn't entirely sure that Fuentes would remember him. He picked up the receiver and started punching in the number.

Dialing Mexico City was like dialing Oak Park these days; after a minimum of long-distance noise a female voice cooed in his ear, "*Panamérica Financiera, ¿en qué puedo servirle?*"

Dooley took a breath and dived in. "*Quisiera hablar con Ramón Fuentes. Dígale que le llama Dooley, el consejero de seguridad del senador Cruz Zamudio.*"

He had to repeat his name, but she went away with a click and in less than a minute Fuentes came on the line.

"Mr. Dooley, this is a surprise." He pronounced it "surprice"; accent apart, his English was actually pretty good. "I heard that you left town. Ernesto was telling me the other day he can't find a good man to replace you."

"I did leave, that's right. I'm calling from Chicago. I have to confess I used his name to get through to you."

"That's OK. What can I do for you?"

"Actually I'm calling in hopes I can do something for you."

There was a brief pause. "Oh, shit. What is it, the DEA?"

"No, no. You got me wrong. This isn't a warning. Nothing like that."

"Jesus, you escared me. I'm thinking, what is this policeman calling me for?"

"Yeah, I can see how that would be a little alarming. Look, I think I can steer a little business your way, that's all."

"Business?"

"Yeah, I may have some clients for you."

"What kind of clients?"

"The kind you handle. People who have money and want to make it grow and don't want to give too much of it to the government."

"Ah. Now I'm estarting to see your point. Where are these people?"

"Here. In Chicago."

"Friends of yours?"

"Not exactly. Acquaintances."

"And how much money we talking about?"

"Well, not as much as some of your clients probably, but I'd say at least as much as a Mexican senator."

"Aha. And what do they do, what kind of business are they in?"

"Well, gambling mostly. A little of everything. They have diverse interests and they deal in cash a lot."

"I see." In the silence Dooley could hear a faint tapping over the line, a pencil on a desk maybe. "Why me?"

"What do you mean?"

"Well, first, why did you call me, and second, why do these people want me? What are they doing with their money now?"

"I called you because the senator once told me you were the best moneyman in Mexico and reasonably honest besides."

"That's nice of him. I don't do anything with drugs, you know. I don't touch it."

"I understand. As for your second question, these people are in the market for a new financial advisor because their last one retired."

"Voluntarily?"

A sharp professional mind at work, thought Dooley. "More or less. He couldn't take the rough-and-tumble."

"I see." A couple of seconds passed. "Well, you know, I'll need to know more."

"Sure. This is in the very preliminary stages. I need to talk to them again, and if we get to the stage where a meeting is in order, I'll call you. I just wanted to know if you were interested."

"I'm always interested. As long as somebody can vouch for the client. Your word is good enough."

"I appreciate that. If we do get to a meeting, will you want to do it in Mexico?"

A musing noise came over the line. "You know, I could fly up there. I've never been to Chicago. I hear it's a lot of fun."

"It's a barrel of laughs, Mr. Fuentes."

"You can call me Ramón. And say, Frank—you don't mind if I call you Frank, do you?"

"Not at all."

"I'm assuming you'll expect some consideration if this works out."

"I wouldn't say no to a small finder's fee, but I'm not greedy."

"OK, why don't we discuss that when we move to the next estage?"

"Fair enough. I'll give you a call in a few days."

"Good. I'll be looking forward to that. Ernesto misses you, you know. He says he eslept a lot better when you were here."

"Tell him it's my turn to sleep for a change," said Dooley.

"So who is this fuck?" John Spanos poured a healthy measure of ouzo into a glass and shoved it across the desk to the cop. The cop had taken off his cap and laid it on the table but he was still in uniform, the radio clipped to the shoulder of his black leather jacket emitting periodic bursts of indecipherable static. The room in the back of the Halsted Street store smelled of olive oil and candle wax, and through a closed door an argument in Greek could be heard. The cop was a tired and disillusioned man whose face had sagged and lengthened with the years until he looked like an oft-whipped hound. He took a drink and winced as the liquor burned down his gullet.

"Well, he's not a cop anymore. If it's the same guy, he was, once upon a time."

"I thought so. The fucking guy walked, talked and acted like a cop. Except a cop on PCP or something. I mean, he was off his head."

"Well, that sounds like the guy. There's a whole bunch of Dooleys and more than one Frank, but as far as I could tell the only one that fits your guy would be a guy that was a homicide dick till he quit and left town under mysterious circumstances. Eight or ten years ago."

"What kind of circumstances?"

"Well, nobody proved nothing but here's what happened. This guy had a wife, and she got killed. Some deadbeat that lived down the block broke in and raped her and strangled her one night. Total impulse crime, the dumb fuck confessed to it the next day. But they

181

screwed up the case somehow and he walked. Well, it turns out a few weeks later the guy turns up dead in his house. Shot to death. Funny thing, Officer Dooley resigned two days before, turned in his star. They go look for him, he's gone. Left the apartment, left town. They eventually find out he went down to Mexico but nobody ever cared enough to bring him back. I guess they figured the deadbeat had it coming."

Spanos swirled ouzo in the bottom of his glass. "And Dooley's back, huh?"

"My source hadn't heard about it, but it's possible."

Spanos nodded. "Jesus, a rogue cop."

The cop drank and winced again. He exhaled and said, "What's he want with you?"

Spanos leveled an annoyed look across the table. "You heard, right? You know all about my little visit to Belmont and Western the other day?"

"I heard."

"OK, that's what it's about. He thinks I did it. He thinks I killed Ferguson."

The cop nodded, slowly. "You didn't, did you?"

"Aw, fuck, Alex, what do you think? I went through this all with them the other day. I wasn't anywhere near the god damn place."

"'Cause I'd have a little problem with that. A blind eye here and there's one thing, but hey."

"Alex, word of honor, OK? I'm not that fucking dumb, for starters."

"OK, OK. I believe you. What do you want me to do?"

"I don't know, you already did it, I guess. I just wanted to know who the guy was, what the fuck he was up to. Tell me honestly now, would this be some shit the department was pulling, you know, maybe the guy was wired or something, to get me to say something?"

"No, I can't see that. I really can't. That'd be . . . Jesus. They've pulled some dumb shit, but I really can't see that."

"Because, you know, a cop goes down, people go a little nuts."

"I know. You can understand that, right?"

"Sure. I can understand that. But I didn't do it."

"All right."

"I just want to know how much I have to worry about this asshole. I mean, this fucking loose cannon comes into the bar making death threats and all."

"Death threats? You can make a complaint if that's the route you want to go."

"Fuck, I'm a big boy. I just want to know how serious the guy's likely to be."

The cop drained his glass and held the wince for a while this time, looking into the empty glass. "I don't know what to tell you. That story about his wife, you can take it as seriously as you want."

Spanos sat still, his mouth drawn into a thin hard line. "Yeah," he said finally.

The cop picked up his hat, rose to his feet. "Thanks for the pick-me-up."

"OK, thanks for the intelligence. See you Friday night?"

The cop paused with his hand on the door handle. "I don't know, John. I haven't been doing too well. I've had the luck of a northbound deer on the southbound lane of the interstate lately."

"Well, you got a chance to win some back. Your luck's bound to turn."

The cop's eyes rested on Spanos for a moment. "Yeah. Maybe so. See you then."

Giannini's sat at a suburban intersection, next to a gas station and across from a mall, a long, long way from Taylor Street or the Patch. It was a low white building with red awnings and purple neon in the windows and a sign that said ITALIAN SPECIALTIES and KARAOKE MONDAY.

Inside it was dimly lit and overdecorated, the type of Italian place that gave you a plate of peppers and cheese cubes and pepperoni slices to keep you happy while you looked at an oversized and over-priced menu bound in red leather. The decor incorporated clumsily executed murals of vaguely Italianate landscapes with dark wood paneling and chairs that elderly customers had difficulty maneuvering because of their weight. To get to the dining room you had to pass through a lounge with two television sets and a dance floor at one end. There was a band setting up; from the look of their suits with the cute red vests Dooley knew just how they would sound.

He had chicken cacciatore and a Heineken and watched. It looked like a tame suburban crowd and he had to laugh at himself a little; black suits and violin cases were nowhere in evidence. It was a restaurant full of middle-class people, probably mostly of Italian descent and a generation or two removed from the old neighborhood that was now mostly black or gone altogether, wiped out by an expressway. You didn't need a password in Sicilian to get in; they took American Express. The band kicked in and was not quite as dire as Dooley had feared.

Dooley thought the two men in the booth at the back were maybes. Anywhere else he'd have put them down as older working-class guys on a boys' night out and not given them a second thought; they could be Streets and San workers on their bowling night. In fact there was a very good chance they *were* with Streets and San, though whether they actually did any work was moot.

Dooley finished his meal and asked for the check. His waitress was a plump raven-haired woman who had been beautiful not too many years ago. She was hustling, handling five tables and managing to do it without losing her temper. Dooley watched her totaling up his check and said, "Is Mr. Casalegno here tonight?"

She kept writing, frowning in concentration. She slapped the check down on the table and said, "Honey, I got enough trouble keeping track of your chicken without keeping an eye on him. Ask at the bar."

Dooley left her a good tip. The band was loud enough that Dooley had to shout a bit when he ordered a second beer at the bar. He watched three couples lurch around the dance floor and thought about his approach. He remembered Mike D'Amico saying that greed was all you needed to know about wise guys and figured subtlety was probably a waste of time. He didn't have time to do a Donnie Brasco number anyway, hanging out and worming his way into people's confidence; quick and dirty was going to be the ruling principle. When his beer came he shoved a twenty across the bar and repeated his question.

The bartender took his bill to the register and came back with his change. "Who's asking?"

Dooley reached inside his jacket and pulled out a sealed business-sized envelope. "Would you give him this, please?"

"You got a name?"

"For Mr. Casalegno I do. Just give him that."

The bartender shrugged and took the envelope. He went down to the end of the bar and tapped the shoulder of a man who was sitting there watching the band with a look of morose resignation. He passed over the envelope, leaning close to speak to the man. The man looked over his shoulder, scanned, found Dooley. Then he took the envelope away.

Dooley drank beer and waited. The man who came into the bar looking for him was younger than Dooley, and he didn't look like muscle; he looked a lot like the owner's son in a prosperous Italian restaurant. He had on a rugby shirt and he was nicely groomed and even looked pleasant, as if he'd be happy to stop by your table and share a glass of wine. "You the man with all the money?" he said when he stopped at Dooley's place at the bar.

"That's me. Frank Edmonds." Dooley set down his beer and stuck out his hand.

Instead of shaking it the man said, "What's the story?"

"Are you Angelo Casalegno?"

"No."

"Well, the money's for him. Is he here?"

"What's the money for?"

"I'll explain that to him."

The pleasant looking young man stared at Dooley from a distance of a foot and a half for another five seconds or so and said, "OK, come on."

Dooley followed him back through the dining room, down the hall past the phones and the rest rooms and around a corner. The man knocked on a door and pushed it open; Dooley followed him into a haze of smoke. The office had a desk and an oxblood couch with a coffee table in front of it and some filing cabinets. The only light came from a lamp on the desk. The desktop was cluttered with papers, pens, a phone, a full ashtray, the detritus of a working restaurateur. On the coffee table was a nearly empty bottle of Chivas, an ice bucket and several glasses. A man sat behind the desk and another one on the couch. The man on the couch was the muscle, a heavy middle-aged bruiser who looked bored at the moment but could no doubt get interested fast. "So what's this?" said the man behind the desk, holding up the ten one-hundred dollar bills he had taken from Dooley's envelope.

The man behind the desk was considerably older than in the pictures Dooley had seen. He had white hair and big black-rimmed glasses that gave him a cartoonish look, dominating a face that age and dissolution had caused to sag into dewlaps. He wore a dark blue V-necked sweater over a dress shirt with the top button undone. The glasses magnified his very dark eyes.

"That's your cash rebate," said Dooley. "That's just a little inducement to sit and listen for a while. You get to keep that whether or not you decide to do business with us."

"Hang on a second, you're going a little too fast for me." He shot a look at the younger man, who had sunk onto the couch next to the bruiser and was lighting a cigarette. The younger man shrugged and the man behind the desk looked back at Dooley. "Who the hell are you, to begin with?"

"You're Mr. Casalegno, are you?"

"Yeah, I'm Casalegno. So what?"

Dooley looked at the chair that was drawn up in front of the desk. "May I sit down?"

"Sit down and start talking."

Dooley sat and crossed his legs. "My name is Frank Edmonds, and I represent a company called Panamerican Finance of Mexico City. We are the best, and I mean the best, investment counselors in the hemisphere. We are discreet, we are worldwide, and we are damn good. We can take your money and put it where the IRS will never get it, and we can make it grow for you. We take cash and turn it into secure bank accounts in places the IRS can't go, under whatever name you choose. Or if you prefer we turn it directly into real goods—real estate, luxury goods, bullion, you name it. We guarantee access and liquidity and most of all security. We don't take on just any-body as a client and we do not, I repeat *do not*, leave loose ends for the IRS or any other federal agency, American or Mexican, to pick up. We do all this for a fee, of course, but I think once you see what we can do for you, you'll consider it money well spent."

Angelo Casalegno stared at Dooley for a while and then said, "What the fuck are you doing here?"

Dooley smiled. "That's the question I'd expect you to ask. I'm here because word reached us of the death of Mr. Herb Blumberg."

Casalegno sat stone still. "Who?"

Dooley put on his most discreet look. "Sir, we know that Herb

Blumberg was handling your affairs. We had dealings with Herb from time to time. When we heard about his death, we figured you might need somebody to take over for him. As I said, we don't take on just anybody, but Herb's relationship with you is all the recommendation we need."

Casalegno stared at him like a man trying to decide whether he has been insulted. Finally he said, "That son of a bitch gave my name out to other people?"

Dooley shook his head. "No. We know about you and Herb the way the FBI knows about you and Herb. It's a matter of good intelligence work. That's what I'm paid for as Panamerican's stateside scout. I have the contacts to find out who's got money and who needs to move it."

The looks traded among the three other men in the room told Dooley he was a long way from making the sale. Casalegno took his time shaking a cigarette out of a pack and getting it lit with a gold lighter. "Contacts. Like with who?" he said.

"Some law enforcement sources, some banking contacts, some miscellaneous information mongers. I'm pretty good at what I do."

"And what you do is poke your fucking nose into other people's business, is that about right?"

"That's exactly right. But believe me, what I know about your business is a lot less than they know down at the Dirksen Building right now. They've picked up your trail in a serious way. What I'm here to offer you is a way to hide some of your money before they scoop it all up in a RICO prosecution. I'm the guy who can walk along behind you with a branch, rubbing out your tracks."

He had hit on the one thing guaranteed to get Casalegno's attention, Dooley could see; his FBI trouble had to be weighing heavily on his mind. Casalegno smoked and glared at him for a while and said, "I'm supposed to just give you my money? What the fuck keeps you from just running off with it?"

"We've got an office in Mexico City. We don't keep the address a secret. We encourage you to visit, in fact. The type of client we deal with, it would be very bad business and possibly unhealthy to lose people's money, so we're careful. In any event we don't expect you to give us anything until you've checked us out. We've never had any complaints."

Casalegno gave out a hollow chuckling sound. "And how do I know you're not from the G or something? You could have a wire up your ass and be getting all this on tape."

"Then it would be entrapment, wouldn't it? They'd never make it stick. But I understand your concern. You'd want references."

"You damn right I'd want references. You'll need the fucking Pope on your side to get me to hand over money to somebody I don't know."

"Well, we don't have His Holiness in our Rolodex quite yet, but I think we can probably give you a name or two you might know. That would be if we get to the next stage."

There was a silence; Dooley made no attempt to interpret the look between Casalegno and the man who might be his son. Instead he smiled blandly at the thug on the couch, who was looking at him without curiosity while working at his teeth with a toothpick.

"What's the next stage?" said Casalegno.

"If you're seriously interested, I call the head of the firm in Mexico City and he flies into town to meet with you. He can lay out our whole package for you and give you all the references you want. Very discreetly, of course. We've found that those hotels out near O'Hare are pretty convenient for fast private meetings."

"They are, huh?"

"So we've found." Dooley smiled again.

Casalegno gave him a long hard look through the smoke and said, "I'm gonna have to think about it."

"Sure." Dooley rose to his feet. "I'd recommend you don't take too much time, though, because they're burning the midnight oil down at the Dirksen Building."

"How do I get in touch with you?"

Dooley read him Roy's number. Casalegno clawed a piece of paper toward him and wrote it down. "What was your name again?"

"Frank," he said. "Just Frank. That's really all you need to know."

19

"I'M STARTING TO HEAR THINGS ABOUT YOU," SAID KEVIN.

The Bears were down by six at the half and Dooley had killed the volume on the TV and gone behind the bar for more beer. Kevin took the one Dooley slid across to him and twisted off the cap slowly, waiting for Dooley to make some kind of response. "What kind of things?" said Dooley, closing the mini-fridge.

"I hear you've been hanging around the OC intelligence guys, asking questions."

"That's right. I have."

They leaned on the bar across from each other. Upstairs they could hear music, something Colleen had put on the stereo, a thumping bass coming through the floor. Dooley looked past Kevin to the TV, talking heads moving their lips in silence. Kevin said, "Why does that make me nervous?"

Dooley looked him in the eye. "I don't know. What do you think I'm gonna do, shoot somebody?"

"I certainly hope not."

"Well, don't worry, I won't."

"So what's with the detective work?"

"I'm a detective. I'm trying to solve a murder."

"So's everyone else in the department."

"They got nothing. They'll never pin it on Spanos."

"You're sure it was Spanos, are you?"

"One hundred percent."

"Is that the dick talking or the best friend?"

"Both. I knew Roy well enough to know just what he'd have done if it was a real stickup, and believe me, he never would have got shot. He got shot because he was set up."

Kevin gave him a long look, conceding nothing. "So what's your strategy here?"

Dooley gave a little shrug. "I'm gonna nail him. He's gonna confess, somebody's gonna rat on him, or somebody's gonna shoot him."

"Yeah, it's that last part that worries me."

"It won't be me."

"You want to explain that in a little more detail?"

Dooley drank beer, watching a 49er pull in a long TD bomb on the halftime highlights. The truth was, he didn't want to explain. Not yet. "I'm gonna get in his face and stay in his face. I'm gonna be a nuisance. He's gonna get tired of it and do something stupid or somebody else is gonna get tired of it. One way or another, something will happen."

"I don't think you have the slightest idea what's gonna happen."

Dooley looked at him. "No, I guess I really don't. That's the interesting part."

After a moment Kevin said, "You want my advice?"

"Sure. You're my big brother, I gotta listen."

"Forget it. Let the department get him. They will, sooner or later."

"I don't think so, Kevin. I don't think they want to bad enough."

"A cop killed on duty? You shitting me?"

"They think Roy was dirty. They got mileage out of the funeral, now they don't give a fuck."

"You're wrong. They'll work it to death. They'll get him."

"They don't have enough. If they did, they'd have made an arrest by now."

"They found the car. They're working on it. Prints and things, you never know. They have a good chance of nailing him."

"You're an optimist."

"You'll just fuck things up. Or get yourself killed."

"If he tries to kill me, I'll kill him. It'll be a fair fight, don't worry."

"You carrying a piece around, is that it?"

"Frisk me, man. I'll hold still."

Kevin's face went hard and cold. "You know, you always had that way, that talent for pissing people off."

"I'm sorry, Kevin. Roy was my partner."

"Don't try and play God, kid. I'm telling you. You really think you're big enough for the role?"

Dooley couldn't come up with an answer to that; he clamped his mouth shut for a few seconds and then said, "I'm gonna nail him. One way or another. I won't kill him. But I'm gonna nail him, I promise you."

Kevin was stone-faced. Finally he said, "I'm telling you, watch your step. I'm not gonna cover for you."

"Have I ever asked you to?"

Kevin tossed his head in the way he had always done to say, That's it, I've done my best and it's your funeral now. He turned away from the bar. "OK. Let's see if the Bears can pull their heads out of their asses this half."

Dooley had changed the greeting on Roy's answering machine to a terse order to leave a message. When he came in Sunday night and punched the button, there it was: *You want to talk business, be at the McDonald's on Harlem just south of Addison, Monday at noon. Get yourself a hamburger and wait.* That was it, but Dooley recognized the voice.

At eleven fifty-six the next day, the lunch rush was just starting and the parking lot was about half full. Dooley had no intention of getting a hamburger, but he locked up the Nova and made for the door. When he was halfway across the lot a horn sounded. Dooley looked and saw somebody wagging a hand at him from the open passenger window of a Caddy Seville. He changed course, and as he got closer he recognized the neat and prepossessing young man from Giannini's. There were two other men in the car, one at the wheel and one in the back seat. "Hop in," said the young man.

Dooley flashed on Mexico for an instant, walking into places he wasn't sure he'd walk out of. "How ya doin'?" he said, opening the door.

They pulled out of the lot and went north on Harlem. The man behind the wheel had gray hair coming out of his ears and shoulders that strained at his leather jacket. The man on the seat opposite Dooley was a little younger, but with the same size and the same attitude evident in his sleepy-eyed look: you're nothing but a little heavy lifting to me. "This is Willie," said the boss's son, pointing over the seat. "And this here's Tony." He clapped the driver on the shoulder.

"Hey, guys." Dooley turned to the front. "I never caught your name the other night."

"I'm Pete. I guess we never got introduced." He twisted to extend his hand.

Dooley shook it. "Pleasure to do business with you."

"Yeah, well, that's what we're gonna talk about."

Dooley waited, but that appeared to be all the talking that was going to happen for a while. Nobody said anything while Tony turned left on Irving and drove west. For half a mile or so they were still in the city; then there were cemeteries on either side, and finally they crossed Cumberland into the forest preserve and there was nothing but trees. OK, thought Dooley, let's think tactics. Step one, run like hell.

Another half mile into the forest Tony slowed and pulled the big Caddy off the road. He crept on the shoulder until a couple of cars had passed and then turned off the road abruptly, onto a barely visible track through the trees. They crawled over uneven ground, weeds brushing the chassis, for a hundred yards or so until they reached a clearing. Tony cut the engine and it was very quiet. Dooley could hear cars whooshing by back on the road, a thousand miles behind him. "We meeting somebody?" he said.

Pete barely turned his head. "Yeah. My old man's gonna join us. You got something else to do?"

"You guys are the only thing on my agenda today."

"That's good." Pete was lighting a cigarette. "We could get out, I guess. Enjoy nature some."

Everybody got out. Dooley took a quick look and saw that it would be tough going in the underbrush; in any event Pete and Willie had moved, entirely casually, to hem him in against the car. Tony came and stood near him at the rear of the car. He offered him a cigarette, shrugged when he declined, and lit up.

Dooley looked at the bare trees and thought how hard it would be to find a body under the new-fallen leaves. Nobody said anything for about two minutes, and then they heard another car coming through the trees. This one was a white Marquis, and when it hove to twenty feet from the Caddy, Angelo Casalegno got out of the back seat. Two men who belonged to Willie and Tony's peer group got out of the front. Angelo Casalegno looked at Pete and said, "Nobody."

"Looks like you're clean, Frank," Pete said. The tone was jaunty but there was no smile with it.

"Was there any doubt?"

"There's always doubt," said Casalegno, coming to stand in front of him. "I don't trust nobody in this business."

"That's wise," said Dooley. "I don't either."

"Check him out," said Casalegno.

Tony ground his cigarette out with his foot and Willie stepped in on Dooley's left. "Take it easy," said Willie as Dooley bristled. "Take your jacket off."

"How come?"

"Just do it, Frank." Pete had lost his friendly manner.

Dooley slipped out of his jacket and Willie took it and handed it to one of the two newcomers, who started going through the pockets. Tony said, "Raise your arms."

Dooley obeyed and tried to keep still as they probed, groped, and patted him. When they were done with his torso Tony said, "Take off your pants."

Dooley lowered his arms, looked him in the eye and said, "We get to that point, we got a problem, brother. I may lose the fight, but you won't forget it. I'll empty my pockets and you can pat me down, but I don't take my fucking pants off for you." Dooley didn't want to fight but he knew you never just lay down for anyone if you wanted to keep any leverage at all.

There was a brief stare-down; Dooley was way past the point of letting a middle-aged tough guy bother him with a look. After a couple of seconds Casalegno said, "Pat him down for Christ's sake. You got any objections to taking off your shoes?"

"Shoes I can maybe do." Dooley kicked them off and then stood rigid as Willie ran his hands up and down his legs, inside and out, while Tony emptied his pockets and tossed the contents onto the roof of the car.

Casalegno watched with his arms folded. "You see, Frank, I been burned before. The nicest guys sometimes wind up wired to the fucking teeth. And the G gets better at this shit all the time. You can understand that, can't you?"

Dooley shook his head and smiled, the good sport. "We wouldn't do business with you if you weren't careful," he said.

"There's nothin' in his wallet," said Tony. "I mean nothin'."

"There was thirty or forty bucks in there," said Dooley.

"I mean no ID. Nothing. It's empty." He waved the wallet at Casalegno.

"You don't carry ID, Frank?" Casalegno looked amused.

"Not when I think I'm about to get rolled. What do you need my real name for anyway? All you need is to talk to the man in Mexico. He'll give you all the credentials you want."

"He looks clean," said Tony. He handed Dooley the wallet and said, "You wanna count the money?"

"That's OK, I trust you, Tony." Dooley put his wallet and keys away.

Casalegno stared at him for a moment. "OK, it don't look like you're wired. You could still be trying to set us up. We still don't know who you are."

Dooley tied his shoes, put his jacket back on. He looked Casalegno in the eye and said, "Yeah. It could be a setup. If you're worried about that, all you do is say good-bye. I'm not gonna pester you. I made you a business proposition, you considered it. No hard feelings. Only thing is, I walk away now, you're never gonna see me again. And the G's gonna get all your fucking money while you're looking for another Herb Blumberg. You got a minute to make up your mind."

Angelo Casalegno laughed, a short nasty sound. "I got my mind made up. I'll talk to your man in Mexico. But he better be able to give me a name, someone I can call. You understand? I want a name. Somebody I can go to who can tell me the guy's on the level. I'm gonna want a very discreet and very personal reference. Clear?"

"That's clear, Mr. Casalegno. I'm sure my man can oblige. You want me to call you at the restaurant when I've made the arrangements?"

"Christ, I don't talk business on that phone. You kidding?" Casalegno gave him an irritated look. "You page me. Pete, give him the number." Pete took a notebook from inside his jacket and wrote in it, then tore out the page and handed it to Dooley. Dooley looked at the number and stashed it.

"You page me at that number and be ready for a call-back. And make it a safe number."

"That sounds like it'll work." Dooley swept the gathering with a

197

look. "Fellas, it's been fun. Do I have to hitch back for my hamburger or is a return trip included?"

"You're one of the lucky ones," said Casalegno, making for the Marquis with his gofers in tow. "You got a round-trip ticket."

"I think you can make your plane reservations," said Dooley.

"They're interested, huh?" Fuentes was shuffling papers at the other end of the line.

"They want to talk. How soon can you get here?"

"Lemme see. I can be there the day after tomorrow if you want."

"OK, make it the day after tomorrow. Call me back with the flight info and I'll make you a hotel reservation."

"I'll want to meet with you first. I'll want as much background as you can give me."

"That's fine. They're gonna want to know more too. They're gonna want a recommendation."

"Then I think we're about at the estage where I need a name."

"OK, you'll be talking to a guy named Angelo Casalegno. He's as much of a number one guy as the Chicago mob has these days."

"How do you espell that?"

Dooley spelled it. "I don't know how much money he has, but it's almost certainly worth your while."

"I'm sure. The question is, do I know somebody he'll listen to?"

"If anybody knows the connections, you do."

"Well, we ought to be able to come up with somebody he'll trust."

"I'm sure we can," said Dooley.

Dooley had pumped Mike D'Amico for as much as he could get on the habitat and migration patterns of John Spanos before D'Amico had gotten suspicious and clammed up; taking off from there,

Dooley decided the valet parking guys on Halsted were a pretty good bet. At Greek Islands one of the crew knew Spanos but hadn't seen him; at Roditis he was promised that Spanos would be by any minute, and finally at the Plaka a toss of the head informed him that Spanos was inside.

Dooley wasn't particularly dressed up but then nobody dressed for dinner anymore; he saw a man in cutoffs and a backward baseball cap at a prime window table. He spotted Spanos at a back table and told the host that he was joining him. Spanos didn't see him until he was halfway across the room, and then he stopped chewing and watched him come, his face settling into stone. Dooley pulled out a chair and sat down. "Lamb with artichoke," he said. "I think all these joints along here secretly share the same kitchen."

Spanos swallowed. In a low hoarse rumble he said, "Who the fuck invited you in here?"

"Are you ready to come with me?"

"I'm ready to shove this fucking knife in between your ribs."

Dooley stared at him, drumming his fingers on the white tablecloth. "You don't scare me, John."

Spanos gave the killer look another few seconds and then gave it up. He set down his knife and fork and picked up his wineglass. He drank and said, "Funny, you don't scare me either. You're not a cop. You're just an asshole with a grudge. And I deal with them all the time."

"Well, you're gonna be dealing with me for the rest of your life. But don't worry, it won't be too long."

"Fuck you. If you were gonna kill me, you would have tried it at the bar the other night."

"I told you. I'm gonna wait until I can get away with it. Like you did with Roy."

"I didn't kill him."

"He recognized your voice. That's the only reason he would ever have tried to draw on a man in that situation. He knew you were there to kill him."

The look that passed between Dooley and John Spanos in the ensuing silence erased the last doubts, on both sides. Dooley knew an innocent man would not have let the silence stretch on, and he could see Spanos knew now that no denial was ever going to work. "So," said Dooley at last. "Here's what it comes down to. I'm going to kill you, but it may take me a while. Then again, maybe not." Dooley pushed away from the table. "Enjoy your dinner, friend. Each glass of wine may be your last."

Spanos watched him stand, a sour flushed look on his face. Just audibly over the pleasant murmur and tinkle of the restaurant he said, "You got it backwards, Dooley. *I'm* gonna kill *you*."

Dooley smiled. "I guess that makes it a fair fight then, doesn't it?"

20

Eighteen stories down, Lake Shore Drive was still humming, little toy cars sweeping past with their lights playing over the ribbon of pavement. The Drive was never empty; somebody was always going someplace. The noise that rose up to Spanos was the prolonged sigh of the city itself, vast and exhausted.

A fucking head case, a wack job, thought Spanos. But is he dangerous? Spanos had dealt with plenty of cops, but none had ever worried him quite as much as Frank Dooley, precisely because he wasn't really a cop. He was an ex-cop head case, off the rails and off the map. Spanos had not liked the jolt he'd gotten seeing Dooley walk into the restaurant; he hadn't liked that at all.

So far, thought Spanos, he's all blow and no go. If he was serious he'd have done something serious by now. He knows he's got no power, no leverage, nothing. So he gets in my face and provokes me. He wants me to make a mistake.

So I do nothing. I ignore him, ride out the storm. Half the secret of life is riding out the storm, keeping your mouth shut and trusting the lawyers.

But son of a bitch, the man is an irritant. I'm being stalked, is what I am. I'm starting to understand what broads go through.

So here we go again. What do we do? Spanos leaned on the balcony rail and shook his head. Already the horizon was starting to lighten a little; the sun would be up before too long and he hadn't slept. Fuck the man, he was getting very seriously on Spanos's nerves.

Behind him steps sounded softly. He cast a look over his shoulder. Stacy came onto the balcony, hair tousled, robe clutched around her shoulders. She put a hand on his shoulder. "Baby," she said.

"Go back to sleep," said Spanos sourly.

"I couldn't." Stacy leaned her head on his shoulder, put an arm around his waist. "You want to come back to bed, try again?"

Spanos twisted, grabbed her arm, shoved her away. He wanted to backhand her with her big puppy eyes, feeling sorry for him. He wanted to throw her over the rail. He opened his mouth to snarl at her, saw the look on her face, remembered Joe Delvecchio. He relaxed his grip. "Nah, forget it. I got too many worries tonight. You caught me on a bad night."

Stacy smiled, tentatively, putting all the vulnerability and submission she could into it; Spanos could see right through it. "You let me know if there's anything I can do."

Spanos looked out into the immense emptiness over the lake. He filled his lungs and let it all out again. "I gotta deal with so many assholes," he said.

Together they watched the horizon start to go faintly orange. "Have you ever made love on a balcony?" Stacy murmured. Her hand was inside his robe.

Spanos felt things stirring. This was maybe going to work after all. He closed his eyes for a moment. He snapped them open immediately, because the first thing he saw was the mocking face of Frank Dooley, looking at him across the table.

He swatted Stacy's hand away and wheeled away from the rail. "Leave me the fuck alone," he said.

"Sooner or later he'll be back. That's where you come in." Spanos took a drink of coffee out of the Styrofoam cup. He had gotten it at the deli and slipped a word to Terry, out of earshot of his mother,

202

then gone to sit in his car parked on Harlem. Three minutes later Terry had come to join him.

"You want like, a bodyguard, you mean?"

"Something like that. Just to keep him out of my face. I was thinking a baseball bat might be the thing. A couple of smashed kneecaps, maybe a little skull fracture, I know that would make me reconsider. That could make me get religion."

"I could get into some creative mayhem."

"Now, I don't know. Is the guy really armed, that's the next thing we got to consider. That night at the bar, was that a bluff?"

After a moment Terry said, "I could get a piece."

Spanos drank coffee, looked across the seat at the kid. "So could I. But there, you're taking things to a different level. We gotta consider, are we ready for that?"

"Fuck, if he's got one."

"Well, that's the big question, isn't it? Does he?"

"He killed a guy before, you said."

"Yeah. That's true."

They were silent for a few seconds. "Why don't you just take him out?" said Terry, not looking at him. "Have somebody do it, maybe."

Spanos had asked himself the same question. It ought to be getting easier. The answer seemed to be that Dooley didn't have the look of an easy victim.

"I've thought about it. But let's try the Louisville Slugger first. The trick is to find the son of a bitch. That's where we play detective. We'll out-detective the fucker."

"He's a detective?" Terry scowled out the windshield.

"He was. That's what I hear, anyway. He had to leave town in a hurry after he killed a guy."

"Jesus, and he skated?"

"Well, that's cops for you. They're not gonna go after one of their own."

"That's outrageous."

"Yeah, well, welcome to the world, kid. Anyway, what I did was, I figured the guy is a friend of Ferguson's, right? And he just got back in town? So what's he gonna do, where's he gonna stay? I had Ferguson's number and I figured it was worth a try. I call and what do I get? The voice on the answering machine sounds a hell of a lot like our pal Dooley."

"No shit."

"And of course I had Ferguson's address because you don't take a bet from a guy unless you know where to find him. The thing is, do we go over there and sit outside all day waiting for him? How patient are you? I got a feeling it's quicker to just wait for him to show up at dinner. But that makes things harder, because then he's choosing the time and place."

"Yeah."

"So there you go. There's the problem. You interested in helping out?"

Terry shrugged. "I'm interested. I owe the fucker, remember?"

Spanos reached for the ignition key. "I remember. I was hoping you would, too."

Jim Ferguson stood among cardboard boxes in his son's apartment and wondered if he could finish the job. There were things a man shouldn't have to do, and cleaning out a dead son's apartment was one of them. He had told Theresa he would take care of it, wanting to spare her the ordeal; she was having a worse time than he was. Mandy had offered to help but she worked all day; this morning Jim had decided it was his job, and it was time.

The apartment was silent; the first time he had been here, Roy had had the TV on, blaring in the background. His son had gotten him a beer out of the fridge, held it out grinning, joking about a housewarming party, like a kid in his first apartment instead of a forty-five year old man coming off a bad divorce. For a second Jim Ferguson was unable to move, immobilized with a heavy heart. He had learned all about that expression, that almost physical sensation when grief becomes weight.

He heaved a sigh and moved down the hall; Jim Ferguson knew how to batten the hatches and tough it out when he had to. The thing was, he shouldn't have to at age seventy-nine; after surviving North Africa and Anzio and a near bankruptcy with four kids to feed and a coronary, it seemed like an old man ought to be due for a break.

He had put everything into boxes the previous day and it was time to start loading the station wagon double-parked out front. Moving slowly on creaky knees, conscious of the unreliable heart pulsing in his chest, he began moving boxes up from the kitchen.

He heard steps on the landing; he'd left the doors propped open downstairs. He set a box down on a chair with a grunt, and looked up to see a young guy in the doorway, a big strapping kid in a Hawks jacket with black hair and a chin that could use a shave. The kid was just standing there looking at him.

"Can I help you?"

"Yeah, I'm looking for Frank Dooley."

Jim leaned on the back of the chair, waiting for his back to stop hurting. "He's not here."

"I got the right place? I heard he was staying here."

"Yeah, that's his stuff over there." Jim pointed to the neat pile of bedding and clothes in the corner. "But he's not here now. I don't know when he comes and goes. He's just here for a few days." After a pause in which his heart sank Jim said, "It's my son's place, really."

The kid nodded. "You Roy Ferguson's dad?"

Jim stared at him. "Yeah."

"That's tough about Roy. That's really tough, man. I was sorry to hear it."

"Yeah, it's tough. You a cop?"

"Not yet. I'm going into the academy next month. Dooley was gonna take me out to lunch and fill me in on some things."

"Well, looks like he forgot, maybe." Jim bent to his labor again, lifting the box off the chair and stepping toward the door. "Excuse me."

"Lemme take that." The kid took the box out of his hands. "I'll help you out. If you don't mind my hanging around a bit to wait for Dooley. That your wagon out front?"

"Yeah. Hang on, it's locked up." Jim followed the kid down the stairs and unlocked the back of the station wagon. "Thanks a lot."

"Think we can get it all in one load?"

"Christ no, I'm gonna be doing this all day. And I'm gonna have to hire somebody for the furniture."

"Well, look. I'll run stuff down the stairs and you load, OK?"

"Jeez, kid. You don't have to do that."

"I got nothing better to do. Start with the kitchen stuff?"

"Might as well."

Jim watched the kid go back in the building and remembered when Roy was young and eager, going into the academy, and thought about everything he had lost in a chain reaction of tragedy: grandson, favorite daughter-in-law, and now finally son. He hoped to God he was the next one in his family to die.

In four quick trips they had the wagon loaded. The kid worked like a mule. Jim tried to give him a few bucks but the kid laughed at him and shoved them away, wiping sweat off his forehead. "Nah, forget it," he said. "Put it away."

"I gotta lock up," Jim said. "I don't know if I can let you wait inside."

"Nah, I'll wait down here on the steps. I'm starting to think Dooley's blown me off anyway. Gimme the key, I'll run up and lock it for you. Be right back."

The kid was back in less than a minute, handing him the key. Driving away, Jim could see the kid in the mirror, waiting on the steps in front of the building. He looked like a damn good kid.

Like Sean, like Roy. Jim wanted his boys back so bad he could cry.

Dooley was flashing on a Mexicana flight from years ago, standing in the crowd with Consuelo waiting for her parents to come off the plane; with a foot in both countries they had practically been on a shuttle for a while. After her death they had retreated to Mexico for good.

Not much had changed; the crowd was still mainly Mexican, waiting for relatives coming up the pipeline. Mexicana was upper-bracket, a long way from thirty-hour truck rides up from the border, but a lot of these people had started out that way.

Fuentes came through the door from the gangway with a patrician air among the cowboy hats and Selena look-alikes. His suit was tan, his black beard was neatly trimmed; he had an overcoat draped over his arm and a briefcase in his hand. He spotted Dooley and smiled. "Frank." They shook hands. "I like the beard."

"I had it in Mexico."

"You did?"

"Just trimmed it a little." Fuentes puzzled over the new look while Dooley steered him through the crowd. "I put you in the hotel just across the street. That way you don't need to worry about taxis and things. Ten minutes after you check out, you're on your flight."

"But I wanted to see the city."

"We can do that tonight. Tomorrow is business. You'll want to talk to these people and make a quick getaway."

"A quick getaway. Why does that worry me?"

"I'm just being security conscious. You won't want to hang around."

Fuentes was frowning. "I think we need to talk."

"We got all evening." Dooley wasn't looking forward to it; he had mixed feelings about people like Fuentes. In a place where the line between tax avoidance and tax evasion was even fuzzier than in the U.S., Fuentes had been socially acceptable, just barely. On one hand Dooley's attitude was ruthlessly cynical and on the other people like Fuentes gave him the creeps. The bottom line was he needed him and he had to be cordial.

The O'Hare Hilton had a black marble check-in desk, potted palms and huge purposeless urns, with acres of carpeting and ranks of professionally obsequious personnel chosen for their grooming. "So this is Chicago," said Fuentes in a tone of wonder, looking out the window of his room at vast stacks of parking levels. "Al Capone's town."

"This isn't Chicago. This is just Airport. But you're looking at a place where more than a few bodies have turned up in car trunks. People that knew Capone are still around."

Fuentes turned, looking serious for the first time. He was a dark, not very handsome man, improved as much as could be by skillful hair management and good tailoring. "And that's who we're going to talk to?"

Dooley grinned. "As soon as we can arrange it."

Fuentes wanted to see Chicago; Dooley took him to the Green Mill. The last time he'd been in, it had still been dark and decrepit and absurd with its murky rococo decoration, essentially unchanged from Capone's days. Now it was brighter and cleaner, and judging from a quick glance at the clientele Dooley figured it had been caught flat-footed by a trend. But they still had a bar to lean on and they still had whiskey, and Fuentes's eyes glowed like a child's as he looked around the place.

"I used to come here a lot when I was a cop," Dooley said. "Come two o'clock on a Sunday morning when the other bars closed, it would fill up with wasted Indians. Two-ten, two-fifteen, the side door would open and in would come the entire Sioux nation, chased out of the joints down on Wilson."

Dooley could see Fuentes framing the anecdotes he was going to dine out on already. "Amacing," said Fuentes.

Dooley gave him another minute to gawk and said, "So. Mr. Casalegno."

"Yeah, Mr. Casalegno." Fuentes hunched over his bourbon. "I made some phone calls, found a couple of people who are willing to recommend me."

"That's good. He's very suspicious."

"Can you blame him? You know what kind of estuff the IRS can pull these days?"

"I can imagine."

"But I have a client in New York who says he knows Casalegno. And I just made half a million dollars for this guy in platinum futures, so he's going to say nice things about me."

"That's good. It wouldn't hurt to have more than one name to give him."

"Sure. There's another guy in Las Vegas who used to be in Chicago. He says he knows Casalegno too."

"Let me give you a third name."

Fuentes had never quite stopped being suspicious, Dooley could see. He was used to being wined and dined and set up for snow jobs, and he could see another one coming here, though he covered whatever he didn't want to show very smoothly by taking on more bourbon. "Who?" he said.

"The clincher. Give him your guys and then give him a name for me. Or better yet I could just let it slip. Tell him you've already done some work for a guy here in Chicago. About, say, ten million dollars' worth."

Fuentes's face went blank. He stared into his drink and said, "Why would I want to do that, Frank?"

"Well, I guarantee you it will get his attention."

Fuentes shook his head and gave him a puzzled look. "But it's not true."

"No, it's not. But it would be very useful."

"What's going to happen when he checks it out? What's the guy going to say?"

"He's going to deny everything. But you'll be back in Mexico by then."

It didn't take Fuentes long to tumble to it; he raised his glass as if to drink but stopped, shook his head and laughed, set it back on the bar. "That's a very dirty trick, Frank."

"Well, this is a very dirty guy we're talking about. And I owe him a big one. If you need an inducement I'm prepared to offer you cash for the favor. Ten thousand dollars for one little lie."

Fuentes looked at him with furrowed brow. "It's that important to you?"

"It's that important."

"Then I'll do it for free. Provided you can convince me I can get away with it. I take no risks."

"Fair enough. I saw you bring a laptop off that plane. I imagine you could probably cook up some documentary evidence tonight if you work at it a little."

Fuentes looked around the bar, his gaze finally coming to rest on Dooley. "And I always thought you were a nice guy."

"What can I say, Ramón? Nobody's judgment is infallible."

Dooley had to park two blocks from Roy's place, down on Addison. If you were lucky enough to have a garage to rent, this neighborhood was livable; if not, who the hell needed it? Dooley was tired and a little drunk. He cut over a half block south of Roy's to go up the alley and went quietly up the back stairs. The apartment was dark, and it echoed more than before when he let himself in; he knew immediately that Roy's dad had been in. When he turned on the light he saw that the boxes that had been on the kitchen table were gone.

His time was running out; maybe it was time to think about his next move. Dooley was depressed by the empty place, Roy's traces disappearing. He wanted to talk to somebody, anybody. He'd fucked things up with Andrea and he wasn't quite sure how; he was wearing out his welcome in this town. He moved up the hall in darkness, despondent, the loneliest man on earth.

He paused at the entrance to the living room, feeling for the light switch, sensing the greater emptiness, sensing something else? When the light flicked on the first thing he saw was the reflection in the front windows, somebody winding up.

The floor creaked and here came the bat and Dooley's reflexes took him forward, telling him to get inside the swing. He ducked and charged and the blow just caught his shoulder, doing no real damage as he jammed the batter like a fastball on the fists. His head went into the hitter's chin and knocked it back as Dooley drove with both legs. The batter had the sense to let go of the bat and grab Dooley's jacket as he fell, pulling Dooley down on top of him. A hand went for Dooley's throat but he was quicker; he had both hands in the face already, feeling the rough stubble, catching a nostril, finding one eye with a thumb.

Dooley pressed, jamming the eye back deep in the socket, and somebody screamed; tree-trunk arms knocked him away but he had the advantage now and he came back with a knee to the crotch that ended it right there. The kid in the Hawks jacket let out a roar that ended in a rattle and rolled into a fetal position, his back to Dooley, not knowing what to grab next.

Dooley scrambled away and found the bat; he'd left the Walther in its hiding place under the sink before heading for the airport but the bat was going to be enough. He made it to his feet and stood ready

Sam Reaves

to hack, watching the kid try to crawl. "*Jesus, my eye,*" the kid squeezed out.

Dooley stooped to grab the kid by the hair. He tugged him to a sitting position and slammed him back against the wall. The eye seemed to have won the battle for priority; the kid slumped against the wall with one hand over his right eye and the other stuck out in front of him, waiting for the next blow. "All right, all right," he said, in a high panicked tone. "OK already."

Dooley watched him for a moment, panting. "Gimme a reason not to split your *fucking* head open," he gasped. The kid's uncovered eye opened enough to look up at Dooley.

"Don't hit me again."

"That's two out of three," said Dooley. "I win."

"OK, OK. You win."

"You never ran into anybody who fought that dirty, huh? You come at me like that, I'll do whatever it fucking takes." Dooley shot out a foot and bounced the kid's head off the wall again. "Say it again. Tell me who won."

"You did."

Dooley waited until the kid could look at him with his good eye again. "I got a message for Spanos," he said. "You listening?"

"Yeah."

"Tell him if he wants me to come get me himself. Tell him he's a yellow cocksucker. Tell him sending *you* is child abuse. You got it? He wants me, he can come talk to me himself."

"OK. OK. Fuck, you put my god damn eye out."

"Be grateful I left you one. Now get up."

"I can't."

Dooley grabbed him by the hair again and pulled. The kid came up to his knees. "*All right.* I'll get up."

The kid made it to his feet and stood, shaky, leaning a shoulder on the wall, eyes squeezed shut. "How'd you get in here?" said Dooley.

212

The kid let out a long breathy moan before he could put the words together. "The old man. I helped him move stuff out and unlocked the back door when he wasn't looking."

"I oughta break your fucking knees just for that."

"Don't hit me."

"Say please."

"Please don't hit me."

Dooley watched him for a few seconds. His heart was kicking out the front of his chest but he was starting to come down off the high. "I'm gonna drive you to a hospital," he said. "You're gonna tell 'em some bullshit story and I'm never gonna see you again. Is that clear?"

The kid rolled along the wall, steadied a little, facing Dooley now with his hand over the hurt eye, looking at Dooley with the other. "Yeah. OK."

"I don't know why the fuck I'm bothering with you. How old are you?"

"Nineteen."

"Jesus. Why aren't you out chasing girls or something, instead of doing shit like this? Fuck Spanos. Fuck all those guys. You think that's a life?" Dooley went to the door and opened it. "Move."

The kid stumbled down the stairs, one hand on the banister. Dooley came behind, trailing the bat. On the first floor the door was on the chain and an old man was peering through the gap. "I called the police," he said, his voice breaking with tension.

"I *am* the fucking police," snarled Dooley, and for one splendid instant he believed it again.

21

ACCORDING TO D'AMICO, SPANOS HAD A FAVORITE BREAKFAST PLACE at State and Division, an easy walk from his apartment on Lake Shore Drive. Dooley waited in the car, half a block away, until he saw Spanos come around the corner, stop at the newspaper box outside the restaurant, and take the paper inside. Dooley got out and locked up the Nova. His shoulder and a knee hurt a little when he moved; he was getting too old for the rough-and-tumble. He was now officially living out of the car, having cleared his possessions out of Roy's place and spent the night on a couch at Kathleen's house. He'd found another message from Andrea on the phone machine, asking him to call, but he wasn't going to talk to her again until it was all over.

Spanos was in a booth by the window; he had a cup of coffee in front of him and the *Sun-Times* open to one side. He didn't look up until Dooley was on top of him. "Top o' the marnin' to ya," said Dooley as he slid into the booth.

Spanos's nostrils flared; he stared across the table and Dooley thought for just a second that he was going to come across it. "Get out of my god damn booth," Spanos said, very quietly.

In a jaunty tone Dooley said, "Where's your bodyguard? A man in your position ought to be more careful about exposing himself." In the silence a bleached-blond waitress arrived with a menu. Dooley smiled at her and took it. Spanos hadn't moved. "Let me tell you something," Dooley said, opening the menu.

"No, you listen," said Spanos. His voice was a throaty rumble.

"I meant what I said. I'll kill you. You been warned. This is the last time."

"Was that a warning last night, sending Junior with his whiffle-ball bat?"

"I don't know what you're talking about."

"Maybe you don't. He's probably still in the hospital. I took him to Illinois Masonic. I'll tell you what I told him. You want to talk to me, you want to take a swing at me, you want to kill me, here I am. Don't send somebody else. That's chickenshit."

Spanos maintained the stone face for a few seconds longer and then vented a laugh. "You're so full of shit you slosh when you walk."

Dooley smiled again, serene and in command. "No bullshit, John. Your time's almost up. You keep giving me last chances, here's one for you. You get up from this table and come over to Area Three with me, and I won't kill you. Say no again, and you won't live out the week. And that's a promise."

They stared at one another until the waitress came back with her pad. Spanos let her stand there for a second, leaning back with a smile on his face, before saying, "I'll take my chances."

Dooley shrugged. He handed the menu back to the waitress, giving her a big smile. "Sorry, I can't stay. Could I just get a cup of coffee to go?"

Fuentes's suite had a sitting room with a round table in a corner, a coffee table in front of a sofa, a mini-bar and enough chairs to handle a small crowd. Fuentes shoved chairs here and there and stood regarding things from various angles before deciding to greet Casalegno in the armchair at the head of the coffee table. "We estart casual and move to the big table when things get serious," he said. He was in shirtsleeves but his tie was impeccably knotted. His briefcase lay open on the round table with his laptop, up and running, beside it. Dooley laid on a pot of room service coffee and they waited for the phone to ring.

When Dooley opened the door to the suite Tony came in first, scanning, followed by the old man. Casalegno came in scowling, a man who trusted nobody. Fuentes made a ceremony of rising from the armchair, offering his hand first to Tony, who ignored it, and then to Casalegno, who shook it after a second's examination, as if he were worried about psoriasis. "Pleased to meet ya," he growled.

"Pleace, sit down. Coffee?" Fuentes waved Casalegno to the couch and Dooley stood by to pour coffee. Tony went snooping, poking quietly into the bathroom and the bedroom. "I'm essighted to be here," said Fuentes. "I've heard a lot about Chicago but never had a chance to visit."

"It's OK." Casalegno looked like a man in a proctologist's waiting room, expecting the worst. He watched as Tony came back into the room and shrugged, just perceptibly. Dooley poured coffee and then sat down.

"So my colleague tells me you have some money you need to put in a safe place." Fuentes was cheerful and brisk, one leg crossed over the other with hands clasped on the knee.

"Yeah. But I gotta tell you right up front, I'm gonna take some convincing. I mean, I don't know you from a guy on the street, right?"

"I underestand that. I hope we can answer all your questions today."

"OK, number one, who the fuck are you? I hope you don't mind my being frank."

Fuentes gave him a smile that said he was delighted to encounter such refreshing frankness. "Who am I? That's a very esmart question, Mr. Casalegno." The smile went and was replaced by a look of deep seriousness. "I'm the best investment advisor in Mexico, and I especialize in discretion. I keep a low profile, I never advertise, and I have excellent relations with the authorities. This gives me a freedom to maximize my clients' profits that I could never have here in the Estates. I think you'll find that my clients are very happy with my services."

"OK, good. That's where I wanna start, right there. Before we go any farther, I'm gonna need to talk to somebody about you. Your pal here says you got my name from somebody that knew me. I gotta know who, and I gotta talk to him. Savvy?"

Fuentes's smile was wide and bright. "Savvy, Mr. Casalegno. No problem at all. You know a man named Salvatore Giardina, in New York?"

Casalegno's eyebrows went up a fraction of an inch. "Sal Giardina?" He pondered, nodding slowly. "I've heard of him. He one of yours?"

"I think he'll be happy to tell you what we can do for you. I happen to have a phone number where he can be reached, if you want to call him right now."

Casalegno took to nodding again; he shot a look at Tony. "Yeah, OK, I might wanna do that. But he didn't give you my name. He doesn't know me well enough for that."

Fuentes froze with his mouth open and his eyes flicked to Dooley. Dooley said, "Of course. There's another man actually, right here in town. He didn't actually suggest I contact you, but your name came up. And I took the liberty of contacting you on my own initiative."

"And who was that?"

"That was a man named John Spanos."

There was a second of two of total silence; Dooley sat in his armchair and held his breath. Fuentes was staring at him with the perfect look of alarm on his face. "John Spanos?" said Casalegno.

"Yeah."

Fuentes rose and went to the round table and started riffling papers in the briefcase. Quietly he said, "You know, Frank, I didn't get permission from Mr. Espanos to use his name."

"Ah. Mm, well. I'm sure he wouldn't mind."

Casalegno said, "No kidding, Spanos has money with you, huh?"

Fuentes shrugged. "Some."

Dooley sat and watched things happen on Angelo Casalegno's face. "Maybe you should start with Mr. Giardina in New York," he said.

Casalegno said nothing for several seconds. "How much money does Spanos have with you?"

"I can't tell you that, Mr. Casalegno," said Fuentes. "I'm sure you underestand."

"Yeah," said Angelo Casalegno, nodding. "I understand."

Casalegno had disappeared into the bedroom to do his telephoning. Tony guarded the approaches, slouching from window to television and back with his hands in his pockets. He had turned on the TV but found nothing that held his interest. Airplanes screamed into the sky and made the windows rattle. From the bedroom came Casalegno's raised voice, just audible: "I don't care what you're doing. Get your ass out here." Fuentes and Dooley sat at the coffee table, making small talk about acquaintances in Mexico. The hands on Dooley's watch crawled.

Casalegno came out of the bedroom. "Giardina and Stein say you're OK."

Fuentes gave a gracious nod. "Did Mr. Giardina tell you about the platinum group metals?"

Casalegno scowled at him. "No. He said he doesn't know what the fuck you do with the money but it seems to get bigger and he doesn't pay taxes and he can get cash out of a bank in Nassau any time he needs it."

Fuentes spread his hands, a modest man acknowledging a high compliment. Dooley said, "Was that Mr. Spanos I heard you talking to just now?"

"No." Casalegno stood looking at him for a moment. "I called a guy that works with me. I wonder if you know him too."

"What's his name?"

"Vincent Bonifazio. That name ring a bell?"

Fuentes shot Dooley a look, full of innocent inquiry. "I don't think so."

"I think I've heard the name," said Dooley, "but I've never dealt with the man."

Casalegno looked from one to the other, looking for something. When it looked as if he had found it he made a small noise of satisfaction. "Well," he said, "I think he may be very interested also in what you have to say. He's gonna join us in a while."

Casalegno and Fuentes were talking business at the round table, Casalegno rapt with wonder as new vistas of financial privacy opened before him. Dooley was going silently mad in his chair. It was past noon now but his stomach hadn't let him eat any of the room service spread Fuentes had had brought up. His main worry all along had been that Casalegno would go direct to Spanos; once that bullet had been dodged he started worrying that Bonifazio would bring along somebody who'd seen him before.

Dooley tensed when he heard the knock. The two men who walked in were strangers. One was a wicked-looking runt with white hair and strange pale blue eyes; the other was an old heavy, bent and wet-eyed but very much alert. Fuentes and Dooley stood up when Tony opened the door but Casalegno kept his seat. "Vince, Pete. Good to see ya."

"Angelo. Hey, Tony. Who's this?"

Casalegno said nothing. Suddenly there was tension in the room. To Fuentes, Casalegno said, "You ever seen this man before?"

Fuentes shook his head. "Never."

Casalegno turned to Bonifazio. "You know this guy?"

"What the fuck? You heard him."

"OK, have a seat. Just checking."

Warily, Bonifazio sank onto the chair Dooley had vacated. "What the fuck is this? What's this shit about Johnny?"

"That's what I wanna know. Funny thing, I was talking business with these two gentlemen and his name came up."

"OK, who are these *gentlemen?*"

"These are the money people. We were talking about money. And surprise, surprise. Mr. Dooley here just happened to mention John Spanos."

Bonifazio looked at Dooley. Dooley watched his face change, going from wariness to sudden and profound suspicion. "How in the fuck do you know John Spanos?" said Bonifazio.

"I introduced him to Mr. Fuentes," he said. "He had some money he wanted to move."

Bonifazio's lizard eyes flicked back and forth between them. Dooley could hear the wheels turning, could hear the tumblers falling into place. Bonifazio narrowed his eyes and asked the question, the big one, the really important question. "How much money?"

Fuentes put on a show, the man of principle backed to the wall. "I can't tell you that."

Now the look was between Bonifazio and Casalegno. "Son of a bitch," said Bonifazio.

Casalegno gave a grim smile. "You see why I got interested?"

Bonifazio looked as if somebody had spit in his face. He even wiped a hand over his mouth. Then he looked at Fuentes and said, "How do I know this is straight? Who is this greaser fuck? Who is this asshole here?"

A cool silence reigned. Fuentes raised an eyebrow at Dooley. Dooley looked at Bonifazio and tried to look affronted. Casalegno said, "People vouched for him. Giardina in New York, Jimmy Stein out in Vegas. I talked to 'em."

Bonifazio sat nodding, eyes flicking back and forth between Dooley and Fuentes. Fuentes cleared his throat. "I get the impression this is a surprice."

Casalegno laughed. "Yeah. It's a surprise."

"I'm afraid we made a mistake. Mr. Dooley should have checked with him before he told you."

"No, he didn't do anything wrong. I asked you for references, right?"

Fuentes shrugged. "I'm thinking it might be time for me to go across the estreet and catch my plane."

"No." Bonifazio shot a finger at him. "You're gonna sit right there and look Johnny Spanos in the eye and say what you just said to us."

"Hold on," said Dooley. "Ramón has to get back to Mexico City tonight. He's got his reservations made and his flight leaves in an hour and a half. And you can see the position I put him in. I just divulged some confidential information and had it blow up in my face."

"That's your tough luck. And his. Nobody's leaving until Johnny has a chance to defend himself."

Dooley looked at Fuentes, who was starting to look genuinely distressed. Fuentes tightened his lips and said. "Give me one moment, please." He got up from his chair and went to the round table. He stood and pecked at the laptop, frowning. Finally he said, "I shouldn't show you this, but I have to catch that plane. Take a look."

First Casalegno and then Bonifazio stood up and went to the table. Fuentes stood aside and Casalegno stooped to look at the screen. "What the fuck is this supposed to tell me?" he snapped. Fuentes pointed at two or three places on the screen. "Holy shit," said Casalegno. He beckoned to Bonifazio.

The runt stooped in turn. "What? Like I'm supposed to know what this means?"

Casalegno pointed. "It means that fucking Greek's been robbing us blind." The two Italians straightened up and looked at each other.

"Ten million bucks?" said Bonifazio.

"Can you print this out for us?" said Casalegno to Fuentes.

He shook his head nervously. "I don't have a printer."

"Son of a bitch." Casalegno came away from the table. He looked at Dooley, he looked at Fuentes. He stuck out his hand. "Ramón, it's been a pleasure meeting you and it's gonna be a pleasure doing business with you. I think maybe I can arrange a little trip to Mexico next month."

"I look forward to it. Give me a call and we can talk about the best way to move currency. I could even send one of my especialists up to help."

"Sounds good. Better go catch that plane." Casalegno watched Dooley as he stood up. "You're here in town, right?"

Dooley let out a deep breath. "I'm based here, that's right. I travel around a fair amount."

"Well, I may see you around. Do me a favor, will you?"

"What's that?"

"Try and do a little better at keeping your mouth shut about me than you did about Spanos."

"I stand corrected, Mr. Casalegno."

"We're gonna have a little talk about that, I think," said Fuentes, giving Dooley a very convincing look of displeasure.

"We better go get you checked in," said Dooley, frowning at his watch.

Bobby Marino was watching the blonde behind the desk and discreetly picking his nose when the pay phone behind him rang. He flicked a ball of filth onto the carpet and got up and lumbered over to the phone. An idler who apparently had nothing better to do than answer ringing pay phones was already reaching for it. "That's for me," said Bobby. The idler looked at him and got out of the way fast. "Yeah," said Bobby.

"A blond guy with a goatee and a Mex in a suit with a beard are on their way down," said Vincent Bonifazio in his ear.

"A suit with a beard?"

"A Mexican with a beard, you idiot. In a suit."

"Oh. OK. What do you want me to do?"

"The Mexican's getting on a plane. I'm interested in the gringo. Follow him."

"How did I do?" said Fuentes, his leather soles tapping on the tiles of the long concourse.

"You did great. I think you got a new client."

They walked another fifty feet or so. "What's going to happen to your friend Mr. Espanos?"

"He's going to have some explaining to do."

Tap, tap, tap, tap. "I just helped you kill a man, didn't I?"

"Is your conscience bothering you?"

Fuentes said nothing until they reached the gate. Then he turned and said, "I never thought I had one. I'm finding out I do."

"If it's any help, Spanos killed my best friend."

Fuentes nodded gravely. "I guess that's OK, then. In Mexico, we would just go and shoot the guy."

"That did occur to me," said Dooley. "But I like this better."

"So what are you gonna do now?"

"Right now? I'm gonna be real careful to lose that human canine that followed us over from the hotel. Don't look right away, OK? I don't want him to know I spotted him."

Fuentes was looking at Dooley with something approaching awe. "Ernesto told me you were good. I didn't know how good."

"I think we're going to find out how good I really am in the next few hours," Dooley said.

"Well." Fuentes grinned. "Lots of luck."

"I appreciate that," said Dooley. "Give Ernesto my best."

Dooley pulled in at the Marriott and parked. He passed a hand over his face; he was tired as hell. He'd spent the whole evening driving around the city after shaking the clumsy tail. He'd gone as far south as 18th Street, looking for Consuelo again, grabbing a bite to eat at a taquería she'd taken him into once, driving by her parents' old apartment. He'd driven back north and gone into a movie, then walked out halfway through. He'd almost stopped at Kathleen's but driven on by at the last second, not wanting the small talk. He felt like he was reviewing his whole life in Chicago, right on the edge of another big change, he had no idea what.

The whole thing with Spanos had left him empty, washed out, with none of the satisfaction he thought he ought to feel. He'd finally decided he would come up here and tell Andrea it was all over, but now he wasn't sure he even wanted to talk to her. He almost drove away again but he was tired of driving around and he decided at the very least a drink wouldn't do him any harm.

The bartender glared at him as he came in. "If you're looking for Andrea, you're too late."

"What?"

"She quit."

It took Dooley a second to process it. "You're kidding me."

"I wish I was. She quit on me in the middle of her shift, walked out and left me with a room full of people. I don't know what's so god damn funny about it."

Dooley couldn't help it; he was grinning. "What's funny is, it took her so long."

"Yeah, well, if you see her, tell her thanks a lot from me."

"I'll be sure to tell her, you bet." Dooley left.

He got back in the car and drove again, a little faster now. The house on LeMai was lit up behind the curtains. Dooley leaned on the doorbell and he didn't have to wait long. "You did it," he said when she opened the door.

Andrea smiled as she stepped back to let him in; she didn't seem surprised to see him. "Yeah. It came on me all of a sudden. I just slapped the tray on the bar and left. They sending the U.S. Marshals after me?" She sounded different somehow; she'd lost that tentative uncertain manner he'd seen these past weeks.

"I think your pal's happy to keep all the tips. I doubt you'll ever work for the Marriott Corporation again, though."

That made her laugh, and Dooley realized he hadn't heard Andrea laugh in a long, long time. Even more amazing, she threw her arms around him, just like that, out of the blue. Dooley squeezed back and they just stood there swaying for a few seconds. Then Andrea pulled away just enough to look at him, and said softly, "Thanks for waking me up."

"I didn't do anything. You were ready."

"You were there, that's the important thing. I'm glad you came back." A smile flickered but the look on her face was grave.

"Well, hey. Can I take you out for a drink to celebrate?"

Andrea looked at him with wide gray eyes long enough for him to start getting the message even before she said it. "You could take me back there to the bedroom, if you wanted to," she said softly.

Dooley took a deep, deep breath and let it out slowly; sudden joy was something he'd forgotten all about. "OK," he said.

22

DOOLEY WOKE UP NEAR DAWN. A LITTLE LIGHT CAME IN AROUND THE blinds to show the ghostly outlines of an unfamiliar room. Andrea's head was nestled in the crook of his arm, her breath warming his chest. She moved a little when he shifted and he wondered if she was awake too. He tightened his embrace and ran a hand softly over her hair; her lips tensed in a kiss on the skin of his chest. Dooley closed his eyes. This is what I came home for, he thought. All these miles, all these years, to wind up here. He could feel Consuelo someplace close by; she didn't mind, she couldn't, no more than Roy would. People passed on, and the ones who were left had to go on making the best of it in a world with a lot of rough edges. And sometimes good things happened, like finding the one person on earth who knew just precisely what it was to hurt the way you did. He kissed the top of her head, gently. A long way up in the night a jet rumbled, going someplace far away.

Peace, thought Dooley. That's what this is. I knew it had a name.

Spanos's beeper went off as he was driving up the diagonal on Grand Avenue. It was a number he didn't recognize, and he almost decided to let it slide until he got to the deli, but he spotted a bank of pay phones at a convenience store up ahead and pulled into the lot. It was a dark day with a lowering sky and a touch of ice in the wind; the city looked dirty and cold. Spanos threw some coins in the phone and punched in the number.

"Yeah," said somebody at the other end, and Spanos recognized the *yeah* of Vincent Bonifazio.

"What's up?"

"Forget the deli today. We got a little problem we need to discuss. Come over to the body shop. How soon can you make it?"

Spanos scowled into the wind. "Fifteen, twenty minutes. What's the problem?"

"I'll fill you in when you get here. We got a possible crisis coming up."

"What the fuck, what kind of crisis?"

"I'll tell you all about it. Just get your ass over here."

Spanos hung up and stood watching traffic for a second or two; sudden crises and changes in routine always went right to his stomach. Spanos had read about high-stress occupations and laughed; nothing an investment banker had to face could compare to the constant worry about pissing off a man like Vincent Bonifazio. Spanos went over everything that had happened in the last week and decided his ass was covered. He got back in the car.

The overhead door of the body shop was down; the place looked closed. Spanos parked around the corner. He walked back and went in through the storefront. The garage was lit by fluorescent lights up near the high ceiling; there were two or three cars in there but nobody working on them. Spanos walked toward the little cubicle in back and saw Bobby Marino step out of it with a cup of coffee in his hand. Bobby flapped a hand at him and wandered back inside.

Spanos came into the office and saw the whole brain trust, such as it was, gathered around the desk. Bonifazio sat behind it, with Pete Bianco looking vacant on a chair in the corner and Gino Alberti leaning against the filing cabinet. "Jesus," said Spanos. "Looks like the fucking Oval Office in here."

The first alarm went off when Bobby closed the door behind him. Spanos turned and gave him the eye and got a face full of hot coffee. He shouted and raised his hands, leaving himself wide open for the pile driver to the gut. Spanos sank to the floor trying hard to find some air somewhere; he felt hands on him, pulling him up, and then a chair was rammed into the backs of his knees. He sat clumsily, then keeled over forward and came to rest with his head on the desk before he managed to draw a breath.

"You don't sound too good," said Bonifazio. "You oughta be able to afford better health care, all that money you got put away in Mexico."

Spanos drew painful breaths with his head on the desktop, thinking *Mexico, Jesus Christ, Mexico*? "Huuuuh," he said.

His head was snapped back, Marino's fingers in his hair. Bonifazio was smiling. "I didn't quite catch that, John. Wanna try again?"

"What the fuck are you talking about?" Spanos squeezed out.

Bonifazio flicked a look over Spanos's shoulder; Spanos's reactions were a split second too slow to avoid the chop on the back of the neck that made everything into bright lights and a curtain of pain. When Spanos recovered he came off the chair suddenly, twisting and flailing. "Hit me again motherfucker and I'll tear your heart out," he snarled, missing everybody and falling over the chair. Marino caught him and threw him against the wall. He looked up to see Gino with a good two-handed grip on an iron bar that would make an eggshell out of his skull.

"Easy, John," said Gino. He looked apologetic but he gave the bar a little waggle.

"Sit down," said Bonifazio. "Now you know what's what, talk to me. Tell me about Mexico."

Spanos sat. He wiped coffee from his face, shook it on the floor, drew some deep breaths. He stared at Bonifazio the whole time. "Vince, you gotta help me a little. I swear to God I don't know what the hell you're saying. What the fuck is in Mexico?"

Bonifazio just looked at him, a man looking at a dog that has soiled the carpet. "Ten million dollars is in Mexico," he said. "That's what the computer said."

"What fucking computer? You lost me, Vince."

"The one the Mexican had."

"What fucking Mexican?"

"What was his name, for Christ's sake? Pete?"

"Fuentes," said Pete from the corner.

"Yeah. Your buddy Fuentes. The one you gave ten million dollars to."

"I didn't give no fucking Mexican no ten million dollars, Vince. I don't know where you're getting this shit."

Bonifazio was silent and Spanos hunched his shoulders, waiting for the next blow. "We saw it on the computer, John. Right there in black and white."

Spanos knew he was talking for his life; unless he could get to the bottom of this massive fuck-up he was trunk music. "When? Where? Where'd this god damn Mexican come from? What'd he tell you?"

"Casalegno knows him. He's a money guy. Angie has money with him, and he found out you do too. Ten million dollars, for Christ's sake. Where the fuck did it come from, Johnny? The cocaine, is that it? You work out something with your nigger friends after all? You been bringing coke into good white neighborhoods and taking the money back out of the country?"

Spanos peered across the desk at him. "Who told Casalegno I have money with this Mexican guy? That's fantasy."

"We're gonna need that money, John. We're gonna need account numbers or whatever it takes to get it. You know the rules."

"But's a *lie*, Vince! It's smoke, it's bullshit!"

"Angie doesn't think so. He talked to people in Vegas and New York about the guy. He's legit."

"But who the fuck *told* you I have money there? I never *heard* of the fucking guy."

"Who told me? Your buddy, the guy that introduced you. What was his name? Frank something."

Spanos stared openmouthed; he sat stock-still with his jaw sagging and heard the name reverberate around the inside of his skull. "Frank?"

"Yeah. What the fuck was his name, Pete? Frank what?"

"Shit, I don't know."

"Dooley," said Spanos quietly.

"Huh?"

"Frank Dooley."

"Nah, that wasn't it."

"What'd he look like?"

"What'd he look like? What the fuck difference does that make?"

Spanos pounded the desk. "It's a setup, Vince. I been knifed in the fucking back here. What did the guy look like?"

Bonifazio gave him a good hard five seconds' stare. "Young guy. Maybe your age. Blond hair, little beard, what do they call it, a goatee."

Spanos laughed, a single violent expulsion of air. "Motherfucker," he said.

"What did you fucking call me?"

"Find him," said Spanos. "Before you do anything you'll regret, go find him."

"I guess I haven't had much of a life the past couple of years. All this time I've lived a five-minute walk away, I've never eaten here." Andrea was looking around the restaurant as if she'd never been in one before. In front of her lay the remains of a large breakfast: eggs, ham, pancakes.

"Don't get out much, huh?" Dooley polished off his second cup of coffee.

"I haven't wanted to. Go to work, sleep, hang around the house.

Do the necessary shopping, have dinner at my parents' house once in a while. I've just been kind of numb for a long time." She looked across the table at Dooley and he could see something new and luminous there. "But I think that's over now." She covered her hesitation with a sip of coffee. "Is it too early to ask what your plans are?"

He stared at her gravely. "No. I just can't give you an answer. My plans only extended up to last night. Today's a whole new ball game."

She was amused. "Oh, you planned it, huh?"

"Not us. That was a total surprise."

"Come on."

"Really. When I walked into that bar last night, taking you home was the last thing on my mind."

"So what happened last night that was planned?"

Dooley played with his coffee cup, looked out the window. "I think I took care of the guy that shot Roy."

Silence. "What, you mean you can prove he did it?"

"No. But I know he did it."

"Then what do you mean you took care of him?"

"I mean I think he's gonna be in the papers in a couple of days."

Andrea was staring at him with those wondrous gray eyes, but they were a little troubled now. "Frank, did you kill him?" she said finally, just above a whisper.

"No. I won't have to. Somebody else will take care of it."

She frowned at the tabletop. "I'm afraid you're going to have to explain that a little better."

Dooley thought about it; he was talking a lot, but if he couldn't tell her, who could he tell? "OK, I'll start with a war story. From Mexico days."

"OK."

Dooley leaned closer to her, hands laced on the table. "In Mexico once," he said. "I had a situation where my client was being extorted by a local bad boy, a guy who was connected to the the García Abrego drug mob. Your basic protection racket—Pay me and nothing happens to your car—except the car here was a fifty-employee machine shop, the man's livelihood and the economic mainstay of the neighborhood. The local cops were no help because their yearly cost-of-living adjustments came straight from García Abrego. So what do I do?"

"I don't know."

"All I had was the fact that I was a *puto gringo*. That's all I survived on for eight years down there, mystique and bluff. I knew wherever I went, people's first thought would be that I was DEA. So I ran with it. I go to the guy, the bad guy, and I pull my piece on him and arrest him, no legal basis for it in the world, pure bluff. He's indignant but what's he gonna do, I got a nine-millimeter on him. I march him out to the car in handcuffs, had to borrow a pair of handcuffs from a friendly mope at the local *policía*. I put the guy in the car, drive him out in the country and tell him to stay away from María. More bullshit. I picked the name out of the air. I knew the guy had a reputation for hitting on the local girls, I make up a name. He says who's María, I say you know who I'm talking about and you keep your hands off her or I'll put a bullet in your head. I undo the handcuffs and leave him by the side of the road. He has to hike back into town, steaming. He's pissed off at me now, but so what? I lay low for a couple of days, and sure enough. Forty-eight hours later he's dead."

"Why?" Andrea said, intent.

"What does everybody else see? The local drug dealer gets picked up by the DEA and then released. Why? He had to swing a deal, right? So now he's a liability. Bam. So long, amigo. His own people took care of him. He's off my client's back."

Andrea stared, exhaled, shook her head. "Where'd you learn to think like that?"

Dooley was staring out the window, seeing nothing. "I don't know. I just lived on the edge down there. There's a gambler's expression, don't gamble with scared money. That means you can only risk it if you can afford to lose it. Well, down there somehow it seemed like there was nothing I couldn't afford to lose. Maybe it was a death wish, after Consuelo, something like that. All I know is I just never thought twice, I looked at a situation and said hey, if I get in this guy's face he's gonna cave. And it always worked."

"So that's the war story. What about last night?"

Dooley picked up his coffee cup, suddenly reluctant. He drank and said, "Essentially, I framed the guy. I made it look like he was holding out. That's the fastest way for a wise guy to get in trouble with the higher-ups, not to pass on their cut of the profits. And I made it look like he was holding out big time. I ran a little scam on the higher-ups."

Andrea was having trouble digesting things; Dooley could see her starting to wonder about the man she had just slept with. "That's really nasty," she said.

"Yep. I wouldn't call it as nasty as shooting a man in cold blood with a sawed-off shotgun, though."

She blinked at him. "I'm not arguing that."

"I talked to Spanos. Three times. I told him he could come in with me and make a full confession. He turned me down."

"You're a hundred percent sure he's guilty?"

Dooley almost said yes right away, but something in her eyes stopped him. He looked at Andrea and knew this was somebody he couldn't lie to; what he'd come into in the last twelve hours was something that could only survive in a bullshit-free environment. "Ninety-nine," he said. "Maybe ninety-eight."

They looked at each other for a long time. Finally Andrea looked away out the window. "That's close enough, I guess."

"You're on parole," said Vincent Bonifazio. "You're hanging by a fucking thread until we get five million dollars or you prove it's all bullshit. You try and leave town, we'll find you. I swear to God I'm gonna watch you night and day, I'm gonna be sitting on your fucking doorstep. You can run but you can't hide from me, Johnny."

"Why in the fuck would I run? Everything I got's right here. What I'm gonna do is, I'm gonna find this piece of shit and haul him in here and he's gonna tell you the truth."

"Fine, you do that. When I hear it from him I'll believe it."

"Vince, you can check it out yourself. The son of a bitch has been coming after me for days. He came right into the Plaka and got in my face. He came into the place I have breakfast at. You can go ask 'em yourself. They saw him. Ask Nick down at the Plaka, he'll remember. Go to the—what the fuck's the name of the place?—Monday's, at State and Division. Ask the waitress with the bleached-blond hair. She knows me, she'll tell you, she saw him. It was just yesterday. I'm not making this shit up, Vince."

"Go, get out of my sight. You got three days to come up with my five million dollars."

"Or Dooley. I bring you Dooley. I shove a gun in his fucking ear, he'll tell you the truth."

"OK, bring him in. I hear it from him, I'll believe it. Now get the fuck out of here."

Spanos turned, stuck his finger in Bobby Marino's face. "You. You hit me, you cocksucker. I won't forget it."

"It's just business, John. For Christ's sake." Marino stared in wonder.

"OK, it's business. You better not try that business no more. You understand?"

"*Johnny.*" Bonifazio's voice froze everybody. "I told him to hit you."

"Yeah. I know. I won't forget that either." Spanos kicked the door open and left.

From the body shop in Melrose Park to the deli on Harlem was a quick five-minute drive at the speed Spanos took it. He parked at the corner and went into the shop. Terry was behind the counter in a white apron, wrapping up a sub. He had a thick bandage over his right eye.

"Come on, kid, we gotta talk," said Spanos, muscling a customer aside. Terry looked up at him and said nothing. From the far end of the counter his mother gave Spanos a look of outrage. "Come on, this is more important than a sandwich. Let's go."

"Leave him *alone*!" Laurie was brandishing a knife, coming up the counter toward Terry, her face distorted; the female of the species protecting her young. "Get out of my shop!"

Spanos reached over the counter and grabbed Terry's arm. "Now." He tugged Terry toward the end of the counter.

"Just gimme a second, Ma. I'll be back." Terry was letting himself be pulled.

"I'll kill you if you don't let go of my son!"

Spanos let go. "Move, kid."

Terry came around the end of the counter in a hurry. "If you go with him, don't bother to come back," screamed his mother. Customers gawked. Spanos pushed open the door.

On the sidewalk he grabbed Terry's arm again. "Get in the car." He hustled the kid to the corner and they got in. "What the fuck happened to you?"

"Dooley damn near took my eye out."

"I thought you had a fucking baseball bat. Why didn't you beat his head in?"

Terry gave him a one-eyed shamefaced look, a little shake of the head. "Those little fuckers are fast sometimes."

"My God, I can't believe I'm hearing this coming out of your mouth. You let him take you?"

"He's vicious, man. Son of a bitch fights dirty."

"All right, shit. You found him, anyway. We're gonna go find him again."

"Uh-uh, man. I'm through. I got one good eye left. Till the eye's better I'm out of it. I'm fuckin' living on Tylenol."

Spanos looked at him from on high for a moment and then said, "OK, fuck it. Go back in there and help your mama make sandwiches. Bye-bye. I'll take care of it myself, I guess."

"Sorry, man. He just fuckin' took me, that's all. He's a bitch."

"OK, don't worry about it. I shouldn't have sent a boy to do a man's work, I guess. Good-bye."

With his hand on the door handle Terry said, "I don't think he's gonna be sitting there waiting for you. I'd move if I was him."

"I'll find him."

"You want something that might help you?"

"What?"

"While I was up there I listened to his phone messages. There was one from a broad. Sounded like a friend, come see me, that kind of thing. And she left her number. Might be worth checking out."

Spanos stared at the kid. "You write down the number?"

"I memorized it. I got a head for numbers."

Spanos reached over and slapped Terry on the shoulder, then reached into a pocket for a pen. "Kid, you did all right."

23

THE PLAKA WAS EMPTY; A WAITER IN A WHITE SHIRT WAS LAYING OUT silverware and another one was folding napkins at the bar. Laughter and the clanking of pots came from unseen regions. The sun shone in through the south windows and made it look like a cheery place to have lunch. "We're not open yet, sir," said the waiter at the bar when Vincent Bonifazio came in. "Eleven-thirty we open up." He sounded Greek.

"I'm not here for lunch. I need to talk to your manager, the owner, whatever." Bonifazio planted his feet and made it clear he wasn't moving. The waiter gave him a three-second assessment and slid off the bar stool. "What the hell do you eat in a Greek restaurant?" said Bonifazio to Pete Bianco as the waiter wandered toward the back. "What's Greek food, besides gyros?"

"Beats the hell outa me. Octopus. I think they eat octopus. And they drink turpentine."

"Turpentine?"

"S'what it tastes like to me."

The man who came to talk to Bonifazio was in shirtsleeves but his trousers were half of a nice suit. He had an impressive head of graying hair. He too assessed Bonifazio as he approached, and he looked a shade apprehensive. "What can I do for you?" He halted at a cautious distance.

"You know John Spanos?" Bonifazio wasted no time.

The man with gray hair looked at his two visitors and seemed to grow even more cautious. "John Spanos? Yes, he comes in here to eat." He had a deep voice and the same mild Greek accent.

"That's what I hear. I also hear he had a little trouble in here the other night."

Now the waiter at the bar had caught it, the hint, the faint odor of menace in the air. "What kind of trouble?" said the man with gray hair.

"I understand a man came in while he was having dinner and started harassing him. This would have been—oh, two or three nights ago."

The owner frowned, bewildered. "No. No, I don't think so."

"A guy with blond hair and a little goatee, like." Bonifazio caressed his jaw, miming the beard.

"Yeah, I remember," said the waiter. "Couple nights ago, yeah. I waited on Mr. Spanos. I remember the guy coming in. But he didn't harrass nobody. He came in, sat down for a minute, got up and left again."

"You hear what he said?"

The waiter shrugged. "No. He seemed glad to see Mr. Spanos, though. He kind of smiled, they talked for, I don't know, really just like a minute, and then the guy left."

Bonifazio looked at Bianco, who blinked back at him.

"Is there some problem?" said the owner. "Did Mr. Spanos make a complaint about something?" He was desperately trying to figure out if he was talking to a lawyer, though Bonifazio looked like no lawyer he had ever seen.

"No," said Vincent Bonifazio, suddenly full of cheer. "I just heard a rumor, that's all. Just trying to help out a friend. Hell of a nice place you got here." He reached out and gave a very puzzled Greek a friendly slap on the shoulder.

Out on the sidewalk Bonifazio looked up and down Halsted Street, lively with rumbling trucks, and shook his head. "So the girl at the breakfast place says Spanos smiled at the guy, here they say the guy looked glad to see Spanos. That sound like harassment to you? Getting in his face? Threatening him?"

"Not to me it don't."

"No. Sounds pretty friendly, don't it? Sounds like pretty good buddies. You wanna know something?"

"What?"

"One thing and another, I'm pretty fucking tired of Mr. John Spanos."

Spanos phoned from a 7-Eleven on Harlem. "Lemme talk to Alex," he said to the woman who answered the phone. He sucked on a cigarette while he waited, filling his lungs to bursting and holding it in. What he really needed was a drink but he had to stay right on top of things today.

"Hello?" said Alex.

"Spanos here. You gotta help me out. I know you're off today but I need a quick favor and I need it bad."

"Ah, mm. What kind of favor?"

"Listen. You got that book at the station, right? What do they call it, the crisscross book. I give you a phone number, you give me the address, right?"

"Right."

"So I need an address. And I need it fast."

"Jeez, I'm not going in today. That's a hell of a thing to ask me today."

"Alex, I ain't got time to fuck around. I need that address."

"I could get in a lot of trouble."

"OK, forget it. See you around. You'll be hearing from George about that, what is it, six grand or so?"

"Now wait a second, hang on." A sigh came over the line. "I'll have to make a special trip."

"Do it. Lemme give you a number where you can get me."

"That's all you need, the address?"

"That's the only thing I need, Alex. Be a pal and get it for me."

"Boy, I'd like to get the fucking money if I could. Put his head in a vise, squeeze him until he coughs it up. Crank it till his eyes pop out." Bonifazio was pacing today, his eyes on the floor of the little room behind the deli, five steps across the room and back again.

"I don't know, Vince. What's he gonna do, write us a check?" Pete Bianco stared at the end of his cigar.

"How the fuck do I know what he's gonna do? He sees his options, he'll cough it up. Give us an account number, hand over a key. How the fuck do I know?"

"That could be tricky. The way these things operate, you might have to fly to the Cayman Islands or something to get anything. They hide it pretty good."

"What do you know about it?" Bonifazio halted in mid-stride. "Don't tell me you got your own Mexican. You stashing it away somewhere too? Am I gonna have to put your fucking head in a vise?"

Bianco shrugged. "I hear stuff, that's all. Gimme a break."

"So what are you saying? I let him keep it?"

"I don't know what I'm saying. I'm saying it could involve a lot of work."

"Fuck. How could I fucking let the guy get away with ten million dollars? I shoulda seen the fucking signs. He dropped enough hints. Always pushing to get involved with the niggers. Son of a bitch, he was right, too. That's what fucking hurts. Ten million dollars, Jesus Christ. Can you believe you can make that kind of money in drugs? I'm telling you, Pete, the country's fucked up. It's down the fucking toilet."

"So what are you gonna do?"

Bonifazio halted, his pale blue eyes fixed on Bianco. "We gotta clear it with Angelo. I gotta get the OK. Spanos is too big now. I'm tempted, but I gotta clear it."

They stared at each other in silence. Bianco nodded once or twice. "OK. It's past noon. He oughta be up soon."

"I'm sorry, I didn't get no call," said Siminowicz, into the phone. "I don't get a call beforehand from Casalegno, you don't get a piece."

"What is this?" said Spanos. "The fucking Brady Bill? I gotta wait five days or something? I need a god damn piece."

"Sorry, man. I don't give 'em out to just anybody. You can understand that, right? Security. That's how I stay in business."

"But you know me."

"Sure. I know lots of guys. But there's only one or two that give the OK."

"I'll give you top dollar, cash on the barrel. I'll pay a premium. I need it now."

"Sorry, bud. Them's the rules. And following the rules is what protects me. It's just like the military—you don't draw a weapon without authorization."

Spanos swore into the phone. "You can't help me, huh?"

"Well, you want me to call Casalegno?"

"No, don't do that. Don't do that." Spanos thought about calling Jumbo, going through the whole nerve-jangling process of dialing pagers, waiting by pay phones, driving into shit neighborhoods, all over again. "Look," he said. "You gotta know somebody. You're not the only guy selling guns in this fucking city. Can you give me a name? Somebody that'll sell me a piece, fast?"

Siminowicz was silent for a few seconds. Spanos had just about decided to hang up when he spoke. "There's a guy in Crete."

"Crete?"

"Yeah, it's down south. You know where Balmoral race track is?"

"I know where the fuck it is, it's a long way away is where it is."

"Sorry, man, that's where the guy lives. He's got guns, if that's what you want."

Spanos exhaled into the phone. "OK, what do I do?"

"I'd have to call him. He won't sell to a stranger."

Spanos closed his eyes, the headache pulsing inside his temples. "Would you do that for me?"

"I can call him, yeah. What are you gonna need?"

"Something for personal defense. I don't care about silencers, any of that bullshit. I want something that'll put a hole in someone."

Siminowicz made a noise into the phone that might have been a laugh. "I think he can provide that."

They went back to Andrea's and back to bed; holding each other there were no doubts, no second thoughts. Dooley wanted to tell her everything that was in his heart but found that this heat, this touch, this kiss was clearer than words. This was a language that said everything there was to say. Afterward they slept.

In the late afternoon they went out. Dooley had one thing on his agenda: stay the hell out of everyone's way. Twenty-four hours before, he had thought it might be a good time to go out of town for a while. Now there was Andrea.

He wanted to take her out, do the town, take in some dinner and a movie maybe, just be together. He felt like a kid on his first hot date. He wanted to do something dumb like buy her a drink at the top of the Hancock Building, but the sky was too low; the overcast would start at about the fortieth floor. He wanted to walk along the lakefront with his arm around her. He didn't want to think about gangsters this evening.

He thought about the odds of being spotted on the street and decided that as long as he avoided Greek Town his chances were pretty good. They got in Dooley's car and went. He took her to O'Rourke's; he had to stop and look it up in a phone book on the way because he had forgotten it had moved off North Avenue. They had a couple of pints of stout and Dooley got sentimental, the Irishman in him stirring. He told her stories about his father. When they came out they smelled of smoke and it was dark already. Dooley drove skillfully, jockeying through the traffic, reaching over to grasp Andrea's hand at stoplights. He pointed out places where things had happened to him: as a cop, as a young guy out on the prowl. He felt like he had finally come home.

For dinner they cruised the Loop for parking and then walked around: Dooley liked the feel of it, a real big-city downtown with a lot of early-evening bustle, lit-up windows, a chill in the air, and the Christmas lights up already. Binyon's was gone—since when? Dooley caught sight of the Berghoff sign and knew where he wanted to have dinner. For Dooley it had always been a special-occasion type of place; he had been in his thirties before he realized that serious diners looked down their noses at it. Fuck 'em, thought Dooley. He still liked the high ceilings and the wood paneling and the waiters in black jackets and long white aprons and the sauerbraten and the creamed spinach. He liked the beer.

They were waiting for dessert when Dooley finally put it together, her vacant looks and forced smiles and long silences. He'd been doing all the talking and she had been working too hard to listen. "You don't like it, do you?" he said into a silence.

She knew exactly what he meant and gave him the first fully open look of the night. "It bothers me, I'm sorry."

Dooley shrugged. "You think he doesn't deserve it?" he said.

She had to think for a while. "I think he deserves to die. But I'd rather see it happen after a trial."

"Sometimes that's not possible."

"Because I think people deserve the truth."

"What do you mean, the public?"

"Yes, the public. But him, too. Is he going to know why he's getting killed? And if he doesn't, have you really avenged Roy?"

Dooley sat there looking at her and realized the rage was gone. He felt for it for a second or two but it was gone. The desserts arrived but neither of them had much appetite. Dooley picked at his apple pie and shoved it away. "The criminal justice system is a very imperfect machine," he said. "I've seen that from the inside out. It failed me with Consuelo and it's failing with Roy. It fails all the time. I guess I'm just sick and tired of that failure."

She reached across the table for his hand and he loved that look on her face; he'd been waiting for it to come back all afternoon. "Frank. If anybody knows what you're feeling, it's me."

"Yeah. I know."

"All I want to say is—I'm sorry, maybe I shouldn't say anything."

"No, I'm listening. Say it."

It took her a few seconds to find the words. "I don't know much, but one thing I've decided is that truth is like oxygen. You can't live without it, you smother and die without it. You can't have a marriage without truth, I found that out. And I don't think you can have much justice without it, either."

"Boy, tell that to the lawyers."

He knew that was irrelevant and she ignored it. "Roy told me something once. He said you lose a few if you go by the rules, but you win in the long run because it's the rules that make it a system instead of a gang."

Dooley nodded slowly, staring at the tabletop. He said, "He was a lot better cop than I was."

"I don't know about that. But I know that's where his sense of honor came from, from being the best cop he could be."

"Yeah." Dooley stared at Andrea for a long time and finally he said, "I pitched it all, didn't I? I pitched the good part with the bad. I got rid of the rules and I got rid of the honor at the same time."

She started to cry, looking at him, one tear breaking from the corner of each eye. Dooley was vaguely conscious of the waiter looming briefly and hustling away. "Maybe you can get it back," Andrea said huskily.

24

DOOLEY GOT UP AND WENT TO THE BATHROOM. IT WAS JUST STARTING to get light. He washed and shaved and stared at himself in the mirror for a while. Forty-four and showing every day of it, older but no wiser. He asked himself, What the hell do I do now?

When he went back into the bedroom Andrea was awake, up on one elbow, bare shoulder showing above the sheet, hair tousled. "You OK?" Her voice was faint, anxious.

"I'm fine. Go back to sleep." He sat on the bed beside her, leaned over and took her in his arms, bore her back down onto the pillow. She gave off the heat of an untroubled night under the covers. Dooley had lain awake and listened to her breathing.

"What are you going to do?" she breathed into his neck.

Dooley eased his embrace and sat up. "I'm going to talk to Casalegno."

He got dressed and made himself a cup off coffee and then pulled Angelo Casalegno's pager number out of his wallet. He stood in the kitchen looking at the sheet of paper, running through options. Andrea was leaning in the doorway, in her bathrobe. "Not here," Dooley said. "I'll page him from Roy's. You don't want him getting this number."

She nodded. "I'll come with you."

"No."

"Why not?"

"Spanos knows where Roy lived. Who knows what he's up to, at this point? He could be sitting outside. You're better off here."

She closed her eyes briefly. "OK. Be careful."

"I think we're a little past that point," Dooley said. "But everything you said is right. It's time to start acting like a cop again."

He put the Walther in his waistband, in back. Andrea kissed him and held on to him for a while at the door. He looked into her face and saw nothing but a deep fatalism. She looked as sad as the end of the world. "I'll be careful," he said. He went out into the early morning gray light and got into the Nova. As he pulled away he could see her slowly closing the door.

He let himself into Roy's and walked up the long hallway again, his gun drawn. Anybody that jumped him now was going to get a hole punched in him. When he was sure the place was empty he went to the phone. He dialed Casalegno's pager, punched in Roy's number, and hung up. He went to stand at the window.

He saw people come out of their houses and drive away to work. He saw leaves fall. He stood there and saw the last eight years of his life go by, and resolved that the next eight years were going to be an improvement. He saw Andrea, all the sadness in the world in her eyes. The telephone rang.

"Who the fuck is this?" said Angelo Casalegno.

"It's Frank Edmonds, Mr. Casalegno. I'm sorry to bother you so early."

"Who?"

"Frank. I introduced you to Ramón Fuentes, remember?"

Silence. "What's going on?"

"I got something to tell you. It's pretty important."

"Ah, Jesus Christ. I knew it was too fucking good to be true. What happened, the G get him already?"

"Nothing happened to Ramón. I'm calling you about John Spanos."

"What about him?"

"He was framed."

"What?"

"He was framed. He doesn't have any money with Ramón. That was all bullshit. We cooked it up, faked it. Spanos never met Ramón in his life."

Silence again, and then, "What the *fuck* are you trying to tell me?"

"I'm trying to tell you that Spanos is innocent. He hasn't been holding out on you, at least as far as I know. He's a good soldier."

Dooley could hear the old man's bewilderment over the line. "So who framed him?"

"I did."

"Say that again?"

"I framed him. It was all my idea."

"Why, for Christ's sake?"

"I'm a cop, you stupid son of a bitch. I couldn't nail him for killing Roy Ferguson, so I tried to get him killed." Dooley was tired of talking with these people.

It made no noise, but now Dooley could hear panic coming across the wire. The silence lasted long enough that he began to think he'd lost the man. "Mr. Casalegno?"

When Casalegno answered, there was a new, darker tone in his voice. "You mean this was all a fucking police setup?"

"It was a setup, all right. We'd have had you good, too."

"Son of a bitch. So that fucking Mexican's a phony?"

"Well, you can feel free to go ahead and send him your money, as far as I'm concerned."

"God *damn* it. I can't believe you can get away with something like that in this day and age."

"I'm not getting away with it, you asshole. Aren't you listening to me?"

"I hope they throw your fuckin' ass in jail. I was all ready to give that guy a suitcase full of money."

"Yeah, we know."

Dooley could hear horrifying realizations dawning. "Jesus Christ. That's entrapment. You can't fucking do that. My lawyer will eat you alive in court."

"Don't worry, I don't think it's going to get to court. Look, the point is, you gotta call off the dogs. Spanos didn't cheat you."

"So what are telling me now for?"

In a flash of clarity Dooley saw that complete frankness was useless; Casalegno would never believe the simple truth. "I was ordered to," he said.

"What do you mean?"

"That's all you need to know. I cooked up the scheme, now I have to take it apart."

There was another pause, and finally Casalegno said, "You fucking guys never cease to amaze me."

Spanos checked out of the motel just after eight. He had slept poorly and then had to get dressed in the same clothes again; he hated putting on dirty clothes after a shower. His only luggage was his briefcase with something under five thousand dollars and the 9mm Browning Hi-Power in it. The man in Crete had driven a hard bargain but Spanos still had enough cash to see him through what he expected to be a difficult couple of days.

The motel was a short drive from the Tri-State, out in the middle of nowhere, traffic lights and shopping centers. Spanos spent a minute looking at the map, figuring out which exit to take to get to the address on LeMai on the Northwest side. He figured it was a long shot but it was the only shot he had left. He doubted Dooley would set foot in Ferguson's apartment again.

He laid the map aside and opened the briefcase to look at the automatic lying there. He had shoved thirteen rounds into the magazine the night before. Spanos hoped he wasn't going to need more than one or two of them.

Andrea took a shower and dressed. She had a piece of toast, drank some coffee. She cleaned up, turned on the TV, turned it off again, went and sat at the kitchen table and put her head down on her arms. This was her life; four years of pain and emptiness and then it starts all over, you have someone but his job is looking into the eyes of the beast. He loves the life and he doesn't care that it ties you in knots. Andrea couldn't understand how she'd fallen in with cops; there were no cops in her family and she'd never given them much thought till she'd met Roy.

Roy. Sometimes she loved him and sometimes she hated him and sometimes when she thought about him she just wanted to let herself fall into that deep, deep well and cry herself to sleep; she liked him best when she remembered him with Sean.

Her feelings were all tangled. She'd always liked Frank Dooley and maybe she loved him now; it had certainly eased that deep-seated ache to lie in his arms, but he was just like Roy: he had that attitude and now she had to sit here and wait for him and hope nobody killed him today. She had gotten something back and she couldn't even enjoy it because it might be taken away from her at any minute.

Andrea raised her head and dried her eyes; she blew her nose and went to the sink and got herself a drink of water. She looked out the back window and wondered if Frank would like living here, if he would mow the lawn. She wondered if that was what she wanted. The doorbell rang.

Spanos had given it some thought: telephone first? It could be a colossal waste of time driving all the way up here. The other side was, a phone call was a warning. He had decided to come straight here and take his chances. He checked his hair in the rearview mirror, still feeling dirty and unkempt, and got out of the car. He would read the situation here as best he could and if it was a dry hole he'd try something else. If the woman was leaving messages for Dooley she could at least tell him where to look next.

He rang the doorbell and stood with his head down as if he were deep in thought, not giving any neighbors that might be looking out a window much of a face to see. When the door came open a foot or so he looked up at a sad pair of eyes under nice blond hair. "Yes?" she said. She was mistrustful, he could see, wondering who this guy at the door could be.

"Hi, is Frank here?"

She waited too long, blinking at him. When she finally said, "Frank who?" she had given herself away. "There's no Frank here," she said, starting to close the door.

"Hang on. Frank Dooley? He gave me this address."

The door stopped moving and she was thinking about it, he could see. "When?" she said.

"Yesterday. I got some money for him." Spanos had an instinctive feel for what got people's attention, and this one never failed.

"I'm afraid you've been misinformed," the woman said. The door started moving again.

"Can you just give him the package?" Spanos pulled open the screen door, his other hand going into his pocket, and she hesitated, her attention caught just enough. When his hand came out holding the automatic he had a foot in the door and her frantic attempt to slam it caught on the stiff sole of his oxford. He threw all his considerable weight into the door and she cried out as it caught her in the face and then he was inside.

* * *

Dooley drove back up Lincoln, trying to sort out his feelings. He wished he had something to feel good about, but he wasn't achieving positive things here; he was just undoing negatives. At least he'd stopped Casalegno from sending a lot of money south, out of the reach of the law; his conscience had been bothering him a bit on that score. When he stopped to think about it, he wondered where the hell his conscience had been the last week or two. He had seen gang wars started for personal grudges that wound up taking out two or three innocent people along the way. Where the hell had his judgment gone? He was glad Andrea had come along to throw some water in his face.

The trouble was, when he got it all undone he would be right back where he started, with John Spanos walking around free. Nobody was going to nail him for killing Roy; each day that passed made it less likely. For an instant he thought of the Walther digging into his back and was tempted to just go shoot the son of a bitch after all, man to man: draw, partner.

Andrea. Nothing was worth it if it meant throwing her away. She had brought him home. He turned off Devon down LeMai, impatient to see her, tell her he'd undone it. He pulled up in the driveway and cut the ignition, went up the steps and leaned on the bell.

When she opened the door, Dooley was halfway in before he noticed the gaunt and paralyzed look on her face; his momentum brought him in far enough to see John Spanos behind the door, aiming an automatic at his head. Dooley was so astonished he could do nothing but stand there and stare as Spanos shoved the door closed. "Where the fuck you been?" said Spanos. "You're missing all the fun."

Dooley still couldn't move; he wanted to but he couldn't. Spanos jerked the muzzle of the gun at Andrea. "Back on the couch. Move." She obeyed, looking small and frightened. Dooley could see a swelling, a faint discoloration, on her right cheekbone.

"Did he hit you?"

"The door hit me when he barged in." She spoke very quietly, sinking onto the couch.

"You. Over there." Spanos backed away into the living room, the gun still raised. "Put your hands on the wall. Do it now."

"The phone message. She left her number on Roy's machine. That was it, right? And you had somebody who could look in the crisscross for you."

"You're a hell of a detective, I'll give you that."

"And I was all set to give you a break," said Dooley.

"I said put your hands on the wall." Spanos motioned with the gun. "Over there. Hands on the wall and spread 'em, we'll see how you like it for a change."

Spanos patted him down and found the Walther immediately. He jerked it out of Dooley's pants and backed away. "Well. You came prepared. Hoping to shoot me with this, were you?"

"I still am."

"Well, it's too late for that. What's gonna happen now is, you're gonna tell some people the truth for a change."

Dooley turned. "I already did. I just talked to Casalegno. I told him the whole thing. I told him to call off the dogs."

The look that crossed Spanos's face mixed incredulity and amusement. "Oh, right. Right, sure, you changed your mind."

"Call him. He'll tell you."

Spanos gave out a whiff of laughter. "You just decided to call the whole thing off, huh?"

"Yeah."

"Why?"

"Because I'm gonna enjoy seeing you spend the rest of your life in Stateville. I want to see your face when they sentence you."

"You're still smoking that Mexican weed, huh? Dream on."

"They made a case against you, dumb-fuck. You're going down."

Spanos froze for a second, just a second, and then shook his head. "I don't believe a word that comes out of your mouth. Not a fucking word."

Dooley shrugged. "OK. Anyway, your problems with Casalegno are over. You can leave us alone and concentrate on getting out of town ahead of the cops."

"Fuck you. My problem isn't with Casalegno. My problem's with Vincent Bonifazio. And that's where you come in. We're gonna go see him."

Dooley and Andrea exchanged a look. He couldn't read what he saw in her face. "Fine. Lead the way."

"Hold on just a fucking minute." Spanos walked to the phone at the end of the couch and picked up the receiver, lodging it between cheek and shoulder, shifting the automatic to his left. He punched in a number and after a few seconds said, "Mike, John here. *Spanos*, you moron. Lemme talk to Vince. Well, call him. Page him. Tell him to meet me there. Where you are, what the fuck do you think I mean? I'm on my way. Tell Vince I got Dooley and we're gonna put an end to this bullshit." Spanos slammed down the phone. "Asshole." Spanos backed away from the couch, shifting the gun to cover Andrea. "OK, come over here. You and me go out together."

"Uh-uh," said Dooley. "She's not going anywhere."

"Keep your fucking mouth shut."

"I'm the guy who can call off Bonifazio. She has nothing to do with this."

"She does now."

Dooley looked at Spanos and was afraid he saw already how it was going to end. "Tie her up or something. Tape her to a pipe in the basement, rip out the phone. But she stays."

"Get up, honey, on your feet. He goes first, you walk next to me. We're gonna walk out to my car together, just like we're going out for lunch. Anybody does anything stupid, I shoot you in the head. What do you think the odds are there's anybody on this block looking out the window right now? If I have to shoot you both and drive away, I will. Everybody got the rules clear?" Spanos pulled his car keys out of his pocket and tossed them to Dooley. "You drive."

Dooley caught the keys. Very calm, very cold inside, he said, "You're just piling another felony on top. Cut and run, asshole. You get Bonifazio off your back, you still got the law."

"Shut up. You, move."

Andrea stood up. "Can I get my coat? From the closet there?"

"Get it. You, jag-off. I know you're fucking nuts, but you're not going to do anything to get this lady hurt, right? Anything, any wrong thing you do, I'll kill her. And you gotta know I mean it. So don't try *nothing*. You get in the car and drive, she'll be on the passenger seat. I'll be in back with the gun aimed at her. Anything you do that makes me even a little unhappy, I'll shoot *her*. Then you can try the hero stuff on me, but where will that get you?"

Dooley watched Andrea putting on her coat. "OK, don't get excited. Whatever you do, don't get excited."

Vincent Bonifazio was getting a headache. "He just called. Mike says he's on his way to the garage. He's got Dooley with him."

"Dooley? Who the fuck is Dooley?" Casalegno didn't have a headache yet, but he had been awakened too early and the coffee was doing bad things to his septuagenarian stomach.

"The guy, for Christ's sake. The guy with the Mexican."

"You mean what's his name, the cop, Edmonds."

"His real name's Dooley. He used to be a cop."

"He told me he was a cop."

"According to Spanos, he's not anymore. What the fuck do I know?"

"You know, this guy is, I'm telling you, this guy is getting me seriously pissed off."

"Tell me about it."

"So we gotta think, why is he telling us this, about Spanos? Why is he calling it off?"

"You know why. Him and Spanos was in it together from the start. When the guy let slip that Spanos had put all that money away, they had to control the damage. Spanos got him to make up this bullshit about it being a police thing and how now they're calling it off because they made a case."

"But what if it's true? What if it *was* a setup and they *do* have a case?"

"Then I think you better call your fucking lawyer. But I think it's all bullshit. I think this is Spanos, still messing with us."

A silence ensued while two elderly thugs chewed nails at opposite ends of a phone line. "Boy," said Angelo Casalegno. "Either way."

"Either way," said Bonifazio.

"You take care of it," said Casalegno, and hung up.

25

Dooley honked, and after a wait the overhead door of the body shop rattled up, revealing a large gloomy garage space with a handful of battered cars shoved here and there. A man in overalls was standing by the door; in the depths of the place a torch was sending sparks onto the floor. Dooley drove in slowly and cut the ignition. "Out," said Spanos.

Dooley and Andrea got out slowly. Spanos bounded out of the backseat and said to the man by the door, "Put the door down and then take a hike." He held out his hand and Dooley gave him the keys.

"Take a hike? I got work to do."

"Take a fucking hike. Take Bozo back there with you. It's lunchtime. Take a long lunch. Call before you come back."

You didn't argue with a man of the stature of John Spanos, not even about your own business; the man in overalls shrugged and turned to punch the button that lowered the door. Spanos jutted his chin toward a partitioned-off cubicle in the back corner of the garage. "Back in the office."

Inside the office were a desk, a filing cabinet, a couple of folding chairs, a coffeemaker with the carafe half full, a calendar on the wall. Andrea sat on one of the folding chairs and Dooley took the swivel chair behind the desk. "Sit tight, keep your hands to yourself," said Spanos.

Dooley settled into the chair, scanning the desktop, the rest of the office. His eyes met Andrea's and they looked at each other for a long moment. Andrea blinked at him, looking taut but in control. Dooley had a feeling she wasn't panic-prone and the feeling reassured him. He figured he had some time to work with, maybe a little leverage. He blew Andrea a kiss, just touching the tips of his fingers with his lips. She closed her eyes, just for a second or two.

Spanos stood in the open doorway, watching the two body men down tools and head for the door. A door slammed. Spanos lit a cigarette and turned back into the office. "Where the fuck is that dumbass guinea?" he said.

"Maybe he wrote you off," said Dooley. "Maybe he dropped a dime on you."

Spanos halted in front of the desk and blew smoke at Dooley. "Guys like you, guys with a mouth on 'em. Sooner or later it gets 'em in trouble. Little punk loudmouths, they always get their chops busted in the end."

"That's all we little punks got is the mouth," said Dooley. "And the brains."

"Brains? Look where your brains landed you, dumb-shit." Spanos walked out of the office, hovering just outside the door, looking toward the front of the place.

Dooley watched him smoke. After a minute he stood up, walked out from behind the desk and went to the door of the office. Spanos had wandered a few feet away but when he saw Dooley he pulled the Browning out of his jacket pocket and leveled it at him. "Sit down."

"You know what's going to happen, don't you?" said Dooley.

"Go sit down."

"They're going to kill both of us, you know. All three of us."

"Bullshit."

"No bull, John. They'll kill me for fucking with them and they'll kill you because when you go down for murder they'll be afraid you'll talk."

Spanos let the gun fall to his side. "I'm not going down for no fucking murder." His eyes went past Dooley into the office just as Dooley heard a soft beep behind him. "Hey! Get away from that phone!" Dooley wheeled to see Andrea sinking back on her chair, her hand trailing across the desk. Spanos dropped his cigarette and came stalking toward the office, gun rising.

Dooley barred the way. "You're gonna have to shoot me first."

Spanos halted, the muzzle of the gun a foot from Dooley's nose. "Don't tempt me. Tell her to stay the fuck away from the phone. I see her ass off that chair again, I'll kill her."

Dooley could hardly stand, his knees were suddenly so weak. He nodded, turned into the office. Andrea was on her chair, lips parted, grasping the edge of the seat, white-knuckled. Heart pounding, Dooley made a palm-down gesture. "Easy. Let's take it easy and not make anybody mad."

Andrea nodded. Jesus, thought Dooley, who'd have expected that? Andrea nodded again, whispered "OK."

In the doorway Spanos said, "What, you think you're fast enough to dial before I catch on? Christ, you been watching too much TV. Now sit the fuck over there, the other chair, and don't try that shit again."

Andrea changed chairs on visibly shaky legs and nodded. She was chalk-white. Dooley took her head in his hands, leaned over to rest his head on hers. "Stay cool. Stay cool and we got a chance," he said softly. "We always got a chance."

"I'm sorry," she said aloud.

"Nothing's gonna happen to you," said Spanos. "Not if you sit quiet and don't make waves. You, sit down."

Dooley turned to him. They were out of time; something had to happen before the place filled up with wise guys. "What the fuck, John? You want it in writing? You're a dead man. They can't let you go down. And you *are* going down. CPD's got your ass in a fucking bag."

Spanos stared at him and said, "Which one? Which case we talking about?"

"Both of 'em, asshole."

Spanos laughed. "You got shit, nothing. Zero, nada. It's a bluff and you're the world's worst bluffer."

"Fine. You call the bluff, it means taking your chances with those old dumbass guineas. All they have to do is *think* you're going down and you're history."

Spanos moved in close and stuck a finger in Dooley's chest. "They know I ain't going nowhere. You got nothing on Blumberg 'cause you never had the fucking notebook. And you got nothing on Ferguson because I was too careful. It was a perfect fucking hit."

Dooley got no satisfaction from hearing it; he just looked into John Spanos's eyes and made the decision: try something right now or it was all over. He sighed, turned away toward the desk. The coffee maybe; blind him with a faceful and hope for the best. He dragged his feet a little, edging around the corner of the desk.

Andrea's sharp gasp was the only warning he got; then lights and sound and a head full of pain. He didn't black out but he was helpless for a couple of seconds; he found himself on his knees hanging on to the desk and making a noise in his throat, eyes squeezed shut. "Preemptive strike," he heard John Spanos saying. "You gotta work on your body language, dumb-shit."

Dooley started to pull himself up but Spanos's hand on the back of his head rammed his face into the edge of the desk. Dooley had never known the world could hold hurt like this. He made it to his hands and knees and then the kick knocked him sideways and Dooley couldn't have said whether he heard or felt the ribs break; his whole body knew it.

"*Stop it!*" Now he could hear the scrape of a chair, feet on the concrete, Spanos exerting himself to throw Andrea across the room. She went over the other chair and hit the floor and that helped Dooley rally; he lurched into the far wall behind the desk and clawed his way up it until he was standing.

Spanos had the automatic trained on his face. "That's enough." He was panting with the sudden activity, the gun rising and falling a little with each breath. "Sit the fuck down." He shifted the gun to Andrea, on her ass in the corner. "You, stay right there. It's over."

It hurt Dooley to breathe; when he moved his head his neck creaked and sent fire up the back of his skull. It hurt Dooley to do anything at all but he made it to the chair behind the desk. Pain, he thought. What the fuck's a little pain; nothing I feel is anywhere near what Consuelo went through. Sinking onto the chair made him groan. Andrea was crying, looking at him. "I'm OK," he croaked. Blood was coming from the gash next to his eye, drops splashing on the desk, on his hands.

Spanos laughed. "Yeah, you're in great shape. Tip-top. Just sit there and try not to die yet, OK? Here." Spanos tossed him a roll of paper towels from the top of the filing cabinet.

Out in the garage there was the sound of a door opening. Footsteps sounded, a motor engaged and the overhead door began to go up. An engine purred as a vehicle pulled into the garage. Spanos put the automatic in his jacket pocket and looked at Dooley. "I win," he said. To Andrea he said, "Sit on the chair."

Dooley took a blood-soaked towel away from his face and spoke quickly in a low voice. He could only draw shallow breaths because his ribs hurt so much. "We're out of time, John. They're gonna kill us both. Our only chance is . . . you give me my gun back. With two . . . with two of us we got a chance. We get out of this, I let you go . . . take your chances. Deal?"

"Johnny!" Vincent Bonifazio's voice sounded out in the garage.

Spanos shook his head. "You're dreamin'," he said.

Dooley watched him walk out of the office. He looked at Andrea, back on her chair. "We got a chance," he said softly. "They won't hit anybody here." He was blowing smoke and he knew it. Andrea nodded, tears still flowing but not losing it. He could tell she wanted to come over to him but was afraid to move.

Vincent Bonifazio came into the office. Behind him Dooley saw two men he didn't recognize, along with Spanos. He wondered where they got all these guys, all these old thick-necked dead-eyed thugs. "Well, well," said Bonifazio. "Who we got here?"

Behind him Spanos said, "This the guy that was at the airport?"

"Looks like it." Bonifazio had a suspicious look on his lined, leathery face.

"Well, say hello to Frank Dooley. He's got something to say to you."

"Hello, Frank Dooley. What the hell's wrong with you?" Bonifazio peered at him, the bright little eyes shining.

"He fell down and hurt himself," said Spanos.

Bonifazio nodded, looking at Dooley. "Clumsy, huh? Well, what do you got to say to me?"

Dooley was out of ideas. He looked at the bright red blood soaking the paper towel and said, "I lied to you."

"Oh yeah? About what?"

"About Spanos. He wasn't holding out on you."

Bonifazio nodded, turned to Spanos. "Well Jesus, John. I guess I owe you an apology."

"Yeah, you do. But that's OK. He's got a fucking mouth on him, don't he?"

Still nodding, Bonifazio looked down at Andrea. He stopped nodding and said, "Who are you?"

"I'm with Frank," she said.

Bonifazio looked at Spanos. "Who's this?"

"Like she said, she's with him."

Bonifazio did not look pleased with the arrangements. He looked at the collapsed chair and said, "Sit down, John. I'll be right with you." He made for the door.

"Hang on, I got some things to discuss too," said Spanos, following.

Bonifazio wheeled in the doorway. "I said sit down." Spanos nearly rammed into him.

"What the fuck, Vince."

"Sit." Bonifazio left; in his place one of the bulldogs filled the doorway. "Hello, John," it said. "Have a seat, will ya?"

Spanos lingered in the doorway for a moment, losing the stare-down. He turned and went to set up the chair as the bulldog closed the door to the office. Spanos sat and looked at Dooley, and Dooley could see the beginning of the end in his eyes.

"What about it, John? Think it looks like they're letting you back in the club?"

Spanos said nothing. He stared at Dooley and thought, and whatever thoughts he was having were dark ones. "Fuck you," he said.

"Slide one of the guns across the desk here, quick. They'll search you before they try anything. You don't want to lose both guns."

"Forget it, Dooley. It ain't working. I'll take my chances with Vince."

The door opened and Bonifazio came in. He looked at Andrea and said, "You know—ah, miss, I'd feel a little better if you left. What we got here is kind of a business meeting, you know? And it ain't really your place. I'm gonna have one of my guys out there take you home, OK?"

Dooley wasn't fooled but he wasn't going to spoil it if Andrea was; she shot him a look and he nodded once, trying to tell her to go, take her chances. She looked at him for two or three seconds, and he wanted to tell her things he would never have time to say. He thought about what joy had felt like and was bitterly sorry.

Andrea looked at Bonifazio and said, "I'm not moving."

The old wise guy wasn't used to women saying no; he scowled at her and said, "I don't think I made myself clear."

"I heard you," said Andrea. "I'm not going anyplace." Her arms were folded; the tears had made tracks down her face but she was calm.

Bonifazio called out, "Bobby. Got some resistance here." To Andrea he said, "What do you want to stick around for? There's no reason for you to be here. It's no place for you."

One of the no-necks came in, looking to Bonfazio for orders. "Get her out of here," said Bonifazio.

"It's going to take two of you," said Andrea.

"Andrea. Go ahead, get going," said Dooley. Split them up, he was thinking, and everyone's chances are better.

"I'm staying," she said.

The goon put out his hand to her, waggling his fingers. "Come on, honey. Don't be difficult."

The second thug appeared in the doorway, looking amused. Andrea gave him a glance and then turned to fix Spanos with a look.

"Well?" she said. "Frank's absolutely right, you know."

There was a long frozen second of mutual realization and then John Spanos brought the Browning Hi-Power out of his jacket pocket and started squeezing off rounds, deafening everyone. The man in the doorway had realized what was happening a split second late and crumpled with his gun halfway out of his belt; the man standing by Andrea's suddenly empty chair was far too slow and could only throw his hands up in a futile instinctive gesture before three shots walked up his torso from belly to breastbone, punching him back against the wall. Vincent Bonifazio was unarmed and there was a brief silence in which he spread his arms in a submissive gesture and said plaintively, "Johnny," before he died with his back to the filing cabinet, his face a picture of dismay and two little red buds popping open on his chest. Spanos swung toward Dooley but Dooley had already swept the carafe off the coffeemaker; he caught Spanos full in the face with the black steaming brew. Spanos squeezed off a shot as he twisted away, bellowing.

Still alive, Dooley threw the carafe and shattered it on Spanos's head. Borne on the wings of an adrenaline angel, Dooley vaulted over the desk and kicked Spanos in the side of the head as he spun out of his crouch. Spanos went backward over his chair and Dooley followed, going on nothing but momentum and desperation. Trying to kick Spanos's gun arm he caught the chair instead and nearly fractured his ankle, but Spanos had to get clear of the chair. Dooley had hit the floor somehow; he latched onto Spanos's wrist and twisted; there was a brief contest of strength and then Spanos gave up; Dooley heard the Browning clatter on the concrete and thought he had won but before he could find the handle Spanos was bringing the Walther out of his other pocket. Dooley embraced him like a lover and squeezed tight for dear life, Spanos's arm pinned under his. Spanos rolled him onto his back, fighting for clearance to shoot, crushing him.

Spanos was a big man and Dooley knew he had to lose; he was hurt too bad to last the round. He had drawn what breath he could to scream at Andrea to run when suddenly it was over; a chair came out of heaven and went CLUNK on Spanos's head. Naturally, Spanos's skull transmitted the impact directly to Dooley's face. When Dooley's vision cleared he saw Andrea above him, pulling at Spanos's collar.

Dooley couldn't move; he was paying the price now for that burst of adrenaline. There was no move he could make that wouldn't bring agony, and lying still was no picnic. Andrea heaved Spanos off him with a gasp. Then she grabbed his arm and hauled him to his feet; Dooley cried out but got his legs under him. "Oh God, oh God," Andrea was saying. Her face was drawn taut and there was no color there.

There was a rattling throaty noise from the floor and Dooley looked down and saw Spanos rolling onto his back, eyes open; what did it take to put the fucker out? Dooley could barely stand, but eye contact with Spanos revived him; with great concentration Dooley shook off Andrea's grip and went to one knee to pick up the Walther. He jammed the muzzle in Spanos's mouth, chipping teeth and gagging him. Spanos's hands went to Dooley's wrist but Dooley had the leverage. "I win," Dooley said in a wheeze that cost him all the breath he had left. Spanos's eyes were focused now, looking into his. Dooley knew just what it was going to look like when he pulled the trigger; he remembered seeing the light in Leroy Dickens's eyes go out.

"Frank!" Dooley froze for what seemed a very long moment, feeling Andrea's hands on him and looking into John Spanos's eyes. "Don't kill him! Don't," she said. "We've got the tape."

Dooley couldn't think what the hell she was talking about but he let her pull him away; he still had the gun and Spanos was watching it with attention, elbows on the floor and hands raised. He spat blood and some of it splattered across his chin. "Just like that," croaked Dooley. "Stay right there."

Andrea sprawled across the desk and scrabbled at the phone; she pressed buttons until the little hatch on the built-in answering machine popped open and she clawed out the cassette. "Let's *go*," she said. She hooked an arm through Dooley's and pulled. *"Please.* Let's go."

Dooley's head wasn't up to this; he let Andrea pull him out of the office, guiding him past dying mobsters on the floor. He kept the gun leveled at Spanos until he was out of sight.

Out on the garage floor, staggering, leaning on Andrea, he got it together enough to ask, "What's with the tape?"

Andrea shot him a look, steaming for the door. "Didn't you hear him? I taped his confession."

26

"The phone in there was just like the one at my dad's house. There's a memo button. You push it and it records a memo, meaning anything anyone says near it. You can get up to five minutes on it. I think we might have just made it."

They'd let Andrea stay with him in the curtained-off corner of the emergency room where he lay waiting for somebody to notice he wasn't in the pink of health. Dooley couldn't believe what he was hearing. "But how did you know . . . he was going to confess?" It was getting harder to breathe.

"I didn't. All I was trying to do was leave some kind of evidence. I thought we were going to die and somebody might find it before it got erased. It was just a long shot."

Dooley closed his eyes. "You set them up for Spanos," he said.

"Uh-huh."

"Where did you learn to think like that?"

It was a long time before Andrea answered. Dooley heard somebody crying, hushed voices down a corridor. "I guess it's true, about how the mind gets concentrated wonderfully," she said. "I just saw all of a sudden I had to get them all in one place so Spanos could shoot them."

So much of Dooley hurt that there was no place to go to hide from it. He wanted someone to put him out of his misery. He wanted somebody to tell him what to do. "See if you can find a phone," he said. "Call Kevin."

* * *

The interview room had no windows; out in the hall he heard some-body say it had started to snow. Dooley couldn't work up much emo-tion about it one way or another. With a cervical collar around his neck and an elastic corset around his ribs and stiches in his face and a bloodstream full of wonderful drugs he was happy to be breathing, if shallowly. "You would have to back it up by testifying," Kevin said. He looked like God Himself in his white uniform shirt with the lieu-tenant's bars.

"I know," said Dooley. "I'll testify. I'll tell it all, even the bad parts. I'll plead guilty to obstruction of justice, impersonating an officer, everything. As long as we nail Spanos."

Kevin looked at his little brother across the table. He shook his head. "You really know how to stir up the hornets, don't you?"

"There's more." The way Dooley said it, both Kevin and Andrea stiffened; what was he going to say now?

"I'll plead on the guy in the Century Mall. It was self-defense but I shouldn't have run. I'll take my chances with the State's Attorney. I just want to get straight with the law again."

Kevin's eyes narrowed. Seconds passed. "That was you?"

"That was me. He had a knife."

Kevin was having a hard time assimilating everything he was learning about his little brother. "Why in the hell did you run?"

Dooley gave it some honest thought. "Because it was easier."

The look on Kevin's face went from incredulity to something like awe. "Anything else you haven't mentioned?"

"No, I think that's about it."

Kevin leaned back on his chair. He blew out his cheeks, raised his eyebrows. "You've been a busy boy."

Dooley blinked at him. "I've been an asshole. Ever since Consuelo died, I've thought the law wasn't good enough for me. I tried to be a cowboy."

"I don't think cowboy quite covers it. Cowboys are pretty tame, compared to you."

"Cowboys are a dime a dozen. But the law—to be a cop, you have to have the law behind you. I miss that, I miss it bad."

Kevin stared at him a while, looked at Andrea, heaved a sigh. He shoved away from the table and stood up. "I'll call Matic. You probably got a long evening ahead of you. You're gonna need a lawyer. Want me to call Uncle Ted?"

"If you think he can handle it."

"He's not quite senile yet. He can probably get you out on bond by Christmas. And he's cheap."

"What the hell, call him."

Kevin turned to go. Andrea passed a hand under Dooley's arm and laid her head on his shoulder, gently. Kevin paused in the doorway. He stared down at Dooley from on high, and Dooley remembered his father giving him just this look, many times. "The old man always said it was a mistake to underestimate you."

Terry pulled up in an Olds Ninety-eight and Spanos came out of the convenience store and ducked into the car. "Thanks, kid. I won't forget it. Anybody ask you anything?"

Terry shook his head. The patch was gone and his eye shone gruesomely red but functional. "I think we're clean. What'd you do, take out a wall with your face?"

"Look who the fuck's talking. He did you worse than me."

Terry gunned it out onto Division Street. "Dooley did that?"

Spanos shook his head. "You were right, kid. He's fast. You hear about Vince?"

"The news had it. All it said was they found him dead. You part of that?"

"I was there. Fuckin' Marino did him. Those two been like that for years. I saw it coming. I had to get the fuck out of there fast. I think I got away clean but it's time for a vacation, you know? You get me to O'Hare and I'm outa here for a while. I got some money for you, you been a good friend."

"Shit, John, I don't need no money for this."

"No, I mean it. I won't forget what you did. You been a good friend. You're gonna do real well. You just gotta be careful, know what I mean? You gotta watch out for people you can't trust."

Terry pushed hard through the traffic. Spanos opened his bag and rooted inside. "Listen, kid."

"Yeah?"

"This fucking Dooley."

"Yeah?"

"We both got like, a reason, you know? I mean this fucker's messed with us both."

"Yeah. He's a mother."

"Well, look." Spanos pulled the Browning automatic out of his bag and slid it into the glove compartment. "I'm gonna leave this with you. I can't get it on a fucking plane anyway. It's clean. It's a piece I had for emergencies."

"Uh-huh?"

"What I'm saying is, you might wanna give some more thought to Dooley, take another crack at him, you know? I can give you an address. He's got a woman he's shacked up with."

Terry checked his mirrors, moved over a lane, accelerated. "Yeah, OK. I wouldn't mind."

"He's a bastard, ain't he?"

"I'll take care of him," said Terry.

"You're all right, Terry. You're gonna do real fuckin' good someday."

Terry pulled off the street into an Amoco station. "We're low on gas," he said.

Spanos scowled. "Shit, you gotta think of that before you start. A pro fills it up ahead of time."

"Come on, John, it was pretty short notice, you gotta admit."

"Yeah, yeah, you're right, kid. I'm sorry. Look, lemme give you money for the gas."

Terry eased to a halt at the pumps, behind a van. "No, I got it. Hang on just a second." He got out and slammed the door.

Spanos looked at his watch, took a deep breath. His head hurt, his stomach was giving him hell. He poked softly at the tender places on his face. He caught sight of Terry in the side mirror, running away.

As the door of the van just in front of him swung open, Spanos saw everything and drew breath for a scream he never had time to deliver. Joe Delvecchio raised the muzzle of a pump-action shotgun, shooting fish in a barrel, and Spanos just had time to think, the kid's going to get his own book now.

The celebration had been quiet, a family gathering. Uncle Ted had left first, flush with triumph; Kathleen and Bob had followed shortly. Dooley and his brother had seen the women off to bed and come down to the basement to the Jameson's. Kevin poured two glasses and they sat on opposite sides of the bar in silence, watching the light play with the golden whiskey. "I thought it was kinda touch and go there for a while," said Kevin. "I thought the younger guy wanted to charge you."

"Yeah. They could have."

"They'd have never convicted you. Not with the guy having the knife."

After a silence Dooley said, "I didn't have to kill him. I could have run."

"But then he might have gone back after the girl."

Dooley nodded. "He might."

"You been brought up before the State's Attorney and they declined to press charges. You're in the clear. And I gotta say, I'm glad Spanos got clipped. He cheated the law, but it saved you a hell of a lot of explaining."

"Yeah." Dooley took a sip of whiskey, mused, set the glass down. "Yeah."

"What's the matter?"

Dooley looked up at his brother; he'd been looking up at him his whole life. "I don't think it'll ever be over. It won't ever be right. Not till I stand up for doing Dickens."

Kevin straightened, stiffening with an intake of breath. He shifted his weight, swaying a little. "Now you're talking about a whole different ball game."

"I know."

"That one, they won't be able to avoid charging you."

"I know."

"You could plead, I don't know, plead you were out of your mind with grief or something. But you'd have to do time on that one."

"Yeah, I probably would."

"Forget Uncle Ted. I don't think F. Lee Bailey could keep you out of jail for that one. I mean, there was premeditation, the whole thing, right?"

"I wanted to kill him, I planned to kill him, and I killed him, yeah."

"They'd fucking crucify you. You're gonna be dodging reporters for weeks on this one. Can you imagine, if you pleaded on Dickens?"

"Kevin."

"What?"

"Pop's gone." Dooley was having trouble getting the words out through a constricted throat. "I need you to tell me what to do."

"I can't tell you what to do."

"I'm begging you to. I ducked out of this family for eight years and I want back in. But if there's one thing about the family that means something, it's our honor. And what kind of honor do we have if I don't come clean on killing Dickens? I'm walking around dirty."

Kevin's eyes were blazing under clamped-down brows. His head went down, his shoulders bulled and he said, "There's honor, and there's honor. Far as I'm concerned, when the law failed to convict Leroy Dickens and you went and avenged your wife, you did an honorable thing."

Dooley stared at him. "I don't believe I heard that."

"I don't say it lightly. And I won't ever repeat it. But I was proud of you, Frank, I really was. You think the old man wouldn't have done it for Ma?"

Dooley squeezed his eyes shut, his head bowed. He hadn't wept in front of his brother in forty years but this was going to be close. When he could talk he said, "McPeak knows. He took it easy on me."

"I got news for you. Everybody knows. Thinks so, anyway."

"I'm not sure how long I can walk around this town with that hanging over me."

"I'm not either. Sooner or later it'll come up. I don't think they can convict you, but it'll always be there."

"You know what that means, don't you?"

Kevin took a drink, a lot more than a sip, and sighed. "I guess so."

"It means I have to leave again."

Kevin said nothing. After a while Dooley looked up and saw something he had never seen before. Kevin was trying to hide it, but those were tears at the corners of his eyes. "You won't be the first Irishman who had to go away from his family," he said hoarsely. "See if you can manage that postcard this time."

"You got it," said Dooley.

"Exile," said Dooley. "I guess that's what it is."

Andrea was looking out over the lake, her shoulders hunched against the wind. The snow had all gone away but it was going to be back in force, and soon. Over the distant Loop the dirty clouds were gathering, shrouding the tops of the highest buildings. "It sounds lonesome."

"Yes, it does." Dooley watched her profile, waiting for a sign.

She watched the lake toss uneasily beneath them. "Where are you going?"

"I don't know. Want to come with me?"

She moved closer to him, and he put his arms around her, wincing just a little at the pain. "I don't know if I could do Mexico," she said.

"It doesn't have to be Mexico. It's a big country out there. That's one of the best things about it. There's room for a lot of fresh starts."

"A lot of it's warmer, too, they say." Water frothed and snarled at the base of the pier.

"It would just about have to be."

Andrea raised her face to his. Dooley kissed her. "What are you going to do?" she said.

"I don't know that either. Want to help?"

She pressed her face to his neck. He felt her breath against his throat. "Funny, I couldn't even get it together to move closer to the lake. Now suddenly I'm thinking ocean. Mountains, maybe."

"Hell, we could have both. Make no small plans."

"When do we leave?"

"Well, what are you doing tomorrow?"

They held on to each other for a while as the wind cut at them, impotent and spiteful. "I'll miss this town," she said.

"God," said Dooley. "So will I."